Lawrence Naumoff

was born in Charlotte, North C
University of North Carolina. H
short fiction, including the Tho
a National Endowment for the Arts award. In 1988, following a ten-year break from writing, Lawrence Naumoff published his first full-length novel, *The Night of the Weeping Women*. *Rootie Kazootie* is his second novel. He now lives outside Chapel Hill in North Carolina.

From the reviews of *Rootie Kazootie*:

'A manic tale of humiliation and revenge . . . takes the agonies of sexual betrayal and speeds them up . . . bitter hilarity.'
Independent on Sunday

'Sublimely manic, melancholy novel . . . a scalding mix of humor and brutal honesty . . . there are scenes that rock with feverish emotion, with the unbridled anger and psycho-frenzy of lovers scorned, lovers betrayed . . . a remarkable writer.'
Philadelphia Inquirer

'Wonderfully maniacal, acidic, witty . . . merciless satire.'
Independent

'Funny, original, absolutely fresh . . . hilarious and poignant . . . an intelligent delight.'
USA Today

From the reviews of *The Night of the Weeping Women*:

'Vicious, brilliant, harrowing and hilarious. This is a tragedy on an almost operatic scale, but it is also a wild black comedy; the worse the nightmare gets, the more you laugh. The most frightening scenes are the funniest.'
Independent

'Dark, powerful . . . the style is as homey as apple pie, the subject matter as treacherous as an unlit street. This vivid, commanding novel scorches into your mind, on its every page, the fact that once you have stopped loving, you can never begin again.'
Sunday Times

By the same author

THE NIGHT OF THE WEEPING WOMEN

LAWRENCE NAUMOFF

Rootie Kazootie

Flamingo
An Imprint of HarperCollins*Publishers*

First published in Great Britain in 1990 by Collins

This edition first issued in 1991 by Flamingo,
an imprint of HarperCollins Publishers,
77–85 Fulham Palace Road,
Hammersmith, London W6 8JB

9 8 7 6 5 4 3 2 1

Printed and bound in Great Britain by
HarperCollins Book Manufacturing, Glasgow

Contents

PART I

Caroline Talks

Chapter 1

On the way home, Caroline and Richard passed a pickup truck coming from the opposite direction, and as it passed, a pig rose up out of nowhere in the passenger seat, stuck its head out the window, looked around and then quickly disappeared.

'Did you see that?' Caroline asked.

'I saw it.'

'Was that Edgar in his new truck?'

'I think so.'

'I heard he was riding around with that pig,' she said, 'but I didn't know he was doing it in a new truck.'

'Just forget it.'

'Lucille told me he'd named the pig Lucille, and I thought, damn, he's getting worse all the time.'

'Just stay out of it,' he said.

'And then she told me he was going to send her on that diet bus tour, or whatever you call it, and that really got me upset.'

'Let him alone.'

'She can't help it if she's fat. All the women in her family are fat. He knew that when he married her. He had to have known it. Didn't he?'

'I don't know,' he said.

'You don't know. You do so. You're just saying that because you don't want to talk to me. You're still mad at me about yesterday, aren't you?'

'I haven't even thought about it,' he said.

'Yes, you have. You're doing it right now.'

Caroline had lost her car keys and called Richard at work to bring her his set. This was the second time in two weeks she'd lost a set.

'I know you don't want me to bother you over there,' she said, 'but I can't help it if I lose things.'

'I'm not thinking about it,' he said.

'Everybody loses things. Especially when they get older. It's just part of life. The older you get, the more things you've got on your mind, and the more things you've got on your mind, the less you can handle them. Isn't that right?'

'If you say so,' he said.

'Oh, I give up. I really do,' she said.

'It's not that bad,' he said.

'But, baby, it is,' she said. 'I'm getting to be such a boring person you don't even want to talk to me anymore.'

'That's not it.'

'It must be, baby. I know it is. You don't even have to admit it. I'm turning into one of those crazy women approaching forty you read about all the time.'

'You're all right,' he said.

'I'm not, though. I feel nervous all the time. Everything's changing and I can't keep up with it. You're changing. I'm changing. My body's changing. I've even got hair growing where I never used to.'

'Come on, Caroline,' he said.

'I do. I'm turning into a man or something. I've read about that. Your hormones start drying up and the masculine ones take over. I swear, I'm just a wreck.'

'Just take it easy.'

'The other day in the bathroom, I swear to you, I was on the toilet for fifteen minutes.'

'That's enough, Caroline.'

'I was sitting there and I thought, damn, what's happening? I must have lost ten pounds by the time I got out.'

'Do we really have to talk about that?' he asked.

'Well, we have to talk about something. If it was left up to you, we'd never talk at all.'

'Some things you want to hear about and some you don't,' he said.

'You don't want to hear about anything. I never say the

right things anymore. I just don't, do I? I might as well give up. Nothing I do or say interests you anymore. I can't blame you, I guess. I don't have a very spectacular life. I thought at one time I would, but it's just slipped on by and now what have I got?'

'Don't worry so much all the time,' he said.

'I don't worry. It just sounds like it when I talk. Most of the time I'm real happy. It's just that when I start talking all this stuff comes out.'

'Don't talk then.'

'I knew you were going to say that. Just as I finished that sentence I thought, he's going to say, don't talk then, and by golly you did. You said it. We're turning into Mutt and Jeff or whatever. Who was that?'

'I don't remember.'

'I know. It's Dagwood and Blondie. That's what we're turning into.'

'I don't get it,' he said.

'I don't either,' she said. 'I guess it doesn't fit, really, when you think about it. Still, they were great.'

'Who?'

'Those old comic strips. I used to have this crush on Joe Palooka. Remember the guy with the little house attached to his bicycle. I used to think he was so cute. That's the way things are when you're young. You fall in love with everything. It doesn't work when you get older. You need something else.'

'Yeah,' he said.

'Yeah what?' she asked.

'You need something else,' he said.

'Are you saying you need someone else?'

'No, Caroline. I was not saying that.'

'Then why'd you agree with me so fast?'

'Forget it.'

'You always say that. Forget it. That's your response to everything. That's all right, though. I know you don't mean it. This is just one of my bad days. You know how I get. We've already had a great time. I loved the auction.'

They had been to a farm equipment auction and had bought a cultivator. Cultivators were implements that hooked onto tractors and were used to dig up, the same way a person with a hoe might, the weeds between the rows of crops. Some cultivators could do four, eight, or twelve rows at a time. They hung out from the sides of tractors like wings. This one fit behind the tractor and worked one row only, but could do as much work in an hour as a person could do in two or three days.

The vegetable garden was a big part of Richard and Caroline's life, and was, except for their house in the country between the university towns of Durham and Chapel Hill, just about all they had left from what had begun as a back-to-the-land life away from everything. They had real jobs now, went to town a lot, saw other people, had a bank loan, and so forth and so on, but they still planted a big garden and canned and froze as much as they could.

'Did the old guy die or what?' Caroline asked, referring to the person who had been sold out at the auction.

'He died.'

'I wish they had sold the furniture. I looked around the house before they started. I guess the heirs got that.'

They pulled into the driveway.

'Can I ask you something?'

'What?' he said.

'Can I do the cultivating?'

'If you want to. It's not that easy, though.'

'I know. I watched you do it when you borrowed Edgar's.'

'The steering's loose on the tractor,' he said. 'It's hard to keep it straight.'

'I'll go slowly,' she promised.

'You better.'

'I will.'

He stopped the truck. They got out.

'Still,' he said, thinking about it, 'maybe I better do it. Or at least get it started.'

'Oh, let me. I promise I'll do a good job. You know how I am in the summer when I'm not teaching. I'm just crazy to do things. I love to drive the tractor. Please let me.'

'Okay, then.'

'You rest, okay baby,' she said. 'You've been at that awful job all week and the least a woman can do for her man is let him take it easy on the weekends. Okay, sweetheart?'

'All right. Help me get it out of the truck.'

They dragged it out. It supported itself upright on its tines. Caroline got the tractor, which was an old John Deere built like a huge tricycle. She backed it up to the cultivator and Richard hooked it to the lift.

The lift was called a three-point hitch. It had two arms that came out from the hydraulic housing between the back tires, and a third point to hook onto above the two lower arms. Once an implement was hooked at the arms, it could be raised or lowered for work or transport and the depth at which it operated in the ground could be controlled.

'Be sure and don't look backwards,' he said.

'What?' she asked.

The tractor was popping and hissing and the clutch pulley whirled around, making a racket like gravel rolling inside a hubcap.

'If you turn around to see how you're doing, you'll go sideways and run over the rows.'

'All right.'

He watched her from the porch. He put his feet on the rail. She went up one row and down another. She made clean sharp turns, using her wheel brakes at the end of each row. She pulled on the hydraulic lever just right at the end of each row and the cultivator left the ground and swung into the air at the same time as she swung the tractor around. She kept the tractor in first gear and finished the garden in less than an hour.

Well, she can surely drive a tractor, he thought.

'Shall I back it in, or what?' she called from the shed.

'Go in frontwards. That way, if it rains, the engine will stay dry.'

The shed wasn't long enough to fit the whole thing, the tractor and cultivator, all the way in.

'It'll probably never rain again, anyway,' she said when she joined him on the porch.

'I don't know.'

She put her feet up like his, looking for a moment like a child copying her parent in some exact way. They looked a lot alike, anyway, and could have been mistaken, if not for brother and sister, then at least for cousins. Caroline had long reddish-blond hair, the kind of color people often referred to as strawberry-blond, but unlike most redheads, she had a tanned, olive-looking complexion. She had beautiful bone structure, and she looked good without makeup, which she rarely used. She had high cheekbones and dark eyebrows and, as Richard could have told you if he'd been persuaded to talk about it, there wasn't a mark, a blemish, a mole or a pimple on her from her toes to her hair. She was just naturally good-looking, and though Richard had darker hair, he had the same good bones and skin and natural good looks.

They rested like that, then, with their feet on the rail, looking the same while Caroline let the vibrations and noise from the tractor slowly ebb out of her, and she tingled a little, the way a piano string might do as the sound it made slowly faded away. Then she said, 'Now what?'

'Just take it easy, I guess.'

Sitting on the porch with her husband and working on the land and being home and together was just about as close to heaven as she could get.

'I love my house, you know,' she said.

'Yeah.'

'I know it's not a big house and people always ask me why we built such a small house, but I think it's just perfect.'

'Uh huh,' he said, and looked out at the road and listened to a car coming from far away.

'No one wants to stay simple or modest anymore,' she said. 'It's like some old idea that's gone forever. Everything's got to be big and fancy and everything's got to be a big show. I hate that. I hate people who live like that.'

'Uh huh,' he said.

'I like the way we live. It suits me just fine.'

'That's good,' he said.

'Some people can't take it, you know. They have to go shopping all the time, buy things, have fancy cars, get the latest hair style and all that junk. They never get satisfied. They're always looking for something else. I like the way we are. It feels right, you know?'

'Yes.'

She changed positions by sitting on the rail and putting her feet on the chair.

'I want to do something special for you today. I could make a pie. Would you like that? A chocolate pie? Would that be good?'

'I don't know. Maybe.'

'I guess it's too hot to get into baking a pie. How about something else. Chocolate isn't good for you, anyway. It makes you nervous and gives some people a headache.'

'Is that right?'

'It is. I read about that in the paper the other day. I was also reading this article,' she said and stopped when she saw he had closed his eyes. 'Are you falling asleep?'

'No.'

'Okay. I was also reading this article about what Americans really eat, you know, and it's like people eat snacks and junk more than anything. More than real food. You know, the sugar content, it was about all that stuff. It said about as many people were drinking Cokes or Pepsis for breakfast as there were drinking coffee. Can you believe that? I still think milk's the best thing for you.'

He didn't say anything.

'I guess you're tired. I don't blame you. I couldn't work over there. I wouldn't, anyway. You know what I'm trying to say. Why don't you go inside and lie down.'

'I'm all right.'

'It is just so hot.'

'Yep.'

'Maybe it'll cloud up this afternoon. When it gets this hot we usually have a thunderstorm. What's that?' she asked, seeing something in the paper.

'It's just something I was looking at while you were cultivating. I was thinking it might be fun. You want to go?'

'Of course I do. It looks hilarious.'

They took his truck, which was in better condition than her car. They had lunch at a barbeque place. The air-conditioning felt so good it might have been worth eating all day long just to stay inside. They ate too much as it was and Caroline was restless once back in the truck.

'I'm too full now,' she said.

'Me, too.'

She sighed and fanned her skin with her blouse, flapping it in and out to cool off.

'I wish we'd gone on and air-conditioned the house when we built it,' she said. 'It's too late now. I hate these decisions that you make and they turn out later to be wrong. I hate that. We could have borrowed a little more then and done it and not even felt it spread out over thirty years.'

'They wouldn't give us any more.'

'Oh yeah,' she said. 'Now I remember those bastards.'

'You sure have taken to cussing a lot these days.'

'I have? Well, maybe I have. Anyway, I don't care. I don't care about anything right now but the heat. Couldn't we buy a window unit?'

'With what?'

'We must have that much money somewhere.'

'I don't.'

'Couldn't we borrow it? Neither one of us is sleeping very well these days. We just lie there and sweat.'

'I don't want to borrow any more money.'

'Of course you're working in the air-conditioning over there. Of course I didn't think about that. That's just like me. I always think about some things but not the right things. Just like I'm always talking about some things but not the right things. You know what I mean? Sure you do. I know what you're thinking,' she said. 'I'm talking way too much and way too fast again. Right? You're thinking there goes Caroline getting out of control again, but I'm not. I know what I'm saying or at least I know what I'm trying to say by not saying it, follow me? I always get this way when you stop talking to me. I always do. The less you talk the more I do. I guess I'm trying to make up for both of us,' she said and stuck her arm out the window and made her sleeve into a funnel so the air went up it and across her body.

'I think it's not sleeping well that's got us messed up,' she said. 'I think that's what it is. I really do. We ought to get a book on sleep therapy and see what they say about it.'

'I feel all right,' he said.

'If you're all right then there must be something really wrong with me,' she said. 'I'm just getting more nervous all the time and I thought I was going to have such a relaxing summer.'

Caroline taught first grade and she loved her children and they loved her. Lately, though, all the other things associated with being a teacher, all the paperwork and the bureaucracy and so forth, had begun to get her down.

'Are you mad at me for being so out of it at the end of the year?'

'No,' he said. 'I haven't even thought about it.'

'Good. What's this mud-bog thing we're going to, anyway? I mean, is it like those trucks with those huge tires you see all over the place now?'

'Not really. It's just stock trucks,' he said. 'Kind of like this one.'

Caroline took her shoes off and stuck her bare feet out the window and leaned across the seat with her head on Richard's lap.

'The floor of this truck is hot as a frying pan,' she said. 'Can I lay like this?'

'Go ahead,' he said.

'I'm not cramping your leg, am I?' she asked. 'Remember

that time we were riding in the car and you got that cramp in your leg and you shot across the car with your leg sticking straight out. Remember that?'

'Vaguely,' he said.

She put her bare feet on the dash and wiggled her toes and then looked at her toenails one by one.

'You used to love my feet. You couldn't keep your hands off them when we got married,' she said.

Richard made a face.

'You couldn't. You used to tickle me and rub my feet for hours. I swear you did. You have this convenient one-way memory,' she said. 'You only remember what you want to remember.'

'I remember everything,' he said.

'Do you remember how much I've always hated Cynthia?' she asked.

'Now we finally get to it,' he said. 'I wondered when it was going to happen. You've been building up to it all day.'

'So?'

'So don't get started on it, that's what.'

'Don't get started?' she asked. 'You're the one who started it by going to work over at her house.'

Richard and Caroline had grown up in the same small town in North Carolina. They had both gone to the same local branch of the state university system in the eastern part of the state. They dated off and on the whole time they were in school, and kept on seeing each other even after Richard dropped out in his junior year.

They married when Caroline finished and got her teacher's certificate, and soon afterwards Richard opened up a one-man cabinet shop. The shop gave Richard, he thought, about as honest a way to earn a living as one could find.

'I told you not to,' Caroline said, continuing on, 'I asked you not to, I begged you not to, but you went ahead and took the job.'

'I didn't have any choice,' he said.

'We wouldn't have starved if you were without work for

a few months,' she said. 'We'd have made it.'

'We would not have made it and I'm not going to sit around living off of you, anyway,' he said.

'I hate Cynthia. She's the only person I've ever hated right off and kept on hating even after I got to know her. I swear she is. She's the worst. She makes my skin crawl. She and all her fancy ways and her fancy, expensive, and so, so exclusive New England college she went to that she just always has to tell you about along with everything else she constantly parades before your eyes. I cannot stand, and I mean *CANNOT STAND,'* she shouted at him, 'to think about you over there with her alone all day long. It's driving me crazy. It is. I can't stand to think about it but I can't stop thinking about it.'

'You want to know what goes on all day,' he said. 'Do you really want to know?'

'I don't know if I can bear to know,' she said.

'If you want to know, I'll tell you.'

'Well, go on, then,' Caroline said. 'Go on and I'll sit here like I'm dead and listen.'

'I walk in the door. She gets up about the time I get there and comes walking through in her bathrobe.'

'Yuck,' she said.

'About the time I get my tools out and start tearing out the cabinets that line that kitchen from wall to wall, and I mean wall to wall, sixty-two feet of them, top and bottom, for a total of one hundred and twenty-four feet, about the time I get started back in on that, I hear the water running in the pipes and she starts her bath. The bath takes forever because it's a long time before I hear the water running out the drain. Then she comes in and chats a little bit and takes her breakfast into the other room where she has made a temporary kitchen-breakfast room kind of thing, and she sits there drinking coffee and reading the paper and looking out the window, and that's about it.'

'What about the rest of the day?' Caroline asked. 'I mean, what do you talk about? I mean, you said, chatting with you. What does that mean?' she asked, madder at that than almost anything because he never chatted with her anymore.

'She just talks. She walks around the room and talks and I keep working.'

'And that's all? What about the rest of the day? I mean, you just described about an hour. You're over there for ten hours every day.'

'Eight.'

'Ten.'

'One time it was about ten. Okay. One time.'

'I don't want to know anymore,' she said, already mad at herself because she had told herself she wasn't going to let on how much this was bothering her. 'I just don't want to know anymore, okay? Just don't tell me anything else,' she said.

'Okay,' he said.

'That's too much already. That bathrobe and that kind of aimless walking around and talking to you. That's too much already,' she said, unable to stop. 'It just is. It's just like Cynthia to have all the time in the world to do whatever she wants. And all the money, too. I bet she wouldn't go to a mud-bog event with you. I bet she wouldn't do that. Would she?' she asked. 'Just answer me that. Would she?'

'I don't know.'

Cynthia was thirty-nine years old. She had a huge house and two children. She had divorced her doctor husband last year and had gotten the house and a settlement large enough to play around with for a couple of years.

'I just want to ask you one more thing,' she said, 'and then I'm not going to say anything else about it.'

'Suit yourself,' he said.

'What kind of robe is it?'

'I have no idea.'

'What color is it?'

'I told you I don't know.'

'I bet you don't. I know you. I know how you are around good-looking women. I know her, too. I know how she coos and preens around men. I know how her voice gets so soft, just so helplessly soft, around men. It makes me want to puke. I swear it does. It makes me want to scream to hear it.'

'Go on and scream,' he said.

'I'm not going to. I'm not even going to think about it anymore. Tell me some more about this mud-bog thing,' she said, trying to get back to the job of making sure her husband loved her the way he was supposed to.

'I showed you the ad in the paper.'

'But tell me, ' she said. 'I want you to tell me about it.'

'You've got these macho types who have four-wheel drive trucks, like you see on the street, and you've got these promoters who go out in a field and dig a two-hundred-foot long pit that gets deeper as it gets longer, and they fill it with loose dirt and then pump water in it for days and then these guys one by one tear their trucks up trying to get from one end to the other.'

'Are we going to try it?'

'This truck isn't four-wheel drive,' he said. 'You know that.'

'Oh,' she cooed, in a soft, Cynthia voice.

'Come on, now,' he said.

'I just don't know those kind of things,' she said in the same voice. 'I just hardly know anything at all.'

Chapter 2

The mud-bog was set up in the infield of an old dirt race-track. The wooden bleachers on the side held four thousand people and were full. Admission was six dollars and the entry fee for the trucks was twenty-five dollars apiece. The prize to any truck that made it from one end to the other was five hundred dollars.

They found a seat and settled down and then Caroline said, 'Get me some peanuts, please. And a Coke.'

While Richard was away, a man in overalls slid in behind them. With him were three sons as big as he was, and in the same kind of overalls, and a tiny, wiry woman who must have been the mother of this tribe. Caroline glanced at them as they shuffled along to their seats and saw that their boots and the cuffs of their pants were caked with dried manure.

'Straight off the farm,' she whispered when Richard came back. 'And I mean, straight off.'

'They're probably just squeezing this in between milking times,' he whispered back.

The announcer called for the trucks to get ready. Each truck stopped as it approached the pit. The driver got out and hooked a long strap to the hitch on his bumper. Then, if the truck did not make it, a tractor could pull it backward and out.

The first truck went into the pit and began spinning. Mud went everywhere. Fifty feet, or about a quarter of the way down, the truck ceased moving forward and began to dig itself deeper and deeper. A judge standing in front and off to the side signaled the driver to let off. Then they measured the distance he had covered, and the tractor, which kept the other end of the strap hooked to it, pulled the truck out.

The people in the bleachers laughed and called and jeered each time a truck mired up.

'None of them are making it,' Caroline said. 'Aren't any of them going to make it?'

'I doubt it.'

After about half the trucks had tried and failed, the audience began to get bored and the announcer called time-out and told everyone he had a special treat for them and introduced a man from California who was going to blow himself up with dynamite.

'He's going to do what?' Caroline asked.

'I've read about this guy,' Richard said.

The man came out in a bright red fireproof suit and got in a coffin in the middle of the dry part of the dirt track in front of everyone. The announcer explained that four sticks of dynamite were under a heavy wooden board inside the coffin on which the man lay. He cautioned everyone sitting close to put their fingers in their ears and to hold on to their children.

'It's got to be a fake,' Caroline said.

'It's not,' Richard said.

The announcer asked for quiet. The crowd instantly became so quiet and still it was hard to imagine that many people getting that still that fast.

On a countdown from ten, the dynamite went off. Almost before they heard it, Caroline and Richard felt the concussion of the blast and saw the man lifted about four feet into the air, and as he lifted, the sound hit them so hard it felt as if they'd been blown up, as well.

'God almighty,' Richard said.

Three men rushed out to help the blown-up man, who stood for a second and then toppled over sideways while the other men tried to hold him up. One of the men talked closely into the blown-up man's face and then they let go of him and he waved to the crowd, which cheered, and then he fell over again and the men dragged him off behind a trailer and out of sight.

'That man is hurt,' Caroline said.

'I think he's just shook up.'

Richard went to get another Coke and some more peanuts, and Caroline thought, I could do that. If Richard leaves me I could go around the country blowing myself up with dynamite and Richard would have to read about me in the paper and see me on television and live with how famous and crazy and wild I'd gotten since he'd left.

The trucks started again. With about ten trucks remaining, the next truck went in the pit and blew up its engine and oil splattered everywhere and at the same time the strap hooked to the hitch came loose and the announcer told everyone that the rules said if the driver didn't get the strap hooked on well enough to stay on he had to fish it out of the mud and hook it back.

There was a lot of laughter and hooting as the driver waded into the mud and fished the strap out and hooked it back and then, with great effort, pulled himself along his truck out of the mud and into the seat and steered as the tractor pulled him out.

Then all the trucks finished and no one had gotten the prize money. The people in the bleacher rose to leave. The announcer asked everyone to wait.

'Don't leave yet. We're going to give away this five hundred dollars yet. We've got a ladies-only special event coming up and you will not want to miss it,' he said. 'For any of you sweet young things, or sweet old things, for that matter, whoever wanted to make five hundred dollars in a quick, legal few minutes,' he said and laughed, 'I'm going to give you the chance.

'The first little gal in the audience who can walk, crawl, swim, or run through this mud from one end to the other will get five crisp one hundred dollar bills when she comes out of it. That's five hundred dollars. Cold cash.'

'This is ridiculous,' Richard said.

'Five hundred dollars is a lot of money,' Caroline said.

There was a general discussion in the stands and the consensus was that no one could make it.

'You've got to stay in the mud, right down the middle,'

the announcer said. 'You can't run along the edges. I believe, I firmly do, that somebody up there ought to be able to make it,' he said and looked hopefully around for a volunteer.

'I tell you what I'm going to do. I'm going to give the first two women what make it five hundred dollars each. You can't beat that. Talk it over with your menfolk and see if they don't think it's a good bet.'

Caroline looked around to see if anyone was going to try it, and when no one did, she turned to Richard.

'No one's going to try it.'

'Of course not.'

'But why. It's not that big a deal.'

'Caroline,' he said. 'You know how sticky red clay mud is? Do you?'

'I know, but like, five hundred dollars. Somebody's just got to try it.'

'No way.'

'Why'd he just say women, anyway? Why not men. That makes me mad. That makes me real mad. That makes me so mad I'm going to go down there and—' she said and Richard interrupted her.

'No you're not,' he said.

'No I'm not what? You don't even know what I was going to say.'

'Just forget it.'

'I was going to say, Richard,' she said, 'that I ought to go down there and kick that man in the teeth, but maybe I'll just do what you were thinking. Maybe I will.'

'Caroline, think about this. For once in your life, think before you act. For once, how about it. Think what you're going to look like down there.'

'I don't care.'

'You're just nuts, Caroline.'

'Oh, really?'

'This conversation is over,' he said. 'Forget it.'

'I'm not going to forget it. If that asshole thinks no woman's got the guts to do that, I'm going to show him.'

'Caroline,' Richard said and grabbed her arm, 'let's go home.'

'Let go of me,' she said and stood up and at the exact same time that she stood up and he grabbed her to pull her back the announcer spotted her and called attention to her and the man sitting behind them tapped Richard on the shoulder and said, 'Let her go, buddy. She's got a right to try if she wants.'

She walked through the path cleared by the people in the bleachers, and as she stepped onto the track, eight other women ran down and joined her.

'This is a gutsy bunch of gals down here,' the announcer said. 'They're going to show us men what they're made of,' he said and the audience cheered. Caroline and the other women put on a little show by jumping up and down and stretching and touching their toes and so forth and then one of the women took off her shoes and when Caroline and the others did the same, people yelled for them to take everything off.

The announcer enlisted the aid of the truck drivers to line the sides of the pit and instructed them to keep the women in the mud and not let any of them run along the harder, dried edge.

'Shove them back in if they try to cheat,' he told them.

Caroline lined up with the rest of them, and it wasn't until she looked down the length of that endless, muddy swamp that she finally got scared. She got that empty feeling you could get when you thought you weren't afraid to fly but when you left the ground you wished you weren't there; that feeling you got when, after pulling out to pass a car, there's another coming right at you and you see you're not going to make it but you can't slow down and you can't get back because someone else has pulled out to pass with you and all you can do is get it over with. That's the way she felt, as if she had decided to kill herself and had jumped but the instant her feet had left the edge of the building she had thought, wait, no, but too late, and the hell and terror of having to live with herself for those few moments as she fell to her death, that's how sick she felt for a brief moment as the announcer gave the signal and she and the others ran in.

She fell immediately, as did the other women, and when she got up and moved deeper into the mud, she found her running became like slow motion, like the effort to run, but in glue. Her hand and leg motions resembled running but she was going nearly nowhere.

She could feel as she struggled for footing that the ground near the sides was firmer and that it was not as deep, but as she veered over that way, and the other women discovered the same thing and moved over there as well, the drivers shoved them back into the middle. When they did this, the announcer scolded the women. When he did, the crowd cheered and laughed some more.

Caroline's face was covered with mud. The mud was filthy, and burned motor oil from the leaking and damaged truck engines floated on it. When she was chest deep in the mud, she accidentally got a mouthful. She stopped. She spit and she gagged and got it out of her mouth.

Oh crap, she thought. What have I done now?

She looked at the crowd but could not find Richard, and thought, why in the hell did I do this. Why?

'Come on, ladies,' the announcer said.

Go fuck yourself, Caroline thought.

'Let's show these men what you can do,' he said. 'We've got a lot of money sitting right here beside me says you ain't going to make it,' he said and held up the bills and flashed them around for everyone to see.

She did try to keep going, as did the other women, but it was bad. For a time, everyone was laughing and cheering and the women and Caroline kept on pulling against the mud in a kind of exhausted swimming motion while the announcer urged them on and told them what he was going to do to them if they didn't make it.

'I'm going to leave all you sweet little things right in there if one of you don't make it through. I swear to goodness I'm going to,' he said, and then, when he heard the laughter, went on further, inspired by the sound of his own voice.

'I tell you, little gals, I'm going to have my boys go get a bunch of hogs and run them in there with you and we're going to fence the place in and sell tickets,' he said, and the crowd loved it. They had these women where they wanted them, and for a while longer it was just about the funniest thing they'd ever seen.

Then, for everyone, the stunt collapsed. The women in the mud stopped moving. The announcer stopped talking. The people in the stands got quiet. It was as if it had gone too far, had crossed over a line that suddenly everyone recognized, and the whole event froze into a hypnotic stillness, like a large painting viewed from a distance.

Realizing something had to be done, the announcer made an enormous effort to bring everyone out of it. He coughed and he cleared his throat and he found his voice again and he made a joke and then he kept on talking and the talking and the jokes and the noise from the loudspeakers brought everyone back. He ordered the men along the sides to pull the women out. They did that, and then the crowd rose to leave, feeling a little better now.

They were able to laugh again and comment on the pitiful sight, but still, down deep, they were uncomfortable. Something had happened. It was time to leave.

Something like a mud-bog was not supposed to end that way. It was supposed to end with a $2,000 engine exploding all to bits and the driver, who had volunteered to do himself in in the same way the man had volunteered to be blown up with the dynamite and the women had volunteered to make fools of themselves, the driver was supposed to get out of the truck and laugh about it all and make everyone feel better. Something had gone wrong.

Richard remained sitting until everyone had left. He walked down the bleachers and across the track and around the back of the mobile home where Caroline stood in a line with the other women. A man in a firefighter's coat and boots stood beside a fire truck and sprayed the women with a gentle stream of water. Another man handed them towels. The women went into the trailer. Richard stood near the other men who were also waiting. None of the men stood very close to anyone else and no one said anything. They had to wait a long time. The women inside undressed and scraped the mud off their skin. They rinsed their clothes out, and squeezed them out and then put them back on, still wet but not as filthy.

Caroline wrapped her hair in a towel and put another one around her shoulders like a shawl.

'Damnit,' she said. 'I thought I could do it.'

He shook his head.

'You don't have to talk to me,' she said. 'I know you think I'm really crazy now. I don't care. I don't care about anything anymore. Just take me home and let me change clothes and then drive me over to the asylum. You don't even have to get out. Just drop me off.'

'Caroline,' he said. 'Just tell me why.'

'I don't know. It seemed,' she said, 'it just seemed for a minute there that I had to do it. It seemed like it was going to be fun. I thought you'd think it was funny, anyway.'

'Me?'

'Well, I thought so at the time. You used to think things I did were funny.'

'We were younger then.'

'I know.'

'That's the kind of thing some strung-out Hell's Angels woman might do, but not you, Caroline. It was just plain stupid.'

'I know it was.'

'You could've died in there. You could've drowned or something.'

'I could not,' she said. 'But what if I had? What if I had started to? Would you have cared?'

'Yes, I would have cared.'

'Would you have pulled me out?'

'Yes, I would have pulled you out.'

'I just wondered. Don't you remember the time I jumped into the inland waterway at Morehead City and tried to swim across to the island and the tide was going out and I went sideways and you ran along yelling at me to look up and see what was happening because I thought I was swimming straight across and you came in after me about the time I realized I was being pulled toward the inlet. Don't you remember that?'

'I remember everything. I already told you that.'

'Well?'

'Well, what?'

'Well, nothing, I guess.'

As they walked to the truck they noticed the announcer coming right at them. He looked up and saw the wet clothes and the towel around Caroline's head and the one on her shoulders and he looked at Richard and then back at Caroline and then right through her and passed by without saying a word.

'Somebody ought to kill that guy,' she said.

It was four o'clock. They drove home. It was the hottest time of the day.

'I could've bought us an air-conditioner if I'd won,' she said.

'But that's the whole point,' he said. 'No one was going to win. No one. They suckered you. It was a sucker deal from the very beginning and you fell for it.'

'Okay. So what? So I'm stupid. You already told me that. You've already told me what a fool I made of myself. What can I do about it now? I don't know how to explain to you. For a minute there I just had to do it. That's all I can say.'

'I'm sure it is.'

'Haven't you ever made a mistake?'

'I sure have,' he said.

'Haven't you ever thought something was going to be one way and it turned out to be another?'

'I have thought that,' he said, 'quite recently as a matter of fact.'

'What do you mean?' she asked.

'Nothing.'

'You mean me?'

'No.'

'You mean us? What do you mean? Tell me.'

'I don't mean anything,' he said.

Caroline's clothes were turning hard as they dried. As they stiffened she thought about turning into a mummy and then she thought about concrete. I ought to just lie down and let someone pour concrete all over me, she thought. Then I couldn't get in trouble anymore. She made herself rigid above the seat so that she was like a board stretching from the floor to the headrest without touching the seat itself. Richard looked at her and shook his head but said nothing.

I guess he'd like me better like this, she thought, and she stayed that way as long as she could. It was a long drive, though, and eventually she settled down into a corner against her door and kept quiet, trying to be good.

Chapter 3

When they got home Caroline cleaned up and Richard watched baseball and then they had supper. At nine o'clock he was still watching television. Caroline was on the porch. She had the light off. She was walking back and forth, slowly, in a dreamy sort of way. Every time she walked behind the chairs, she looked in at him through the open window. After a while she stopped directly behind him.

'If you don't like me anymore, just tell me,' she said.

'What?' he asked. 'Are you talking to me?' He turned around in his chair so he could see her. 'What are you doing out there?'

'I said if you don't like me anymore, just tell me.'

'Go to sleep, Caroline,' he said.

'I'm not sleepy,' she said. 'I want you to come out here and sit with me.'

'Let me watch the show.'

'I hate being jealous,' she said. 'I really hate it.'

'Oh no,' he said and came out on the porch. 'Here it comes again.'

'When you get jealous everything you try to do just goes wrong, but then, a little later, when it's over, you can't believe you acted like that. You think, oh, what was that all about, and you can't believe how crazy you got. It's like this teacher was telling me one day that she hadn't slept with a man in so long she was about to die. She thought, she said, she'd just do anything, just anything to make love one more time, but then she said a couple of days later she chased down this guy she used to know and they made love and she was lying in bed when it was all over and she said to herself, damn, what was all that fuss about?

'I mean, that's the way being jealous is. You just can't stop yourself. You feel like you're going to die from it all but when it's over and done with you sit up in bed and say, damn, what was that all about?'

'Now Caroline,' he said.

'I know you don't love Cynthia,' she said. 'I know that. I know you probably don't even like her that much, maybe a little, I guess you do a little, I guess you always have, but the thing is just your being over there all day is too much for me. It really is. And I've been thinking about it and I was wondering if there wasn't some way you could sub out the rest of the job and let's us go to the beach or up to the mountains. I was thinking after we got back today that you ought to consider that, really, because I know what she's up to. I know what kind of woman she is and I know you, and I don't like it. It makes me feel like the time when we were dating and you didn't call me for a week and I thought I just sat home every night thinking what'd I do what did I do wrong, only I didn't let you know it, did I?

'I never let you know anything back then. I just played it cool and I guess that was what you liked about me, playing it cool and having to chase me down and me such a wild young thing, you must have thought, and liked that about me, but all the while I'm sitting at home dying because you won't call me. But there I sat. I didn't say anything about it because that was the kind of act I had back then and you liked it, but I can't do it anymore.

'I'm getting like Marlene, I guess. The more I think about it, the more I think I am turning into Marlene, who you never met so you don't know what I'm talking about but I'm going to tell you, because Marlene, who was my cousin, was like this woman for whom everything was a giant crisis and who went too far with everything she did.

'She went too far in love and she went too far when she got mad. She just couldn't stay in the middle. She just couldn't stay in between things. She had to be out on the edges of things. When she was in love she had to be more in love than anyone else had ever been. When she slept with somebody she gave them everything she had so they thought they'd died and gone to heaven. They all wanted to marry her. Every man she ever went out with wanted to.

'She was married three or four times but every one of them went bad because whenever they did anything wrong Marlene went crazy and pretty soon all the men left her and she ended up just wandering around in bars sleeping with every man in town. She was doing it to get back at her husbands. Of course it doesn't make sense but she was sleeping with all those men to get back at men, if you follow me, and it just drove her nuts and that's how she ended up in prison.'

'What?' he asked.

'She'd just left her last husband, this was when they lived down in South Carolina just over the state line where there were those little one-room bars because you could drink down there but not up here so it was kind of like your typical border town and there was this guy who just kept after her all week. He kept trying to get her to go out with him but she wouldn't do it. She'd always leave with someone else but she always came back to this same place because Marlene being Marlene couldn't stay away from trouble. Pretty soon this guy came up behind her and put his hands around her and on her breasts, kind of like this, kind of like making his hands her bra, and he held her for a few minutes. She told me all about it when I visited her one time. He held her not for a few minutes I mean, but a few seconds I guess, just long enough for her to realize who it was and slip away, but he had kissed her on her neck while he held her and she said that made her madder than anything, the way he kissed her, like it was supposed to really turn her on or something and she just snapped, she said.

'She told the guy to wait there and went off and found this other man and told him he could have her if he'd help take this guy out somewhere and dump him on the side of the road. That's all she started out to do but after they stopped out in the middle of nowhere at this old fertilizer plant, which she described as this truly awful-looking place like something out of a bad dream, she knocked this guy out with a pipe and they tied him up to a post and set him on fire.

'She said it wasn't until he was burning and screaming that she started feeling bad about the whole thing and wished she hadn't. She said after he quit burning he fell over to the side and he looked up at them and said, help me, help me, like that. She said the guy's hair had burned off and his skin had melted down his face and he was trying to talk out of this melted hole where his mouth had been and she said she just freaked out and left.

'But the guy lived, somehow, I can't imagine what he looks like now, and she and this other guy had to go to prison and that's where I saw her, a long time ago, only I haven't seen her or heard from her in years, because when she got out she went up north and disappeared.

'And when I get like this I think about Marlene. I think, now Caroline, you can't be like that. You can't let everything throw you like that. You just got to know everything's going to be all right. You can't go around worrying about everything that might go wrong before it does go wrong. You know what I mean?

'See, I'm trying to tell you something now but as usual I'm not getting to it very well. How do you say it? How do you tell someone that you love them so much when you've already said it so many times before? How do you make it real? Do you know what I mean, baby? Come on, sweetheart,' she said, 'look at me. At least do that.'

She stood behind him and rubbed his shoulders.

'I'm so worn out. I just wish we could do something really great this summer. I wish we had enough money to go off somewhere and do nothing, like we used to. But we can't. I know. We've got house payments. We've got bills. You've got your work. I know. But I wish we didn't. Sometimes I even wish we'd never bought this land and built this house.'

Their house sat on fourteen acres of land. Four and a half

acres were cleared and nine and a half were in woods. Behind the house was Richard's shop, which was about the size of the house but looked like a barn. There was a porch on the front of the house and the house faced the road but was set back a hundred and fifty feet.

'I don't really mean that,' Caroline went on. 'It's just that once you get started you can't stop. Your life changes. What began as this simple life turns into a mess. Everything takes off and takes you with it.

'You know what there ought to be,' she went on. 'There ought to be some kind of setup where you could go to the bank and say, listen, I know we said we'd pay you $714 a month for the rest of our lives, but see, we really want to take this trip and sort of travel around and do nothing for about a year, because we love each other, see, a lot, and we really don't want to hurt your feelings, you know, but just for a little while you're going to have to do without your money. Okay?

'And there'd be this setup, where you could do it. And then everything would be better. You could get your life back together. Don't you see, honey,' she said and rubbed his shoulders, 'that it's getting that time in our life where we have to be really careful, if you know what I mean. I know you do. I know you know what I'm talking about. I don't have to say any more about it, okay?

'I feel better now. I really feel pretty good. Some people say a mud bath is good for your skin. I guess not one with motor oil and grease mixed in, though. I guess not. Still, who knows. That may turn out to be the funniest thing I ever did. You never know. That may be the end of it all, Caroline's swan song or whatever you call it, when forever afterwards Caroline will be different, and everyone will say, hasn't she changed, isn't that something how Caroline's changed, and you won't have to worry about me anymore, nor for a day. I'll be so perfect people will at first mistake me for someone else, and I won't cry anymore because there won't be anything to cry about, not one thing, and everything I ever did that was wrong or stupid will be gone and I won't have to think about it ever again. Okay? Won't you like that? Isn't that what you want?'

'Well,' he said.

'I know it is. Don't you have this perfect picture of a woman you've always carried with you somewhere and that you and everybody else is always looking for? Don't you have that? I do. I have it and I want it every day. My perfect little picture of my life, I mean.

'That's why,' she said, and took a breath, 'Cynthia's not in it. She's not in my picture and she's not in yours. She better not be, anyway. Because you know what? She's a fake. A goddamn fake. That way she acts, the way she thinks men want her to be, that whole business is such a goddamn rueful and vicious act, in that, you see, you have to feel sorry for her and hate her at the same time, because she's the Venus's-flytrap of the female race, the poison mushroom that looks good enough to eat, and you need to know it, even if you hate me for saying it, you need to know it and that's all,' she said, and pulled his head backward so that he had to look at her.

'That's all I'm going to say about it. That's it,' she said and let him go and went inside and he stayed there with his feet on the rail and his hands in his lap and looked out across the road, more than a little shook up.

Chapter 4

Cynthia, the bane of Caroline's existence, had a difficult night. She'd been restless. She'd had a headache. She'd been lonely. She needed aspirin for her headache but she'd thrown that and all the other medicine away a few months ago as part of her new life. She needed Richard for the rest of what had ailed her, and now, after a long shower, she waited for him.

She was as nervous as she'd been when she'd been sworn in at the courtroom and had to profess she was leaving the marriage of her own volition and that the legal aspects of the divorce had all been handled to her satisfaction.

She had just been through the worst year of her life, desolate and racked with guilt and the sense of failure that the one thing she had worked hardest of all on had failed and she'd had to abandon it and thank God the two children had been protected from most of it, except what she couldn't hide in her face.

She brushed her long hair and braided it and let it hang. She'd always been a strange character for a doctor's wife, bohemian and eccentric and definitely at a loss on the golf course or in the beauty parlor, two places she had never been and never intended to go, though her ex-husband played golf every Thursday afternoon and all his friends' wives had the latest bangs or no bangs, short or long, frizzy or flat hairstyle.

Still, marrying a doctor right out of college had been a heady thing to accomplish, and there was that sense of his doing good for humanity, not counting at least some attraction to all that money. How could one ignore it? One could not, but could, at least, spend it in a sensible and interesting way. It had seemed right for so long, even though the last few years had been awfully dry and bitter, not from any one great act of treachery or deceit, but from the accumulation of living a lie, she guessed, as she thought about it over and over, from giving up her life for his and for pretending it was all okay.

She looked out the window when she heard a car going by and watched it make the turn at the top of the road. Her house was large enough to fit Caroline and Richard's into the garage. She was fixing it up and she was going to sell it and move into something more in line with how she felt, small and contained and less cluttered, a more simplified and modest life, was how she described it to herself.

The house, set outside Durham on what used to be ten acres of farmland until they bought it and built the house on it, after which it became more like an estate, was worth a fortune now, probably three or four hundred thousand dollars, and it was all free and clear, and the thought of that much money depressed Cynthia as much as it excited her.

No doubt another doctor from Duke would buy it. They seemed to be the only people around making enough money to live that way, and no doubt he would bring along a wife and children who would know just what to do with the place, something she had never figured out but had merely gotten into buying things to fill up the rooms, a job that had taken her years, actually years, and had worn her out more than raising the children or putting on the social version of herself for her husband's friends. She had shopped herself out. She didn't ever want to see the inside of an antique store or have to ask the price of another primitive piece of furniture again.

So, that would be over, anyway, and all she had left to do now was to replace the cheap cabinets that the original builder had installed without their knowing they were prefabs and that the veneer would eventually ripple up and the Formica would peel off the overhang and the knobs would strip loose from their screws and fall off so that you had to claw at the doors and drawers to get them open.

While waiting to sell the house, she could begin to sell the furniture and the knick-knacks, and then she could concentrate on Richard.

She had met Richard long ago, when he'd come over on the recommendation of a friend, to build and install some bookshelves. She had liked him immediately and had felt a strange homesick longing and kinship to his simple way of life and his quiet style.

Later she had had Richard and Caroline over for supper, and at first she liked Caroline as well, as much as she liked Richard, but eventually she began to think Caroline was nuts and that it was Richard, really, to whom she was deeply attracted.

Being committed and determined to be a good and faithful wife at the time and a good and faithful mother, she just kept all this attraction and unrest to herself, and waited, hoping something would happen and that whatever it was, it would cause Richard, little by little if that was what it took, to become interested in her.

It hadn't mattered at that time if it took years for him to figure out she loved him. She had time, then. Now that she was single, though, she was ready.

Just after she and her husband separated, she had two boyfriends in quick succession. They drank a lot, they went places, they spent a lot of money. Both of them were doctors who were also divorced. They were interesting and attractive men, but they left her feeling used and empty and rotten.

During a particularly bad time after it was over with these two men, a friend told her about a woman she should see. This woman was a counselor who had all the right degrees, but she was also something of a psychic.

The woman looked at Cynthia closely. Every time she talked to her, she stared into her eyes, and later, after a few visits, when their time together was coming to an end, she told Cynthia that she, Cynthia, had one eye that was slightly larger than the other, and that people who had eyes with this characteristic were seekers of the truth, and she told her to look for something that was to come in her life that would be more real and truthful than what she had been involved with.

Cynthia waited a couple of months, then, with no boyfriend, and then hit on the idea of redoing parts of the house and selling it, and she called Richard and when he walked in the door, pow, she was just knocked over, completely and totally knocked over. She realized what she'd been waiting for then, and why she had decided to remodel the house and sell it. It had been to find him in her life once again.

Now she was wild with expectation, but at the same time she was sorry for what she knew Caroline must be going through if Richard had told her about them this weekend the way he was supposed to and had promised to.

'I couldn't do it,' Richard said after he came in and Cynthia had asked, not hugging him or touching him but just standing back across the room asking.

'But why?'

'Because she's lost her mind, that's why. I mean, she must know, even though I've never said a word to her, what's getting ready to happen and she just lost it this weekend and I couldn't tell her. I just couldn't.'

'What did she do?'

'She went out in front of a couple of thousand people and jumped in a two-hundred-foot-long pit of mud and tried to swim across it, for one thing.'

'I don't get it,' Cynthia said.

'It was at the mud-bog I told you about.'

'Oh yes.'

'They had this, oh hell, it doesn't matter. Just leave it that she volunteered for this stupid thing and made a fool of herself and, other than that, she just kind of talked nonstop all weekend, telling me stories and this and that and asking me if I remembered all kinds of things about us, and all that kind of stuff.'

'Did she ask about me?'

'Sort of. Every now and again. I just ignored it.'

'I'm so worn out with waiting and sneaking around,' she said. 'I want everyone to know about us.'

'We just have to wait.'

'I don't want to wait much longer.'

'What do you want me to do?'

'I want you to tell her.'

'It's not that simple.'

'I know it's not that simple. I've been through it myself, remember?'

'Yeah, but you just told him you wanted him to leave. And he's not Caroline. Not by a long shot.'

'Well, if you're scared of her,' she said, 'please forgive me for asking.'

'Come on, now. Let's just slow down for a few days.'

'I guess that's all we can do.'

'Let me get the cabinets in and everything finished up over here, at least.'

'And then I can sell it. I hate this place. I just want to go off with you and live in a nice simple little house and forget all of this.'

'I don't have a penny to my name,' he said.

'Would you quit bringing that up? You know anything I have is yours. I couldn't care less about all this money. It makes me nervous. That's all it does. You can have it all.'

'I don't want it.'

'I love you, Richard Miller,' she said, 'because I believe you really don't give any more of a damn about it than I do.'

She was truly crazy about him. She had changed her entire wardrobe in his honor. That morning she was wearing a cowgirl-styled blouse and a long, fringed skirt and suede boots with flat heels. She was tall and still looked good and thought she must have held up about as well as any woman thirty-nine years old.

'I've got to get to work,' he said and gave her a friendly shake.

'And I've got to get to town. What do you want me to bring back for lunch?'

'You know I've brought my lunch. I can't very well walk out of the house without it.'

'I know, but we can give it to the birds. Let me bring us something like, let me see, some smoked bluefish. How's that sound?'

'It'd be all right.'

'Or a pizza? Would you like that better?'

'It doesn't matter.'

'Well, I'm going then,' she said.

'All right.'

'Aren't you going to hug me, at least?' she asked and pouted her lips at him.

He was driving her mad because he wouldn't sleep with her until he was gone from Caroline. She admired the hell out of him for it, but at the same time it was driving her bananas and a good strong hug and a kiss made her weak all over, as if her legs didn't have any muscles.

'Oh me, oh my,' she said after he let her go. 'How much longer can I make it like this?'

'You're all right,' he said.

'I'm all right,' she said. 'I'll just keep telling myself that. I just will,' she said, walking out the door. 'I'll just keep trying to remember that.'

By the time she got back, all the overhead cabinets were down and Richard had carried them out to the horse barn.

'This place looks weird,' she said, walking into the empty room. 'I never knew the kitchen was so big.'

'It won't be when the new ones go back. It'll be the way it was.'

'That's all right. Someone else can have it.'

She spread a red cotton cloth across an old pine table in the dining room next to the window and set the places for them, and took out the fish and a container of German coleslaw and two hard rolls.

'What is German coleslaw?' he asked.

'I don't know, but it looked good.'

They ate and then sat together in the middle of the couch with their feet on the coffee table.

'My breath smells,' she said.

'I can't smell it.'

'Let me brush my teeth.'

'Just be still, will you.'

'All right,' she said and curled up against him. 'I'll do anything you say.'

'Your children are going to be mad at you, selling their home.'

'Well, they'll have to accept it.'

'Why don't you ask Clark if he wants to buy it back?'

'You've got to be kidding.'

'It makes sense he might,' he said.

'I guess it does, in a way. He loved the place more than I did.'

'Well.'

'Maybe I'll tell him about it just before I list it.'

They kissed and rolled around on each other and swooned away the time like teenagers making out after school.

'I've got to stop,' he said.

'Why?'

'I just do. I've got to get back to work.'

'All right, but one more thing. Are you going to try to tell her again tonight?'

'I will try. I promise you that. I will try.'

'If you do tell her, call me or come right over. You've got to, okay. I know she's really messed up and I feel so sorry for her, but you've got to look out for yourself.'

'I know,' he said.

'If what you say is true about her, you can't spend the rest of your life like that.'

'I know.'

'It's not fair for a woman to say I'm crazy and it's up to you to keep me going. It's just not fair. She's got to solve her own problems.'

'Okay.'

'Not facing up to things just makes it worse when you finally do.'

'All right,' he said.

'I don't want to see her hurt, but I want you to have the kind of life you deserve. I really do, baby. And I want to give it to you.'

'I like the sound of that,' he said.

'I wonder what we ought to do after I sell the place.'

'I don't know.'

'We could do anything. We could go anywhere. We don't have to stay around here. We could live anywhere we wanted.'

'Well, I've got my business, you know.'

'I know you do, but if there was some really wonderful place to live, couldn't we go there? If we found some really wonderful place. Couldn't we?'

'I guess, but where?'

'I don't know. I'm just dreaming.'

'Well, let me get to it, then,' he said and went back to work.

Chapter 5

That evening when Richard got home he still had his lunch in the truck. He parked at the shop and threw the sandwiches into the woods. He came in with the empty bag.

'What'd you bring the bag home for?' she asked. 'You never bring the bag home.'

'I just did.'

'I wonder what that means. Suddenly one day your husband walks in with the empty lunch bag when he's never done it before and what does it mean?'

'It doesn't mean anything,' he said.

'Okay.'

'Did you have a bad day, or what?' he asked.

'Oh no. It was really exciting.'

'Good.'

'You want to hear about it?' she asked.

'Sure.'

'You want some apple juice first?'

'That sounds just right,' he said.

'On ice?'

'If you want.'

'I love apple juice on ice. Something about making it as cold as possible makes it good. Here. Anything else?'

'Not right now.'

'Well, first off I didn't cry all day,' she said.

'That's good,' he said.

'It is good,' she said. While she talked she whirled around in front of him again and again, as if the whirls were the pauses between thoughts. She was wearing a thin cotton dress which you could nearly see through. 'It's good because that was part of my plan for the day. I was going to wake up and do something and not just sit around and worry about your being over there all day. So that's what I did.'

'Good,' he said.

'I worked in the garden while it was still cool. We'll soon have so many tomatoes I'll never get them all canned. I thought it would be too dry for them, but it seems like it's not. Anyway, after that, I got hot, so I tried to watch a little television, but there was nothing on. I mean nothing. Absolutely nothing. Then I thought, why not go see a movie and sit in the air-conditioning. You wouldn't care if I went alone, would you?'

'No.'

'I mean, I've never done it before but I thought you'd probably think it was all right but when I looked in the papers there was nothing on I wanted to see.'

She danced around a little more, and did a kind of leap across the room, like a ballet dancer.

'But then I thought, well, I'll just go to the mall and stay cool there and go shopping, so that's what I did. Only I didn't buy anything. I just couldn't make myself buy anything so I just walked around. It made me feel good to walk around for a little while and then I saw all these old people doing the same thing and that made me feel bad so I left.'

'That's quite a day, so far,' he said.

'Oh, there's more, see. Later, after I left I thought, well, I can't go home empty-handed, I've got to have something to show for the day, so I went to the smoked-fish shop and thought I'd buy us something really special for tonight. I started to buy a pound of smoked bluefish but then I remembered you don't like it so I went to the new fresh-fish market and bought us a half a pound of scallops and a half a pound of shrimp.

'And then I got some wine. I went to the store and stood in the aisle wondering, red wine with meat, white with fish, and was that the right order or not and I couldn't remember so I got us some expensive white wine and said to hell with it,' she said and showed him the bottle and whirled around again like a dancer.

'Then, after that, I rushed into the grocery store because the shrimp and scallops were sitting in the hot car and I bought some paper towels and stuff like that and loaded up the car and drove off but as I was heading out of the parking lot all these people were beeping at me and waving at me and pointing at me and guess what?'

'You'd put something on top of the car and you were driving off with it,' he said.

'That's it,' she said and climbed up on a chair and jumped off so that for a moment her dress opened up like a parachute. 'That's really it. I had put the paper towels on top and drove all the way across the lot with them there and they never even fell off.'

'That's amazing,' he said and got up to leave.

'What's amazing,' she said, 'is that that's what my life has been reduced to. Goddamnit,' she said and flopped down into the chair on the other side of the table.

Uh, oh, he thought. Here we go. He returned to his seat.

'Is it my fault that nothing ever happens to me? Is it? I mean, you live in this sort of vacuum once you get married where nothing ever happens, where the most exciting thing you can tell your husband at the end of the day is a story about paper towels on top of a car. Isn't that something? No wonder you don't love me anymore. No wonder you don't pay any attention to me. I can't blame you, I guess. What do I do? Nothing. I have nothing to offer you anymore. I'm thirty-six years old and I'm going crazy and who can blame me. Who can blame me for not knowing what to do with myself anymore? Who can blame me for still wanting children even though you're so against it, and who in the hell can blame you when I go along with it and take those pills every day as if my life depended on them when in truth,' she said and dug them out of her purse and threw them at him, 'it's your life that depends on them. Your stupid, selfish life that depends on them.'

'Are you finished?' he asked.

'No, I'm not.'

'Well just sit there for a minute and take it easy,' he said. 'Have some of this juice.'

'I don't want any.'

'Well what do you want?'

'That's just it. I don't know. I don't really want children. I mean I do, but not if you don't. Don't you understand? I like what we have. I'm not compaining about that, not really. What I can't stand is this new thing.'

'What new thing.'

'This new thing, this new way you live with me, like you're living with me because you don't know what else to do. You know what that makes me feel like. Do you?'

'Just cool off,' he said.

'Don't tell me to cool off. Don't tell me anything when it doesn't matter to you what I do as long as I don't give you a hard time. All that yesterday. Everything I tried to tell you and it hasn't made a bit of difference. I mean, for you to sit there and tell me to cool it.'

'I didn't say cool it. I said cool off.'

'I don't give a hoot which one it was. I'm trying to tell you that living like this is killing me. It's making me crazy.'

'Is that what's doing it?'

'Oh, you want to fight, do you?' she said and stood up.

'No. I don't want to fight, Caroline. Sit back down.'

'I will not.'

'What do you want me to do?'

'What do I want you to do? You really want to know? I'll tell you. Just look me in the eye and tell me one thing. Just do it. Tell me whether you and Cynthia have made love. Tell me. Go on.'

'The answer is no.'

'You swear?'

'I swear.'

'I believe you,' she said quietly, and for a moment Richard thought it was over until she turned around and screamed at him, *'THEN WHY DON'T YOU MAKE LOVE WITH ME?'*

'What?' he asked.

'Do you know how long it's been? Do you know?'

He shook his head.

'It's been a month. The last time was just after I started my period and now it's over again and you haven't touched me. I'm going nuts. You want me to play with myself or what? Is that what you want? That's all that's left except to find a boyfriend and I don't want to do that. I only want you. Don't you know that? Can't you see it? Do something, for God's sake. Don't just sit there. Do something.'

'Like what?' he asked, trying to be as still as he could until she was finished.

'Like come over here and kiss me.'

He stayed where he was.

'You can't move? What's wrong? Don't you remember what it's like. Don't you remember how? Do I have to show you? Is that what you want? I guess it is,' she said and pulled up her dress. 'Do you see that?' she asked. *'NO UNDERWEAR,'* she screamed. *'NO PANTIES,'* she screamed at him and he looked out the window to check if anyone could see in. 'I don't care who sees me. I'll run around the yard like this if I have to. Is that what you want?'

'Just put down your dress and relax, okay?'

'I'm not going to. If you're not going to make love to me, I'm going to go in the bedroom and make love to myself. You hear me? You think I go around every day without panties? I don't, you fool. I did it for you. You were supposed to notice. You were supposed to come in and hug me and feel me and notice. Oh hell, I give up,' she said. 'I can't compete. You must be doing something with her. You must.

'Oh, I know what a lady she is. I know all that. I know how proper and composed she is. Cynthia would never act like this. She would never run around the kitchen screaming and yelling at her husband because she has probably never lost her temper in her life because she's so damn perfect she wouldn't have had to. She's one of those women who knows how to get men to do what she wants without ever raising her voice. She probably cries a lot, though. Does she cry for you? Does she cry and pout and weep for you?' she asked.

'I don't know,' he said.

'You don't know. You don't know anything. You think I didn't see you throw your lunch in the woods? You think I didn't see that? You think I'm so dense I don't know that means you and she had lunch together? Good gracious, how stupid must you think I am? Really.

'Can she even cook? I doubt it. I bet she bought a bunch of stuff and brought it home. Didn't she? Answer me. Is that what she did? You don't have to answer me, then. I know it is. You're done for, you know that. If you fall for her, you're a dead man. I swear you are. You won't last a week. How are you going to support her? You think you can bring in the kind of money she needs? Just think about it for a minute. Like you're always telling me. Think about it. If you imagine she's going to support you, forget it. *FORGET IT,'* she screamed. *'DON'T JUST SIT THERE LOOKING AT ME LIKE THAT. I KNOW WHAT I'M TALKING ABOUT.'*

'No you don't.'

'Don't get me madder than I already am. I'm going to throw this bowl of shrimp all the way across this room into the wall. I am going to be forced to do that.'

'Go ahead.'

'No,' she said. 'I won't. Nope. There must be some other way to make you see what's going on. There's another way to get out of this.'

She opened the screen door to let more of a breeze in the house. After a few moments, the flies discovered the door was open and started buzzing in.

'Are you finished now?' he asked.

'Why?'

'Because I want to take a bath.'

'Go ahead,' she said.

'Thank you,' he said.

After she had killed all the flies she could find, she walked around the room using the flyswatter like a swagger stick, swinging it back and forth and popping it in the air while she talked to herself.

'I've got it,' she said when Richard walked past the doorway on his way to the bedroom.

'What?'

'I'm going to work with you tomorrow.'

'No you're not.'

'Yes I am. I'm going to work with you every day until you're finished. I don't know why I didn't think of this earlier. It's got to be the best idea I've had in weeks,' she said. 'It really does.'

She laughed and skipped around the room while Richard stared into the closet, not trying to decide what to wear to look his best but more like trying to decide what a person wore to his own funeral. It mattered what you wore on your last day on earth, just like it mattered whether you had on clean underwear when the ambulance took you to the emergency room and the nurses peeled off your clothes. You wanted to look as good as you could, no matter whether your life ended alone and quietly and peacefully or torn in half by two beautiful women.

Chapter 6

Caroline woke up early. Richard was still asleep. She slid over against him. He hugged her and began to wake up.

'I did it again, didn't I?'

'It's all right,' he said.

'I'm sorry.'

'Don't worry about it.'

'You slept like a log,' she said.

'I was tired.'

'Me, too. Don't get up yet. This is such a nice time to be together.'

'All right.'

'Kiss me. Just a little one, okay,' she said.

'Like that?' he asked.

'Just like that,' she said. 'See?'

'See what?'

'If you didn't love me, you couldn't kiss me like that.'

'I guess.'

'I'm nervous,' she said.

'You don't have to go.'

'Yes I do. But I'm still nervous. But I'm going. Even if I am. Because it's the right thing to do, and when you know you're doing the right thing, you can do anything.'

They got up. She made breakfast and they ate and then she leaned against the warm oven where she had baked the biscuits.

'Of course, I was just thinking, knowing you're right doesn't make it any easier.'

'Nope,' he said.

'I mean, if we had slept all night and I had gotten up this morning and you hadn't kissed me like that and done what you did in the middle of the night, I might not be so sure.'

'What are you talking about?' he asked. 'I didn't do anything in the middle of the night.'

'Yes you did.'

'What?'

'You rolled over and held me. You haven't done that in a long time. A very long time. You used to do it a lot. I guess it's one of the things that makes sleeping in the same bed so nice. It's no wonder my parents fought all the time and hated each other so much. They never touched except when Daddy got drunk and they fought.'

'As far as you know,' he said and rinsed off his plate and set it in the sink.

'Right. I didn't mean to get into that, though. When you held me last night I was thinking how nice it was and I got to thinking about things that happen in the middle of the night when you are asleep and you've let go and there's nothing in the way of things flowing on out if they want to and I remembered then that time you had the dream about the green thing.'

'Oh yes,' he said.

'You woke up that night and screamed *"WHAT'S THAT?"* and I sat up and looked around and said what?, and you said that green thing and I said what green thing, and you said that green thing right there and then you came out of it and we laughed and went back to sleep and I thought, isn't that nice. Isn't that just about the sweetest thing, to have each other in the night when something like that happened, or when, like, I don't know, the other person comes loose from something and needs to hold on to you. I thought, isn't that just one of those unspoken and quiet and unknown moments that make life rich and full, in a private way, you know what I mean?'

'Sort of,' he said.

'But you see, that's why last night I knew something had broken loose and that this way we've been with each other, just prancing around each other all over the house and never looking up, walking by each other like strangers, that's why I thought as you lay so quietly against me that it was over.'

'We've got to get going,' he said.

'I'm sorry for yesterday. I just had this plan in my mind, about, you know, how things would be when you got home, and when it didn't happen, I got messed up. I'll make it up to you today, though. I really will.'

'All right,' he said.

'I'm ready, then.'

'Let's go,' he said and they walked out. The shop was behind the house and right up against the woods. It had been sided with rough-cut pine boards and the boards had been left natural. In just the right light, toward the end of the day, or early in the morning, the shop blended into the woods and was nearly invisible.

On the side of the shop were two big doors. Caroline opened those doors and Richard backed up the truck. They carried the base cabinets onto the truck bed. The base cabinets were in sections but were still heavy, and for some of the sections it was all the two of them could do to slide them along and into place. Once they were all loaded, they tied them down.

'I fogot to make us lunch,' she said and they started out the drive. 'Back up.'

'We can get something somewhere,' he said. 'Let's just go on.'

'Not a chance. Even if she wants to, that woman is not going to make lunch for me. Not now. Not anymore. Maybe at one time it would've been okay, but not now. Go on and back up.'

A little later Cynthia saw the truck turn into her driveway. She saw someone with Richard but could not tell who it was until he backed up to the front porch, which was about the same height as the bed of the truck, and Caroline got out to help unload.

'Oh,' Cynthia said.

'Oh is right,' Caroline said.

'I didn't . . . ' Cynthia said.

'I bet you didn't,' she said.

'Good morning,' Richard said.

'What do we do first?' Caroline asked.

'Unload everything, I guess,' he said.

'Are you going to be helping today?' Cynthia asked, holding on to the porch post so she wouldn't keel over right then and there.

'Today. Tomorrow. Every day until we've finished,' Caroline said and laughed.

Cynthia still had on her robe and Caroline had on her jeans and old tan work shirt and hiking boots. Cynthia was also barefoot.

'Look out,' Caroline said. 'I don't want to drop anything on your foot,' she said as she grabbed one end of the unit and started out with it.

Cynthia went upstairs and locked the door. She sat on the bed. She put her hands lightly over her face and made a dark and quiet place for herself and she breathed deeply. Then she got dressed.

Caroline grabbed the next unit and carried her end of it with one hand. It wobbled back and forth.

'Just use two hands, Caroline,' he said. 'Don't try to be Superman.'

'How about Supergirl,' she said.

'Look,' he said as they set it in the kitchen. 'You're up, you're down. Yesterday we've got this jumping around screaming and crying . . .'

'I didn't cry.'

'Today we've got Supergirl. How about just staying somewhere in the middle.'

'All right. I'll be good. I just feel great, that's all. What do you want me to do next?'

Cynthia came into the room. She was wearing pants, cowgirl boots and a blue-jean jacket.

'Going out on the range?' Caroline asked.

'I thought I could help, too,' she said.

'I don't think so,' Richard said.

'Well, I could,' she said.

'No. It won't work. Be too many people.'

'Let her,' Caroline said.

'Nope. It just won't work.'

'Then can I see you a minute?' Cynthia asked.

'I've got to use the bathroom, anyway,' Caroline said.

She went in the guest bathroom, turned on the rattling overhead fan, picked up a magazine and started reading, while Cynthia led Richard into the study.

'What is going on?' she asked.

'I wish I knew.'

'Why is she here?'

'She had a fit last night and announced she was coming to work with me.'

'Did you tell her?'

'No.'

'And you let her come.'

'I couldn't stop her.'

'I don't want her in my house.'

'Well, you tell her, then.'

'It's not right that she's here. It just isn't.'

'Tell her.'

'She can't come in my house without asking me. She can't. It's my house.'

'Well,' he said.

'The best thing to do is tell her about us. Now.'

'I don't think that's a good idea,' he said. 'It'd be worse today than yesterday.'

'You won't help me do it then?'

'No way.'

'Then I'll do it by myself.'

'Don't do that.'

'Either you tell her tonight or I'm going to tell her now.'

'I'll do it tonight.'

'You promise.'

'I promise.'

'You've promised before.'

'I'll do it. Just don't start anything.'

'I won't. I wouldn't have, anyway. I'm scared of her. Something about her scares me.'

'I know what you mean.'

'I don't want any trouble. I don't.'
'Neither do I.'
'I'll leave it up to you.'
'I'll do it.'
'I know you will.'
'I'll do it tonight.'
'I just got worried for a minute. My heart sank when I saw her get out of the truck. I didn't know what had happened. I thought you told her last night and she had won you over and I'd lost you. I thought, I've lost him forever now.'
'No way,' he said.
'I'm just so scared sometimes.'
'It'll be over soon.'
'Sometimes I think I've made such a mess of things and then I think of you and how right things will be when we're together and then I know it's worth waiting for.'
'I'm trying.'
'I've been living the wrong way for so long. I never wanted to live like this,' she said and surveyed the room with a sweep of her hand.
'You've been doing all right,' he said.
'Kiss me,' she said.
'Now?' he asked and looked down the hall.
'Please.'
Caroline came out. 'You guys still having a conference,' she called.
'Just about finished,' he said.
Caroline went into the kitchen.
'One more thing,' Cynthia said.
'What is it?'
'I had a dream last night that you made love to her. Did you? Tell me the truth.'
'I didn't.'
'Then don't. If I can't have you, then she can't either.'
Later that morning Cynthia spoke to them for a few minutes, commented on the cabinets and so forth and then left for the day. By five o'clock they were ready to leave. They had installed all the base cabinets and had glued and

nailed the plywood on top of them and were ready to cut and stick the Formica the next day.

'We did a lot, didn't we,' Caroline said.

'We sure did.'

'You sure were quiet, though.'

'I never talk when I'm working.'

'I know.'

'How do you know?' he asked.

'Because I've been married to you for fourteen years, you dope.'

'Yeah.'

'Don't you think I know everything about you?'

'Maybe.'

'I feel great, anyway.'

'That's good.'

'The time just flew. I think this is one of the best days I've ever had. I really do. Look how much we got done. I can't believe it. Just look at all that. No wonder you feel good every day when you come home if you get this much accomplished all the time.'

'I don't.'

'But still, at least it's there. You can see what you've done. It's not like teaching. Well, sometimes you can see, but it's slower, and then, the next year, it starts all over. Oh well, I shouldn't get off on that.'

'Nope.'

'What are you going to do tomorrow?'

'You're still planning to work tomorrow?'

'I sure am.'

'Hang the doors I guess. Glue the top, stuff like that,' he said.

'Good. Can I trim the edges?'

'No, you better not. It's easy to make a mistake on that.'

'I want to use the router, though. I love the way it sounds. It spins so fast.'

'Yeah, kind of like you,' he said.

'That's right. Like me,' she said and spun around and around and whistled. 'Just like me.'

*

She took the shrimps and scallops out of the refrigerator. 'I think they're still good,' she said. 'Let's have them now.'

'All right.'

'You want them fried or sautéed?' she asked.

'You fry the scallops and I'll sauté the shrimp,' he said.

They worked side by side. Being with him all day and having him cooking beside her excited her. She put her arm around his waist.

'See how much I can do for you if you'll just let me,' she said. 'See how good we are together.'

'I appreciate it,' he said.

'If I quit my job I could cash in my state retirement money and we could use that if things got bad,' she said.

'Got bad how?'

'I mean if we went into business together and things were a little rough while we were building it up,' she said. 'That way we could take our time and not have to worry about money for a while.'

'It won't work.'

'It might.'

'Forget it.'

'But see, I've been thinking about it all day long. We can ride to work in one car. I mean truck. Some days we don't even go anywhere because we just work in the shop. We can save money on gas right there. We don't even need my car, really, and then we can save on gas, insurance, repairs, and all that.'

'Caroline,' he said.

'No, listen to me. See, on some days you can stay in the shop and build the cabinets while I go out and measure and talk to the people and all that. That's the part you said you liked the least, anyway. That's what you told me. You always said you'd rather build them and let someone else do the rest of it. It'd be just right for us. It'd be perfect. All the money stays home. Can't you see what a great idea this is?

'It's amazing, isn't it. Out of all this worrying and the rest of it I come up with something like this. That's the way it is.

That's the way it always is. You never know. You just got to be open to the possibilities. That's what people are always saying and there I was acting like such a dope, and then, one day, wham-o, it happens and everything turns around and boom, like that, a whole new thing starts and all I had to do to see it was just see it. Because, there it was. All along, right there in front of me.

'I know, I know, you've got that look on your face but it's not what you think, not entirely, or not exactly, anyway, because what you're thinking is that Caroline's so jealous she wants to tie me up day and night, but that's not so, not really.

'Don't start cooking yet. Let me finish. See, I am the jealous type, but this thing is so much more. It gets me out of teaching. It helps you out of all the things you don't like doing. I get to do them and you get to do the things you like. It's the way we started out, don't you see. It's just so great. At least talk to me about it. At least consider it. Give it a chance, at least do that. We've got all summer. We've got the whole summer to try it out.'

'It would never work,' he said.

'Oh you,' she said and turned away. 'You're going to make me cry again. You're not even willing to think about it?' she asked and turned around again.

'It's just too late.'

'What do you mean, it's too late?'

'It just is.'

'But what does that mean, it's too late.'

'It means it's too late.'

'For what?'

'Listen, Caroline,' he said. 'Just sit down a minute.'

'No.'

'I've got to tell you something you're not going to want to hear.'

'Oh no you don't, either.'

'I do.'

'You do?' she asked, kind of bewildered.

'Yes.'

'How bad is it?'

'It depends. I mean, you know.'

'I can't hear anything bad today. I just can't. I won't have it. Not after the kind of day we've had. I don't want anything bad today at all.'

'Just hold it,' he said.

'Listen, if that idea about working together doesn't interest you, then okay, it doesn't, even though I think it would be great. We could do other things. We could go back to the way we wanted to live originally, and do a little farming, get a few hogs and chickens, didn't you love them, they were so much fun, except killing them. Good God,' she said and covered her eyes in a dramatic way, 'do you remember when Edgar shot that pig thirteen times and it still didn't die? That was the worst thing I ever saw. I heard that pig screaming and saw the look in that pig's eyes for years after that, I swear I did.'

'You might as well stop,' he said.

'I can't,' she said. 'Everything's been so wonderful,' she said and began to cry and rushed over to the sink and washed her face and dried it on the dishcloth. 'I'm not going to cry. I know you hate it. I'm not going to. Whatever you're trying to say can wait. Or doesn't have to be said at all. Sometimes if you just wait, things pass and you find out you'd have been wrong if you'd done what you were planning to. You know that. I know you do.

'And we've had such a great day. I feel so good, just so absolutely good for the first time in weeks. Or months. I don't even know. I'm just all shook loose. My whole body feels good. It's kind of tingling. Don't you know? Can't you tell? Come over and feel it. Come on. Hold me a minute,' she said and she swayed in his arms and then pulled away from him, still swaying back and forth and said, 'Dance with me, baby.'

'Dance with you?'

'Sure. That's exactly what I need right now. Let's do it. Why not? We used to dance together all the time. Do you know how long it's been since we've done that? A long time. A long, long time. I love to dance. It's just one of the sweetest things in the world and God knows Caroline needs something sweet about now. She does. You used to be so good at it. You were the loosest person on the floor. You always were. Let me put on some music and we'll just dance away the night. Let's do that. Let's really do that.

'What do you want to hear? I know. You don't care. I know what you like, anyway. Just stand there and I'll surprise you. There. Don't you love that? Do you remember it? We haven't played that record in a long time. Why haven't we? I wonder about things like that, how things you love to do just sort of disappear from your life, you know, like dancing, I mean, and other things we used to do so much.

'That music is so sweet, just so wonderfully sweet. It really is. Her voice just kills me. I just love it. Come on, baby. Dance me. Hold on to me. Come on. That's right. Don't act like you're scared to touch me. Don't be so stupid. Hold me like you used to. Oh God, it feels good. That music. I swear her voice just goes right through me. It just does. It just makes me want to melt away.

'Move that chair out of the way. Don't let go of me. Just push it back with your foot. There. Kiss me now, baby. Just kiss me and take me away and don't say a word. Don't tell me a thing. Not anything at all. Just take me far away. So far away I'll never have to come back. And hold me tight. Tighter. Just squeeze me until I disappear. Just do it. That's it. That's so good. Oh baby, how I've missed you. How much you just don't know. I get so crazy when I think I'm going to lose you and even though I know those kind of things are not the end of the world, I still get so scared. I've been so lonely. It's like you've been gone away from me even though you've been here all along. You don't know what lonely is like. You don't get that way. It's like being dead or being killed. It really is. It's like I'm dying and can't do anything about it.

'It doesn't matter now, though. What a day. There's just so much going on. How can so much be happening in a person's life. I can't believe it. I want to tell you so much. I just have to. You don't seem to know me. Not like you should. After all these years and you still don't. How can that be?

'I've got to slow down, don't I? Just take me to bed, okay? Just carry me in. I'm yours, you know. That's all I really wanted to say. That's what it's all about. Lie down here beside me.

'I love the night. Talk to me. Tell me things. We'll just stay like this forever, and when we've said all there is to say we'll make a pact that no one will ever know about and we won't have to talk anymore after that, not a word. We'll just sail along, like in the song. We will, my darling husband of all these years, we will,' she said and stroked his face while he pulled her close and when he did, she fell asleep.

For a few hours they both lay in a timeless and exhausted suspension while across the county Cynthia roamed around in her empty house, waiting for the phone call, the lights coming down the driveway, a sign, any sign at all.

Three people suspended in a haze of desperation and tied together forever now by the bloodless coup of the mistaken dream. Who could know, who could ever have guessed that long ago this handsome man and these two gorgeous women in love with life itself would later find themselves stuck in the time warp of the broken life, would later find themselves having to step over the friends and partners they had so sadly discarded along the way?

Who could ever know that such a thing would come out of nowhere like it did, digging itself out of the dirt like locusts coming out of the ground? All the time they were there, hiding until it was time, and then one morning, all that noise and those weird hollow skeletons littering the ground, such a well-kept life until that time. Who could know?

Caroline slept. It would have been difficult to wake her. She was so lost. She had gone so far. She had tried so hard. Nothing had come easy for her. Ever. Glassy-eyed, she slept. Deaf, dumb, and blind, she slept. Boneless and limp.

A little filet of tenderness. A sweetheart of distant dreams. Armless in the empty-arms hotel.

While she slept, Richard stared at the wall in front of him. His mind was blank. Nothing moved on the circuits. He just stared ahead like the picture of a shell-shocked soldier who had wandered into battle thinking he might just do whatever it was he had to do, have a little fun on the side, and then get out, but fourteen years later he was still there.

It didn't have to be this way. Somewhere, it was better. Somewhere, it was true, life was rich and flowed easily and graciously, but not for Caroline. Punch-drunk from too many fights, knocked out too many times by the disappointment of people who moved like crabs with eyes popped out on the stems of jealousy and deceit, Caroline tumbled and fell. In the last minutes of her sleep, she grabbed Richard and held on for a time and then awoke.

'I'm awake,' she said, as if surprised herself.

'I know you are,' he said.

'How long have I been asleep?'

'A couple of hours.'

'It's almost dark,' she said.

'Yep.'

'I don't remember anything.'

'We were dancing.'

'Oh yes. Right. It's coming back now.'

'You want to get up?'

'In a minute,' she said.

'My arm's gone dead.'

'I'm sorry,' she said and moved. 'Is that better?'

'It will be in a minute.'

'I remember now. I fell asleep like a kitten. Boom. I was gone. And then I don't remember anything until just before I woke up. Was I tossing around.'

'A little.'

'I thought I would have been. I had that where-am-I feeling, you know, like when you're driving along and you suddenly snap out of it and don't know where you are?'

'Yes.'

'That's the way it was just before I woke up.'

'Uh huh.'

'Did we eat supper?'

'Nope.'

'Everything's still out, then. I bet the stuff is bad by now. I guess that meal just wasn't meant to be.'

'It might be okay.'

'I doubt it. We can try it, if you want. I bet it's bad, though. I think it might have been old when I bought it, and in hot weather like this you really got to be careful.'

'Let me go to the bathroom,' he said.

'Sure,' she said, 'and when you come back, let's just forget the shrimp and go out to eat.'

'We can't do that,' he said.

'Why not?'

'Because when I get back—' he said.

'What?'

'We have to talk.'

'Oh come on,' she said. 'We don't.'

'We do.'

'But haven't I talked enough for both of us?'

'It's just got to be,' he said. 'It just does.'

Nothing has to be, she thought. Nothing like whatever it is he thinks he has to say. A person did not just have to sit in a chair and let someone calmly approach her and tell her that everything she had ever thought about life was wrong. That didn't make sense, especially when you knew you were right, she thought.

As she wondered what to do, it came to her that if she was not there when he came out, then, quite simply, there could be no talk, and with that, she left the room, went through the dark kitchen and out the back door.

'Where are you,' he called when he came back. 'Are you out there?' he called and went out on the porch. She was there but he couldn't see her. She was standing far out in the yard in the dark. She could see him, though.

'Caroline,' he called and went back inside. He searched every room and she watched him as the lights went on in the rooms, one by one, and he appeared for a moment, passing the window of each room and then out again. She followed him around the house, watching him, but staying in the dark and out of sight.

He went out the back door, and she moved along the edge of the woods and followed him. He turned on the lights in the shop. He walked around it and looked in the truck and under the truck and then started back for the house, leaving all the lights on. She positioned herself halfway between the house and the shop and backed slowly and quietly into the woods and watched.

Halfway to the house he stopped and looked toward the woods and right at her with such an uncanny precision that she got chills up and down her spine. He said, 'Caroline, if you're out there, don't do anything rash. You hear me?' he said and stood for a moment, listening, and then went back inside.

The poor boy thinks I'm going to kill myself, she thought.

A few minutes later he returned with the spotlight that had the heavy six-volt battery attached under it. He shone it around the yard and into the woods.

'Caroline,' he called again.

His voice sounded strange and as she watched him she began to feel sad and the longer she watched him the sadder she felt, and the longer she watched the more unreal it all became, as if she were dead, as if she had died and this was what death was really like. She was still there, yet he couldn't see her. She could see this man, this husband and friend for so many years, but she could not get to him. She could only watch. It was as if he was the lost one, and she could not help him. It was a strange moment for Caroline as she hid behind the tree.

She did not move until he had started into the woods across the clearing and had begun making a circle coming toward her. Then she quietly walked along the edge around to the front of the house and went inside. She sat in a chair and waited. Fifteen minutes later Richard came in and actually jerked back when he saw her.

'Hi,' she said.
'Caroline,' he said, 'you scared the hell out of me.'
'I'm sorry.'
'Where have you been?'
'I was out in the woods.'
He put the flashlight down and sat across the room.
'Babe,' he said, 'I'm worn out. I can't take much more of this.'
'I know,' she said.
'I don't want to hurt you, but I just can't keep it going anymore.'
'Am I that bad?' she asked.
'Don't ask something like that.'
'Well, am I?'
'It's just everything, okay?'
'Okay,' she said. 'I understand.'
'You do?'
'It's been such a strange night,' she said. 'I think I can understand anything right now. Being out there in the woods and watching you gave me the strangest feeling. I was so far away from you. It was just,' she said and tried to make a joke, 'like they say in California, like totally unreal.'
He nodded.
'I mean, there you were, and there was our house and everything and I could see it all, but I was gone, you understand. Just gone.'
She looked over at him and he nodded again.
'Gone,' she said again and then lay on her back on the floor and closed her eyes. 'I'm ready now,' she said.
'For what?'
'I'm ready to die. Go on and tell me what you've been trying to say all night.'
'Caroline,' he said and tried to pull her up. 'Just be normal. For the next few minutes, anyway.'
'I can't. I can't be normal. I never will be able to. Go on and tell me,' she said and crossed her arms over her chest in an X like a corpse and got absolutely still.

'All right. Have it your way. It doesn't matter to me. I've been through everything with you. This is nothing.'

'Go on,' she said.

'Well,' he said, 'I guess as things have turned out Cynthia tells me she loves me and wants me to live with her.'

'Oh really,' she said.

'Yes.'

'And?' she asked, helping him along.

'And I guess that's all.'

'It is?'

'I mean, I guess there's more but there's no need to say it all now.'

She kept her eyes closed and remained still but nodded enough for him to see it.

'I'm sorry,' he said.

'It's all right.'

'Is that all you're going to say?'

'That's all I can say,' she said.

'You don't care, then? I can leave.'

'Would you stay if I said no?'

'I suppose not.'

'Then I won't say anything. Don't make me talk.'

'Have it your way, Caroline,' he said. 'I don't know what to do with you anymore.'

She nodded.

'I'm just going to get a few things and go on,' he said and went into the bedroom while she stayed where she was and listened. A few minutes later he came back and stopped in the doorway.

'Are you going to be okay?'

'Don't ask me that,' she said. 'Don't ask me anything.'

'You want me to leave?'

'Is that what you want?'

'I guess I better.'

'Then do it,' she said.

She heard him go out the door. She listened for the truck. She listened for what seemed like an unusually long time for him to get from the house to the truck but nothing happened. She never heard it start. Then she heard the door open and close again.

He's coming back, she thought.

'I forgot my keys,' he said. 'And my wallet.'

'Your keys and your wallet,' she said quietly as he walked by. 'Oh.'

'I guess I'll be going then,' he said on the way out again.

'Bye.'

'I will have to come back and get the other stuff later,' he said. 'And I'll have to use the shop, you know, for a while, until things get worked out.'

'Of course.'

'I'll call tomorrow.'

'You don't have to.'

'I will,' he said and left.

Chapter 7

People become fixated. They become obsessed with things. It's hard to figure out. Some people were just that way. No one could explain it. Some of the best-looking women ended up with these guys you wouldn't have thought they'd look at twice. You saw it and it made you think. You had to know something was wrong somewhere. But there they were. You couldn't drive them away.

I'll die for you. I've waited my whole life for you. Nothing that ever happened before I met you meant anything. I'm yours and you're mine. Cut off my legs if you have to. Cut off my arms. Do anything but don't leave me.

It was a hard thing to resist. Mostly, though, by the time you figured out what was going on, it was too late. Do this to me, they'd say. Do that. Oh. Oh my. And then you were done for.

The theory of relativity was nothing compared to figuring out these situations. Who could do it? Average Joe on the street? Forget it. Good-hearted and decent men ended up with women just three days out of the asylum. It was hard to know.

Einstein would have pulled out the rest of his hair if he'd had Caroline in the back of the house instead of Greta or whoever he had back there cooking and cleaning and picking up his underwear and cleaning out the tub. If it'd been Caroline, his work would have been on the theory of screaming and crying.

You couldn't tell. They looked so good. Everything always seemed so right. For a moment, there, it was. A little later, though, here came the garbage truck. What? I thought, I mean where'd that come from? All of a sudden the garbage of her life was dumped all over you. Relatives, ex-lovers, neuroses so big they walked around the house like monsters. Cold-as-death looks and screaming fits with cans of baked beans slung across the room. The garbage truck had arrived and you were there. It was hard, then, to get away, but it felt good when you did.

'I never thought I'd make it,' Richard said.

It was the next morning. They were just getting around to talking about it. The night before, they'd spent the whole time demolishing the bed upstairs.

'But you did,' she said.

'It's been hell,' he said.

'But it's over.'

'Almost,' he said. 'Not quite.'

'But soon,' she said.

'You can't imagine what it's been like,' he said.

'Tell me about it.'

'I don't know if I can.'

'But I want you to tell me everything,' she said. 'It will help you if you can tell me about it.'

'I know it will,' he said, 'but I don't think I can. I mean, how do you explain what it was like to be married to Rootie Kazootie? I mean, answer me that.'

'Is that what it was like?' she asked.

'That and more. I swear,' he said, 'I really don't want to get into it now. Or maybe ever. I'm just glad it's over.'

'I know. You don't have to say any more. I've been through it myself, remember.'

'Not like this.'

'Probably not.'

'Let's talk about something else,' he said and wandered into the kitchen. 'Like this mess in here.'

'All right.'

'You know, to finish this off, I've got to go back over there pretty soon and get everything.'

'We should have thought of that before.'

'But we didn't.'

'Isn't there enough to do today without going back?'

'I could finish gluing down the tops,' he said.

'Can I help you?'

'Sure.'

'Then let's do that,' she said, 'and go over there some other day.'

That morning Caroline was thinking of everything that had occurred the night before. She walked around the house talking to herself, trying to remember it and understand it.

Now see, she told herself as she wandered around, if he'd said I love Cynthia and I want to live with her, that'd be one thing. But that's not what he said. He told me Cynthia loves him and wants him to move in with her. That's something altogether different. It doesn't really make any sense, but it certainly isn't as bad as the first.

She took a bath. She filled the tub as deep as she could and lay all the way in the water with her feet on the wall above the faucets.

Of course, it could be worse. What does that mean when you hear, Cynthia tells me. Does that mean a person has to do whatever Cynthia says. Like Cynthia says put your hand on your head. Oops, you're out, you forgot to say Cynthia says. Like that. Instead of playing dead like that I should have said, well, what do you want? Maybe I did say that? I can't remember.

She dressed and walked out on the porch. She balanced on the rail, with her feet out in front and her arms out to the side like a gymnast.

Now you see, Caroline, she went on, you weren't prepared for what you heard, even though you said you were ready. The reason you weren't is that you thought he was going to tell you he'd been having an affair with her and you had all that worked out. There she was, just so perfect for it, all hot and lonely and so, so vulnerable, and you had thought, well, so what. Everybody does it sooner or later. Most everyone, anyway. That's what people say.

That's what the magazines always say.

So you thought, well, I can live with that. If he's going to tell me about it, it must be over and done with and we can go on from there. There had to be some reason he wasn't sleeping with me. What better reason than he was sleeping with someone else.

But this is worse. Cynthia loves me and wants me to move in with her. Whoever heard of such a thing?

She wanted to go somewhere, but she didn't want to go to town and end up in a stupor at the mall, sitting on a bench staring at nothing, and so she thought she might visit Lucille, the woman whose husband had named his pet pig after her.

'Are you sure it's all right?' she asked.

'Come on now, if you want to. You know I never go anywhere,' Lucille said.

'All right.'

'Edgar will just be in and out all day, like he usually is,' she said.

Lucille and Edgar were an older couple who had been good to them when they first moved into the community. Lucille lived in the same house she'd been born in sixty years earlier, and Edgar, who had once worked for American Tobacco in Durham, was retired and more or less farmed the land they had inherited with the house.

'So how've you been?' Lucille asked.

'Just great,' Caroline said.

'Well, you're going better than me,' Lucille said. 'I guess you've heard that Edgar has taken to riding around with the pig. He told someone down at the store that he got up Sunday morning and started off to church with the pig in the car and he said it wasn't until he got all the way there that he realized he didn't have me.'

'I didn't hear that,' Caroline said.

'Oh, he's saying all kinds of things. I can't help it if I've put on a little weight. All the women in my family get fat.

That's the way we are.'

'You look fine,' Caroline said.

'You know how men are. I've been trying to civilize him for forty years now and haven't gotten anywhere.'

'Well, he loves you, anyway,' Caroline said.

'You think he does?'

'He'd have to. Else why would he have stayed with you so long.'

'Maybe so,' she said.

Just then they heard Edgar's truck coming down the drive and both of them went to the window and watched. Edgar drove past the house and right up to the gate that led into the pasture and opened the door for Lucille the pig, who stuck her snout out and sniffed around and bobbed her head up and down as if she were gauging the distance she'd have to fall to hit the ground. She slid out of the seat and followed Edgar through the gate. He locked her in and drove back to the house.

'I thought I saw your car,' he said to Caroline when he came in. 'Where's Richard?'

'He's at work.'

'Are you going to have lunch with us?' Lucille asked.

'Why do you think I came home if I didn't want lunch?' he asked her.

'Well, I just asked.'

'Where is it, anyway?'

'I'm just cooking it now.'

'Well, bring it on,' he said and sat at the table. After a few minutes, Caroline and Lucille got it all ready and carried it in. They sat down across from Edgar. He started eating right away.

'Where's the tea?' he asked with a mouthful of food.

'I forgot,' Lucille said, and jumped up to get it.

'How can you forget the tea?' he asked and looked at Caroline. 'How can she forget the tea when we've had tea at every meal for the last forty-some years,' he said and laughed. 'Isn't that something?'

Caroline nodded.

Just before the meal was finished, Edgar drank from his iced-tea glass until it was empty and then waved it in the air for Lucille to refill it. As she took it from him, he burped. This burp was not the usual kind of burp that might be admired in some cultures as a sign of recognition that the meal had been appreciated. This burp sounded like everything he had just eaten was about to reappear in distressingly altered form, and along with it a terrible and rancid odor emerged and began to drift across the table toward Caroline.

Oh my God, she thought, and had to concentrate to keep her own stomach from churning up.

'EDGAR,' Lucille yelled at him. *'PLEASE.'*

'Well, hell,' he said. 'I couldn't help it. It just came out.'

'Well leave the table, then,' she said.

'I didn't mean to do it,' he said and went to the back of the house and shut the door to his room.

Lucille got the conversation going again and kept on talking, but Caroline began to fade. She felt dizzy. It wasn't so much the smell, which drifted across the room and settled like a heavy fog. It was more like being in the presence of someone turning himself inside out in public, the wretched sight of a man and wife fumigating each other in a sadly laughable kind of intimacy.

So it really wasn't so much the smell that caused Caroline to topple over sideways out of her chair and onto the floor, where she lay momentarily stunned. It was just the thought of what happens to people who continue on when there's not much left except the legal document and the momentum of daily life.

'Caroline?' Lucille called out to her as she saw her tip over and disappear from view.

'Oh me,' she said from below the table.

'Are you all right?'

'Yes.'

'What happened?'

'I don't know,' she said, truly embarrassed. 'I think I was leaning over in the chair and leaned too far.'

'Did you hit your head?'

'No.'

'Your face is all red.'

'I'm fine. Really. I'm sorry,' she said. 'I feel so stupid.'

She set the chair back upright.

'I could've sworn you fainted,' Lucille said.

'No. I didn't faint. I've never fainted before. I just leaned over too far.'

Later Caroline drove home. It was two o'clock. It was cloudy but still hot. There would be a thunderstorm before night came. A thunderstorn and a hard rain were bad on a person when that person was alone. It wasn't the fear of the thunder or the lightning, or the rain pounding on the roof and being blown sideways against the windows, that made a person sad and weepy.

It was being alone in the empty house with the lightning popping and sparking and making the telephone ring and no one there when you picked it up and the thunder crashing and shaking your bones and no one to hold you together. A person could just come apart, just completely come apart on a night like that, unless there was someone somewhere to hold that person together.

It was hard to know whether life was better alone and shaken apart or together with someone even in the reduced circumstances of Edgar and Lucille. A woman could end up alone or she could end up with a man like Edgar.

That night, in the storm, Caroline went outside and stood in the rain.

I could die now, she thought. I was almost dead last night but I didn't quite make it. I could stand here and get struck by lightning and then everyone would feel sorry for Caroline and wonder what had happened. Why was she standing there like that?

I can't tell anyone he's left, she thought. I just can't do it.

She sat in her car, dripping wet. She left the window down so that the glass wouldn't steam up. She thought that too many things had been left unsaid and that these things needed to be said and so she thought she might just drive over to see Richard and Cynthia and catch them by surprise with a visit on this stormy night.

The more she thought about actually driving over there and confronting them, in person, the harder it seemed it would be to do, and so, instead, she worked up all her courage and called him, which, while difficult, was not nearly as difficult as trying to figure out how to make her voice sound when Cynthia herself answered the phone.

She paused for a moment while Cynthia said hello one more time, and then made her voice as close to normal as she was able.

'Could I speak to Richard please?' she asked.

She really wanted to tell Cynthia what to do with the telephone receiver, where to place it in relation to the rest of her body, and that if she weren't interested in doing it herself, that she, Caroline, would be more than happy to do for her.

Cynthia put Richard on the phone.

'What is it?' he said.

'Oh, well, I was just calling kind of to see if the phone was still working,' she said. 'The lightning almost struck it or something. It was ringing, you know, a whole bunch of times. I kept thinking it was you.'

'Yeah,' he said. 'I forgot to call.'

'There's a kind of buzz on it now. Do you hear that buzz?'

'I can hear it,' he said.

'It must be on our phone here.'

'It must be.'

'We got four-tenths of an inch of rain,' she said. 'I looked in the gauge just after it stopped.'

'That's a big rain.'

'And then I dumped it out,' she said. 'Just like you always do.'

'Uh huh,' he said.

'I wasn't even sure if you were there,' she said. 'I thought, well maybe he just rode around and went somewhere else. But I called, anyway.'

'Yeah. I'm here.'

'Are you going to come see me?' she asked.

'I've got to come over tomorrow,' he said.

'Good.'

'I've got to get some stuff out of the shop. And pick up a few things.'

'Okay. I want to talk to you when you come,' she said.

'All right.'

'What time are you coming?'

'In the morning. Sometime.'

'Okay, but like what? Like early, or what?'

'I don't know. Midmorning, or something.'

'I'll be here,' she said and they hung up.

Now Marlene, she thought, would be real mad about now, and would be thinking crazy things. She'd be thinking how many different ways she could kill Cynthia and all the things she could do to her. She'd think she could strangle her, real hard, because Marlene would hate Cynthia as much as I do, and she'd think, well, if she didn't strangle her enough to kill her but just crushed her up real bad she'd never be able to talk. She might not ever be able to swallow again, either, and she'd have to have one of those tubes and electric voices to make words with.

Those were the kind of things Caroline tried not to think about as she struggled through a restless night, waiting on morning. She didn't let it bother her, not too much, anyway, that Richard always got up early and was out of the house and going before nearly anyone else in the world even woke up and that he had said he might not be there until midmorning, which meant maybe he was going to sleep late. All of that was nearly too much to not have to think about on a suffocatingly humid and steamy night with the tree frogs and crickets going like mad and the moon shining right in her window, right on the bed, illuminating her in that eerie and distant light so that she appeared to be a creature who had been transported to this planet, or an unsuspecting human being who had been selected for a visit by aliens from another world.

Chapter 8

'I'll be back in a couple of hours,' Richard said. It was eight-thirty in the morning and he had been awake for an hour while Cynthia slept. When she finally stirred, he washed and began dressing.

'But wait,' she said. 'I'm going with you.'

'Oh no,' he said. 'No way.'

'But I want to,' she said.

'I don't think it's a good idea.'

'But why?'

'Because Caroline's over there, that's why.'

'Do we have to spend the rest of our lives afraid of Caroline?'

'I didn't say I was afraid of her. I just said it wouldn't be a good idea.'

'Well, I'm not afraid of her either and I want to go with you. You never let me ride in the truck. I wanted to ride in it to town yesterday and you wouldn't take it.'

'It's too hard to park in town. That's why we took your car. You can ride in the truck any time you want.'

'I want to now.'

'Except today.'

'I don't want you to go without me,' she said and went over to him where he sat in the chair and knelt down between his legs and laid her head on his chest. 'I want to do everything with you. I thought that's what this was all about.'

'It is. I mean, we can. But it's just like before. It's just that Caroline needs time to get used to things.'

'But you said she was calm when you finally left.'

'After a while she was. After she wore herself out.'

'I still want to go,' she said.

'Okay, then. I guess we've got to face it sooner or later.'

'It's the right thing to do,' Cynthia said.

'If you say so.'

Meanwhile, Caroline had awakened at seven, having fallen into a deep sleep sometime in the early morning. She started cleaning the house even before she got dressed. The house was filthy. Bales of dust had accumulated under the beds and chairs and couches. Cobwebs spanned the corners of the crown molding she and Richard had put up in every room in the house. She remembered thinking when they started that it would take forever to cope and fit all those joints. The toilet was discolored and the tub and sinks had hair all over the place, and as she cleaned she thought to herself, maybe I have been a little out of it to have to let things get this bad and not even notice. Maybe that was part of it. He never did like a dirty house.

As she cleaned and walked around the house, she looked at herself in passing every mirror. What do I look like now? She tried to catch the casual glance at herself as if unsuspecting and unconsciously she could have been able to see herself as anyone else might.

Then, after breakfast, at nine o'clock, wearing a skirt and a short-sleeve white cotton blouse, she waited on the porch until nine-thirty and when he hadn't come by then she put on a pair of work boots and walked out to the shed and cranked up the tractor. She let it warm up a minute and engaged the hand-operated clutch lever, which was situated to her right and forward of her, about even with the steering wheel, and let the clutch spin with the rest of the engine so it wouldn't wear out, just like Richard had taught her. When she thought the hydraulics were good and warm, she pulled that lever and lifted the cultivator up and backed the tractor over to the bush hog. The bush hog was the large rotary mower that hooked behind the tractor and was so called, she had been told, because it could mow small bushes and saplings, as well as grass, if that's what you wanted to do with it.

After she unhooked the cultivator, she backed up to the

bush hog, hooked it up, and started mowing the little field they had never fenced in or even sowed into pasture, and after that, the yard. When she was nearly finished with the yard, about eleven o'clock, Richard drove up in the truck. She parked the tractor and started over to meet him. Halfway across the yard she saw that Cynthia was with him.

She closed her eyes. That is my seat in that truck, she thought. Cynthia cannot ride in my seat in my truck with my husband coming up my driveway to my house.

She watched them drive past the house and back to the shop. Cynthia looked toward her and waved a little back and forth wiggle of her fingers.

'Do you see what she's wearing?' she asked Richard, and giggled.

He nodded and she followed him into the shop. Caroline stood in the middle of the yard and stared at them. She had in no way thought that Cynthia would come with Richard. She had not even once thought about it the whole night long while she had, she guessed, thought about everything else.

I won't look at her, she thought.

She closed her eyes and walked toward the house until the house screened her from the shop and then she opened them and went inside and sat in the living room facing the front of the house.

'See,' Cynthia said as she and Richard loaded the overhead cabinets and the rest of the materials onto the truck. 'She didn't do a thing. She isn't even going to come back here.'

'Don't bet on it,' he said.

'She isn't.'

'Maybe you're right,' he said and looked toward the house to see where she was.

Caroline moved sideways in the chair so that her feet were across one arm and her body against the other. She looked at her boots, which had fresh-cut grass stuck to them, and she took them off and set them beside the chair and then took her socks off. Then she looked down at the boots and her skirt and thought, how stupid can anyone look. Work boots with socks sticking out the top of them and a skirt and blouse and out there on a tractor riding around like some fool and there they drive up and see me and why don't I ever know anything before it happens.

'I'm going to get some stuff out of the house,' he told Cynthia who was still in the back of the truck.

'Should I come with you?' she asked.

'No. It won't take a minute. Let's not push it too far.'

'Okay,' she said. She'd already won. She could give a little.

'Just finish tying off everything.'

'How?' she asked.

'Make sure nothing's going to fall out. Just tie it off and then tug on it and make sure it's secure.'

He walked down the drive to the house. He noticed the weeds in the field had been moved and looked around at the rest of the yard. He saw she'd even gotten the tight spots mowed where she'd have had to back into them a dozen times to get everything cut.

'Anybody home?' he called and went in the kitchen.

'I'm here,' she said and closed her eyes, afraid to see Cynthia standing beside him.

'You did a great job mowing,' he said.

'It needed it,' she said.

'What's wrong with your eyes?'

'Nothing.'

'Well, why are they closed?'

'They're just closed.'

'You haven't been crying again, have you?' he asked and looked at her face but couldn't tell for sure.

'Nope. I told you I wasn't going to cry anymore.'

'Good.'

'Did you sleep well?' she asked.

'Come on, Caroline. Don't get into it, okay?'

'I didn't mean to ask that,' she said. 'I mean, not like that. It just came out kind of by habit.'

'Open your eyes, how about it.'
'I might see something I don't want to see.'
'She's not here. She's back at the truck.'
'Oh,' she said and opened her eyes. 'Hi,' she said.
'I've got to get a bunch of clothes and stuff.'
'Okay.'
'Then I'm going to leave. Just stay there. Don't get up. I appreciate you being so calm about everything.'
'I can't get up,' she said. 'I hurt my back.'
'When?' he asked and went into the bedroom and started packing.
'Hooking up the bush hog. I couldn't get it lined up right.'
'It's hard to hook up,' he said from the other room.
'I finally had to use a pole and swing it around.'
'Uh huh,' he said.
'See, I wasn't planning on mowing but I had already cleaned the house. Did you notice?'
'It looks good,' he said.
'And then I was just sitting and waiting on you and when you didn't come right away I wanted to do something and that's why I was on the tractor dressed like that. I mean, I know it looked stupid. I wonder what anybody thought riding by on the road who saw me. I know it doesn't matter, really, what you wear and what other people think of you, but still, I mean, like, what did you think when you saw me?'
'I just thought, there's Caroline. I didn't think anything, really.'
'Cynthia did, though, didn't she?'
'I don't know.'
'I bet. I bet you don't. I wonder what she did say. She probably laughed at me. She probably did. She better not have, though. She's dead meat if she did, I can tell you that,' she said.
'Take it easy, Caroline. Just take it easy.'
'Oh I am. I couldn't do anything anyway,' she said. 'My back's too sore. I'll probably have to go see a chiropractor or something.'

'Uh huh,' he said.

'I don't want to, though. They might crack me up and make me worse. They do that, sometimes. I read about that once, in the paper, about this lawsuit,' she was saying as he walked out with two suitcases.

'Is this yours or mine?' he asked, holding out the typewriter in its case.

'Well,' she said, 'I never thought about it. It's ours, I guess.'

'I mean, can I take it? I need to be able to type out my bills and stuff.'

'Sure. I don't need it,' she said.

'Thanks.'

'You sure are all business about this,' she said.

'There's no other way to be,' he said.

'I guess not.'

'Listen,' he said and put the suitcases down and sat across from her. 'I don't know how all this got started or anything, or when it got started, but I swear, I just wanted to say, and I want you to believe me, that I never started out to hurt you. I never meant to. I never wanted to. Things just happen. You have to go along with things. Things change, and then that's it. They're changed.'

'Not really,' she said.

'Well, that's the way it seems to me.'

'That's just what people say.'

'It's neither here nor there,' he said. 'I'm going on now.'

'But wait just a minute more,' she said. 'I still want to talk to you. I was planning to all morning. I don't care if she is waiting out there. I don't care at all. Let her wait. I want to tell you something I thought about last night.'

'I don't want to hear it,' he said.

'No, this is really nice. You're going to like it.'

He sat down.

'I was remembering Silas, and that thing he told us that time, just before he died.'

'What in the world are you thinking about him for?' he asked.

'It just came to me. Do you remember? About a year before he died we had visited him over at his farm. He said, it's funny you came to visit today. Today is my boy's birthday. He'd be thirty-one years old today. When he said that, we hadn't even known he'd had a son. Then he told us that his son, his only child, had died at birth thirty-one years ago, and every year around that time he just got the saddest and most melancholy feeling and then he'd look at the calendar and realize it was his son's birthday again, and every year on that day he went off by himself for the whole day and thought about his boy and the life they would have had together.

'And I thought about that last night because it's so true for so many things and for so many people, don't you see, that when you lose something that's a part of you it's never gone. Not really. Not ever,' she said and looked over at him as he sat with his head down. 'And don't you see that there was Silas, that primitive old Quaker farmer living in the same house right there where he had held his dead son in his arms and later carried him out to the family plot and buried him next to his grandparents, and then later the son was joined by his mother and, much later, by Silas himself, there was Silas, a voice from the past, a person who had lived and died in a world that doesn't exist anymore. I thought last night, there he was, talking to us again, and telling us something.'

Cynthia blew the truck horn. Caroline slapped her face and sunk down in the chair.

'I guess it's not to be,' she said. 'I guess it's not.'

'I've got to go,' he said.

'I know,' she said and stood up and groaned from her hurt back and then tried to be perky. 'I know you do. I just wanted to tell you about remembering Silas. I didn't mean to get so morbid today. I wasn't planning to at all, really. But then, see, I didn't know Cynthia was coming with you and I thought we were going to have time to talk, because, you know, there's just so much to say. But I see it's not going to work and that's okay. I can live with it. I can. I'm not going to bother you. I'm not. I'm really better now than I've been in a long time. I'm not going to kill myself or do anything like that. So don't go around worrying about it. I'm just going to sit here and think about things and make it through the summer. I don't even know if I'll teach anymore. Maybe I won't. Maybe it's time to do something different. I don't know. I'll see. Give me a hug, anyway, before you go.

'Thanks. Oh my back is really sore. That hug felt good to it, though. You know, that kind of hurt so much it feels good. I know what,' she said as he started to leave. 'Just one more thing. Mash me that way you used to that always made my back feel better. Couldn't you just do that before you go. It won't take a minute.'

'I don't know, Caroline. I've really got to get going.'

'Just a minute. It'll make me feel so much better. If you don't I'll be walking around like a cripple for days.'

'All right,' he said and glanced out the window and saw Cynthia beside the truck. 'Just a quick one.'

She lay down on the floor on her back. She pulled her knees up to her chest and held them there with her hands.

'Well, pull your skirt down, anyway,' he said as he stood over her.

'Well, Richard,' she said, 'it's not as if you've never seen me before.'

He pulled her skirt down over her legs and covered her up the best he could and then he leaned on her with his hands and mashed his weight against her, so that her legs compressed and her back stretched and flattened out.

'Oh God, baby,' she said. 'That is wonderful.'

'Just a minute more,' he said.

'Stretch my legs out now,' she said. 'Just pull them back over my head.'

'Caroline,' he said.

'Just for a few seconds. Just stretch them back real hard. There. Try to make my toes touch the floor over my head. Oh. Oh, my goodness. That's it,' she said as the back door slammed and Cynthia walked into the room and saw

Richard leaning over her on the floor with Caroline's skirt pulled up and her legs back.

'Excuse me,' she said.

'Oh,' Richard said and pushed himself up from the floor. 'Caroline hurt her back and I was stretching her muscles for her.'

'What are you doing in my house?' Caroline said.

'Coming to see where Richard was.'

'Well, you get out.'

'You came in my house.'

'So what?'

'I didn't tell you to leave. I didn't act like this to you.'

'I don't give a goddamn,' Caroline said. 'I'll tell you anything I want.'

'Yes,' Cynthia said in a soft voice, 'you probably would.'

'We better go,' Richard said.

'YOU GET OUT OF HERE,' Caroline screamed and shoved her backward into the kitchen. She shoved her so hard she fell against the table in the middle of the room and knocked it sideways and the chairs beside it fell backward and onto the floor.

Caroline rushed in after her and pushed her against the counter while Richard grabbed at Caroline to stop her.

'LET GO OF ME,' Caroline screamed.

'DON'T YOU TOUCH ME AGAIN,' Cynthia shouted.

Caroline pulled loose from Richard and shoved Cynthia into the screen door and out into the yard and onto the ground.

'STOP HER, RICHARD,' Cynthia screamed.

'GET OUT OF MY HOUSE AND OUT OF MY YARD AND DON'T EVER COME BACK,' Caroline yelled.

Richard got in between them and faced Caroline. He put his arms on her shoulder and pressed her downward, as if to plant her in the ground right there, and he said, 'Stop.'

'I'LL STOP WHEN SHE LEAVES,' she said.

'Go on to the truck,' he said to Cynthia.

'I'll have you arrested if you ever do that to me again,' she said and walked away. 'I will.'

'JUST TRY IT,' Caroline yelled. Richard walked her backward into the house. *'YOU'RE A PIECE OF DEAD MEAT,'* she screamed as he backed her in the door.

'You just stay right there,' he said. 'Damn you.'

'Damn me?' she said. 'Damn her. Why in the hell did you bring her in the first place?'

'It just happened.'

'Let her go on by herself,' Caroline said. 'I want to talk to you and I planned to talk to you and I need to talk to you.'

'I don't have anything else to say. I'm going to leave and you're going to stay right here. Don't try to come see me. Just stay right here and forget it and get yourself calmed down.'

'You can't tell me what to do.'

'Just stay,' he said and walked out and went toward the truck, looking back every few feet to make sure she was still there. Just as he got to the truck he looked back once more. She was gone from the doorway and was out of sight. He quickly opened up the hood of her car, removed the coil wire, got in his truck, and drove off with Cynthia.

Caroline had not seen any of this because she had locked herself in the bathroom. She was still out of control and was trying to keep herself from going any further. After she heard the truck drive away, however, she sniffed around where Cynthia had been, walking over the same ground like a dog sniffing out where an intruder had been.

Damn her. Damn that Cynthia. My house. My husband. My yard.

She got so mad again she decided to go over and finish what she'd started. She wanted to beat Cynthia to pieces or die trying.

She put on a pair of jeans and her boots and ran back out to her car. The car wouldn't start, of course, but she hadn't known it, and that just made her all the madder. She screamed at the car. She twisted the key nearly hard enough to bend it, trying to make it start, as if the force of her wrist would somehow kick over the engine and make it fire.

'DAMN YOU CAR,' she screamed. *'I HATE THIS CAR,'* she yelled and kicked the door closed. *'I HATE IT,'* she screamed again and jumped back in and turned it over again and again until the battery began to wear down and die, gurgling and twittering before it did and then nothing. Turn the key and nothing.

'DAMNATION,' she screamed. She jumped up and down on the hood for a few seconds before she gave up and sat on top of the car with her legs over the windshield and her feet on the hood.

How could this happen? How could it? she thought. Nothing ever worked out right. She felt even more miserable than she might have because she had imagined that when she told the story of how the ghost of Silas had visited her it would mean as much to Richard as it had to her.

Damn, she thought. Everybody's just giving up. Nobody lives the way they're supposed to anymore. People have let go of everything.

She wasn't going to do that, she thought. She was going to be the only person still holding on to everything everyone else had let go of.

As she thought that, she looked across the yard and toward the road and the tractor still parked in the front yard. She jumped off the car, ran to the tractor, climbed up and started down the highway to Cynthia's.

Chapter 9

'Don't say I didn't warn you not to go,' Richard said once he and Cynthia were back at her house.

'I hate it when people say that.'

'What?'

'I told you so.'

'I didn't mean it that way,' he said.

'I know,' she said and clung to him as they talked in the truck. 'I know. You were right and I admit it. I was afraid if you went there alone something might happen to you.'

'She won't hurt me.'

'I know that, but I was afraid I might lose you back to her.'

'No chance,' he said. 'I'm so glad to be getting away from there I can't tell you.'

'Let's not work today,' she said.

'Why not?'

'I'm too shook up to be any good,' she said.

'Well, you don't have to,' he said. 'Just take it easy. Go upstairs and take it easy and I'll get everything unloaded and work on by myself. I was planning to, anyway.'

'But you won't be mad at me for not helping?'

'Of course not. I don't mind. I want to finish up.'

Cynthia took a bath. Then she dried off and lay on the bed in her robe and rested. She could hear Richard working downstairs and that made her feel good.

It was eleven miles to Cynthia's house from Caroline's. The old John Deere would only go twelve or thirteen miles an hour, wide open. Caroline chugged on. She pulled over and stopped every now and again to let the line of cars behind her go around, but she kept on. She had the bush hog picked up by the hitch and it swayed behind her as the tractor wobbled down the road, its front end and steering worn and shaking the whole machine. The back tires were as tall as a person and the two front tires, set far ahead at the end of the long narrow tricycle nose of the tractor, were the size of regular car tires. The old green thing puffed and popped with its peculiar two-cylinder sound and Caroline kept the throttle pushed all the way open.

Shortly after she left home, she passed Edgar and Lucille's house. They both automatically looked out the window, as they would to see any car or tractor going by, and came out into the porch when they saw it was Caroline.

'Where's she going?' Edgar asked.

'She didn't even look this way,' Lucille said. 'She didn't even wave.'

'I wonder where she's headed to.'

'Not here, that's for sure,' Lucille said. 'She'll probably never come here again after what you did.'

'Hell,' he said and went back in. 'If she haven't ever heard nothing like that before, she's in pretty bad shape.'

'Some people have a little more dignity than others,' Lucille said, and pretty soon after that Edgar went out the back door and got in the truck along with Lucille the pig, and drove off with her to the store.

Caroline continued on. The black smoke poured out of the exhaust pipe that was mounted on top of the hood in front of her. Behind her, the blades under the mower housing spun so fast that had either one of them come loose just as a car came up behind her it would have killed everyone in the car. She had been in such a hurry to leave she had neglected to disengage the power takeoff to the mower.

About the time Richard finished cutting a piece of trim and the whine from his miter box subsided, he heard, coming from a long way off, the sound of a tractor just like his. He looked as far down the road as he could to see if it was possible that it was his tractor and, what would be worse, that Caroline was on it.

'Do you hear that?' he called upstairs to Cynthia, who had fallen asleep.

'What?'

All the windows were closed and the air-conditioner was running and she hadn't heard a thing.

'I hate to tell you this,' he said and looked out again just as Caroline pulled back on the throttle and turned into the driveway, 'but Caroline has arrived.'

'I thought you disabled her car,' she said and ran down the stairs to join him.

'I forgot about the tractor.'

'Oh no,' she said.

'There she comes.'

'What'll we do?'

'I don't know.'

'Who does she think she is?'

'She's Caroline, that's who.'

'Well, she can't come in my yard. I'll call the police.'

'No,' he said. 'We'll all end up in the papers if you do that.'

'What's she doing?' Cynthia said, with her voice getting louder and out of control. 'She just ran over my boxwoods.'

Caroline had done just that. After she had throttled down to make the turn, she poured it on again and ran straight through a carefully planted line of boxwoods that had been arranged to delineate the parking area from the yard. As she ran over them, the mower bounced up and down and gave them a flattop haircut. The she throttled back a little just as she entered the azalea bushes and made a wide turn and ended up facing the house and stopped just short of the porch rail.

'Cynthia,' she called. 'Come out here.'

'Look at that,' Cynthia said to Richard. 'Who's she supposed to be, Cowgirl Annie or something, calling me out.'

'We're not coming out, Caroline,' Richard said, opening the door a little and leaning out. 'You're about to get in big trouble. Just go back home.'

'I'm not talking to you, baby,' she said. 'I'm not mad at you. I just want to talk to Cynthia.'

'Man to man,' Cynthia said into Richard's ear as she leaned out behind him.

'I'm not going to do anything,' Caroline said. 'I just want to talk to her.'

'I don't want to talk to you,' Cynthia said and leaned over Richard far enough for Caroline to see her. 'And you better leave my house.'

'You made a big mistake this morning,' Caroline said. 'coming over like that and interrupting me and Richard.'

'There's no more you and Richard,' Cynthia said.

'OH IS THAT RIGHT?' Caroline screamed and jumped off the tractor and onto the porch as Richard slammed the door.

'You shouldn't have said that,' he told Cynthia.

'YOU LET ME IN,' she screamed at them and pushed on the door and saw, through the window, Richard and Cynthia running toward the back of the house.

She ran around also but the back door was locked by the time she got there. Then she walked, quite calmly, back to the tractor.

All right, she told herself, she wants to play rough. I'll show her what rough is.

She drove around the house. The back door was just one step up from ground level. She got the tractor lined up just right and aimed it for the door. If she could keep it straight enough as the front end went up the one step in height, she could bump the door with the narrow part of the tractor and knock it open.

'Now what's she doing?' Cynthia asked as they watched her out a side window.

'I'm afraid to tell you what I think,' he said just as the door took the force of the nose of the tractor.

At the same time, however, Caroline, sitting up high on the seat mounted above the six-foot back tires, got knocked in the head by the overhang of the roof that came out beside the kitchen door. It hit her about the same time she noticed it, and as it grazed her she leaned back and tried to slide under it but got trapped against the seat as she slid down below it and the overhang.

The tractor kept on going.

Oh no, she thought.

'LOOK OUT,' yelled Richard.

He and Cynthia stumbled toward the other side of the room as the entire front end of the tractor broke through the splintered door and entered the house. As it did, the muffler, coming out above the hood, hit the top of the doorway and snapped off.

Oh, help, Caroline thought.

'HOLY SHIT,' Richard screamed.

'STOP HER,' Cynthia yelled at him.

It was an unsettling sight, to put it mildly, for Cynthia to see the front end of a 6,000-pound tractor rolling across her Oriental carpet, the very carpet she had chosen so that all the colors complemented each other and the old pine floor, the deep earth-brown and tan and the reds and yellows, and now, a green, wheezing and roaring monster with oil dripping sat on that rug.

'GET HER OUT,' Cynthia screamed and, in an act of heroism and fearlessness equal to standing up to a grizzly bear as it came through the door of the pioneer home and the woman stands firm to protect her children and her home, Cynthia put her shoulder and her hands against the front of the tractor and tried to push it backward.

'YOU CAN'T PUSH IT,' Richard yelled.

'DO SOMETHING,' she yelled back.

With no muffler in place, the noise of the engine was almost deafening, and the black smoke puffed out against her newly painted ceiling.

Outside, Caroline held on for dear life.

'Richard,' she said, not too loudly, though, as she was mashed up in such a constricted way she could barely get a breath.

It had only taken about two seconds for her to get crammed in below the seat and the steering wheel. In those two seconds the tractor broke through the door. The whole time she kept trying to get her hand up to the clutch lever or at least to the ignition switch but she couldn't do it. She was too jammed down. She was doing all she could just to keep from being killed by the back tires, which had bumped against the outside of the house and stopped the entry of the entire tractor, only allowing the narrow front end to enter about six feet into the room.

The back wheels kept turning. They rolled against the brick on the outside of the house. It looked as if the tractor was trying to climb it. As they turned and caught traction, the whole machine would climb up the wall a few inches and then fall back. It kept doing this, over and over. As it did, it appeared to be jumping up and down in place.

The tractor was working hard. The governor, which automatically sensed the load on the engine, had opened up the throttle. The carburetor was sucking gas and air like a jet about to take off. The tractor just kept pulling, as hard as it could. For all it knew it was trying to drag a harrow up a hill, or take a bottom plow through a stretch of hard ground. It kept trying, just as John Deere intended it to.

Inside the house, Richard and Cynthia were in the middle of internal-combustion hell.

'God durn it, God almighty,' Richard said, over and over again. He could just see through the doorway that Caroline was mashed down and that she could not stop the tractor. 'God durn it, God almighty,' he kept saying as he tried to reach beside the roaring machine to turn it off. The room filled with black smoke and soot and the noise was so loud Cynthia had gone into a screaming fit. She stood in the middle of the room and yelled, over and over, *'STOP HER. STOP HER.'*

'SHUT UP,' Richard yelled back at her, but she just kept on screaming.

'MY HOUSE. MY HOUSE.'

'God durn it,' he said, and ran by her and out the front door.

He had the idea to climb up on the tractor and turn it off.

When he got there, though, he saw the blades of the mower spinning chest-high, and the power takeoff shaft on top of the mower whirling around just like farmers always talked about that wrapped up the sleeve of some neighbor's shirt and then the neighbor's arm, as well, and pulled it off at the shoulder as neatly as popping a fried chicken leg off at the joint.

He could find no safe way up. The low overhang formed a roof over the tractor just above Caroline's head. He saw she could not straighten up, though she was trying.

'Just hold on,' he said. 'I'm coming.'

'Help,' she said.

He peered into the room and got another idea and ran back. Once inside, he saw Cynthia, still standing in the middle of the room, but saying nothing now, only holding her face with her hands.

He grabbed the spark-plug wire on one side and yanked it off and then yanked off the one on the other side. The tractor stopped moving. The motor died. The whole machine rolled back a few inches.

'Help,' Caroline said. 'Help me.'

Around back, the mower blades were still. The p-t-o shaft was still. He released the clutch lever and took the transmission out of gear. Slowly and quietly it rolled out of the house and bumped off the step and onto the ground and stopped. Caroline wriggled back onto the seat and Cynthia cautiously walked out the demolished doorway.

'Oh my God,' Caroline said. 'I did not mean to do that.'

'It's all right,' Richard said.

'I promise you, I just meant to bump it.'

'Don't worry,' Richard said.

He helped her off the tractor.

'I'm so sorry,' she said.

'I can fix it,' Richard said.

'You're going to have to pay for this,' Cynthia said.

'Okay,' Caroline said. 'I don't care.'

'You will care,' Cynthia said. 'You will have to sell your house to pay for that rug.'

'It doesn't matter,' Caroline said.

She stood up and tried to climb back on the tractor but Richard stopped her.

'What are you doing?'

'Going back home.'

'Leave the tractor,' he said. 'I'll take you.'

'What about my door?' Cynthia asked. 'I can't lock it.'

'I'll be back soon,' he said. 'Nothing's going to happen in the middle of the afternoon.'

'What about the tractor?' Caroline asked.

'I'll bring it back later.'

He helped her down and put his arm around her and led her to the truck. She was still shaking, though she was trying not to show it, and actually thought she might not make it to the truck before her legs gave out. She leaned into him and put her arm around his waist, and Cynthia watched them walk off together, and she was hotter than the old tractor engine.

'I didn't mean to do that,' she told him again on the way home. 'I was just trying to bump the door a little and knock it open.'

'You've made a damn mess of everything, Caroline,' he said.

'I know.'

'Why do you keep on like this?'

'I don't know. I don't seem to be able to do right anymore.'

'And you wonder why I'm leaving.'

'I understand,' she said.

'What in the world were you planning to do in the first place?' he asked. 'I mean, you come riding in like some cowboy,' he said.

'Cowgirl,' she said.

'Like some cowgirl, whirl around in the yard and then call Cynthia out like you were challenging her to a fight.'

'I guess it looked kind of stupid, in retrospect,' she said.

'Stupid?' he said.

'Crazy?'

'There're no words for it.'
'Is this worse than the mud bog?' she asked.
'Yes, Caroline,' he said and looked at her. She looked down and bit her finger. 'Much worse,' he said.
'And I thought that was going to be it,' she said. 'I wonder what's next?'
'I don't want to find out,' he said.
'You won't have to,' she said. 'I won't bother you anymore. You or her.'
'Here's your coil wire,' he said and took it out from under the seat. 'I guess I should have let you use the car.'
'Oh,' she said. 'I wondered why it wouldn't start.'
'Right.'
'You must have thought I was going to do something, then,' she said.
'I knew you weren't through.'
'How?'
'How what?'
'How'd you know?' she asked.
'Because I've been married to you for fourteen years.'
'Oh.'
'Fourteen years,' he said again.
'That bad, huh?' she asked.
'Sometimes.'
They pulled into the driveway and parked around back.
'Ouch,' Caroline said as she opened the door and stepped down.
'What's wrong?'
'Nothing,' she said.
'Let me see.'
'No. It's nothing.'
'You're holding your wrist funny.'
'No, I'm not. I just said ouch because my back's still a little out of whack.'
'Come here,' he said and pulled her wrist back.
'Oh, oh, oh,' she said.
'I knew it,' he said.
'It's nothing.'

'You've broken your wrist.'

'No I haven't.'

'I'm taking you to the doctor.'

'No you're not. I can move it. See? You're not supposed to be able to move it like this if it's broken,' she said and moved it by itself back and forth. 'See. It's just sprained a little.'

They went inside. Out of the bright sunlight he looked at her wrist again.

'Run it under cold water,' he said. 'It'll stop the swelling.'

'Okay,' she said.

'You're lucky, you know,' he said and sat at the table while she soaked her wrist.

'How's that?'

'You could've actually been killed back there.'

'I guess so.'

'It scared me, you know.'

'I guess it did. I know I'd hate to be standing in a room and see a tractor crash through my door. I'd have probably died of fright.'

'Yeah,' he said.

'You think that's enough?' she asked a little later.

'Maybe a minute more,' he said.

'Whew,' she said.

'What is it?'

'Hurting a little,' she said. 'But getting better. I shouldn't have tried to move it just then.'

'You better keep an eye on it over the next day or two,' he said.

'I will.'

He got up.

'Are you going to leave now?' she asked.

'I guess I better.'

'Can't you stay just a little longer?'

'It wouldn't be right,' he said.

'Why, it'd be the most right thing you've done in I don't know how long,' she said.

'I better go on,' he said.

'No, don't. You look so tired.'

'I am.'

'Well, stay and rest a minute.'

'I can't.'

'Look. I've got to change clothes. Just wait and don't go until I've done that. At least do that,' she said.

'All right.'

'Come on in here,' she said. 'Wait over here where it's cool. I won't be a minute. These clothes smell like grass and smoke and gasoline and everything else.'

'Okay,' he said.

He was tired. The past couple of weeks had nearly done him in.

Caroline left the door partway open. She walked back and forth a number of times while she changed clothes. When she saw him stretch out on the couch, she sat on the bed in her terry-cloth bathrobe and watched him fall asleep. When she was sure he was completely asleep, she took a pillow off the bed and carried it to the couch and lay on the floor beside him.

It was a sweet moment for Caroline. She watched his face change as he slept. She saw the Richard she used to know. She got as close as she could to him so that when he awoke she'd be the first thing he saw.

'Hello,' she said when he opened his eyes.

'Boy,' he said. 'I must have passed out.'

'You needed that,' she said.

'I guess I did.'

'Isn't it strange?'

'What?'

'How it happened that you're back here now.'

'I don't know if strange is the right word.'

'But you're here.'

'I am.'

'And you fell asleep.'

'So?'

'That made me happy.'

'Falling asleep?'

'I want to kiss you, baby,' she said. 'I don't even care what's been going on. I just want to kiss you and be close to you.'

'You ought to be more careful about the way you tie your robe,' he said.

'You know I was never very good at that.'

'At what?'

'Being careful.'

'No, you were never very good at that,' he said, and they kissed a long time, and later went to bed, and Caroline was, for a while that afternoon, reborn in a sense, the way a person who had died on the operating table and seen her own death and the people all around her and then came back to life, the way that person was reborn, the way she had died that night when she hid in the woods and saw that she had come loose and she had nearly given up, until today, when, in the most unexpected and violent manner, she came back to life, knowing more than when she'd left it those few days so long ago now.

She didn't know, though, that as she slept that afternoon and Richard got up, he had paced around the house and talked to himself, quietly, and walked back and forth past her door and looked at her again and again.

She didn't know that he felt bad for letting her go that afternoon as far as she'd gone, but that he'd found it impossible to tell her no, to hurt her again, to cut her off once more as she climbed out on the end of that sad and desperate limb she seemed to live on most of her life, where she balanced like some beautiful and unknown species of bird, flightless and falling again and again, and waiting, more or less, to be discovered. Waiting, in a way, to learn how to fly, what next to do, how to sing, and all the rest. Waiting all the while, but not knowing it, too far out, way too far out for anyone to understand just what she was.

She did not know, as she slept, that Richard had slowly rolled the truck down the drive and then down the road and did not start it until he was out of range of her hearing. Had she known that, of course, she would have been distressed.

She did not know that he had left a note telling her all the usual things a person says under such circumstances, that he was sorry for deceiving her that day, sorry for this and sorry for that, but so forth and so on, and therefore goodbye. Had she known that, she wouldn't have been happy at all. Not a bit.

But she was. She didn't know a thing, and that was, for a little while, really the best way to live, hidden from the truth and quietly floating along. It was a nice way to be, if you could manage it.

Chapter 10

It was easy to hang a door, really. Most doors came pre-hung in their own jamb; that is, the sides of the door, the pieces of wood onto which the hinges on one side and the latch mechanism on the other were attached, came with the door. All you had to do was slide it in place, plumb it, shim it square and solid and then nail the casing or trim around it.

Some doors, however, came separate from the jamb and you had to mortise the hinges, drill the hole in the door for the latch and get it all lined up, and then do the rest.

There were a lot of different things that could go wrong when hanging a door. As you mortised the three hinges to the jamb, and then did the same with their mates to the door, there was the possibility of their not lining up with each other precisely.

The same thing could happen with the lock and the keeper in the jamb opposite it, and then, when you closed the door, the latch missed and hit the wood. Sometimes the door came delivered to you warped, but you wouldn't know it if you hadn't thought to check before you hung it, and when you closed it, only the top or bottom hit the stop and the rest hung out open like an invitation to the field mice to come in.

Of course, when you were replacing a door that had been removed by a woman driving a 1954 John Deere tractor, you could easily encounter a whole new world of problems.

The rough opening, that is, the opening formed by the framing into which the jamb would be placed, could have been knocked loose or knocked out of plumb and the drywall on the inside and the brick on the outside could have been cracked or busted and crumbled like crackers, and the floor, even with its three coats of hand-rubbed tung oil, could have two filthy black tire marks across it.

It would be mere chance that things would ever be the same again in that doorway, and what person could ever know what had been broken or stained or shaken loose far into the walls or above the header or anywhere at all that he couldn't see or get to without tearing out the entire wall and starting over?

After a shock like that, after a tornado or a hurricane or an earthquake, it was best to move on. Houses changed. People changed, some of them looked the same but weren't. It was hard to tell. A good real-estate agent could sell anything. It was best to move on, if you could.

Over at Caroline's which was west of Cynthia's, another late-afternoon storm was building up. The sky got dark. The wind picked up. The air cooled off and Caroline woke up happy and talking nonstop again, just feeling so good.

'Is that you in there?' she called. She thought she'd heard the refrigerator door open and close. 'Bring something for me when you get a chance. I'm glad it cooled off. I was so hot there for a while. The sun always moves around this window just before supper and I was lying here in my sleep trying to make myself get up and close the shades and then it cooled off and got cloudy and I dreamed I had gotten up and done it.

'Boy, my wrist is still sore. I guess it's lucky I've got a wrist at all. I was so jammed down in there I must have been about the size of one of those circus midgets who come out of those cars, you know, when they have about ten or twelve of them all packed in one of those little cardboard cars. That's the way it felt. I can't believe I didn't see that overhang sticking out. I was so intent on aiming right at the door and just barely bumping it, I guess I missed it.'

She doubled up her pillow with his and leaned against them and covered herself with the sheet.

'Why don't you make some lemonade? I mean some real

stuff. We've got plenty of lemons. I wonder how the name started when you call something a lemon? I wonder where that came from. You know, when you buy a car that's a lemon. Maybe because it's sour. Maybe because you feel sour when you find out you've been had. I bet that's it.

'I remember that time Mother bought those storm doors for the house. This guy came around and was selling them and installing them right on the spot and she'd been watching him all day putting them up on the neighbors' houses and when he finally came to our house and knocked I remembered she was so relieved. It was like she'd been worried she might be left out or that for some reason he might not come to our house because it didn't look good enough, because it was the smallest one on the street and she always felt inferior about that, but anyway, when he finally came and knocked on the door, she bought them immediately.

'They cost five hundred dollars apiece or, God, that can't be right, maybe five hundred dollars for both of them. That's what it was. Anyway, when Daddy got home he nearly went crazy. He nearly tore them off opening and slamming them shut again trying to show her what junk they were and that they didn't cost but about fifty dollars apiece at Sears.

'Anyway,' she said and then paused for a moment as she forgot where she was in the story,'anyway, oh yeah, I was taking about lemons, I remember now. I guess those doors weren't really lemons, not like a crummy used car, but the thing is how bad Mother felt when it was all over. She felt so bad. She just felt so awful. The whole thing had gone sour. For a while there, just before Daddy came home, while that man was putting them up and she was imagining how warm it'd be in the winter without the draft blowing in around the old doors and she was out in the yard looking at them and knowing it made her house as good as everybody else's, for a little while there, she was transformed. It was kind of like, if you think about it, she was in love for a few minutes, for an hour or so there, again, in love with the doors and in love with that man who had come along and changed her life for a little while. It was really like that. I know. I watched the whole thing and thought how happy Mother looked and how nice that man was. They just talked and talked nearly the whole time he was working and she was so happy.

'Here was this man who'd come along and was, you know, in a way, loving her, you know what I mean? Talking to her when Daddy never did. Being nice to her and treating her so sweetly and being so courteous, and so, for a while there, Mother was changed.

'Someone had come along selling storm doors and made my mother happy. Isn't that something? I wonder if she ever thought about it again. I wonder. She never mentioned it. She never talked about anything, really, as time went on. She kind of went into herself and then died. I'm sorry you never met her. She would have liked you. She would have been happy for me. I sure am sorry about that,' she said and got off the bed and looked at herself in the mirror and then out of the window.

'I guess it's not going to rain after all. The other day it rained enough to last for weeks. So it doesn't matter,' she said and walked into the kitchen. 'Richard?' she called. 'I thought you were in here.'

She looked out the door and saw the truck was gone and closed her eyes and shook her head and looked again, like an actor doing a double take, like someone in a Three Stooges film watching in disbelief as Curly gets whacked across the room. That's the way she looked and that's the way she felt as well, as she peered out the front window, still looking for the truck, and then went into the bedroom and saw the note on the table.

A note on a table beside a bed at a time like that was a bad sight. It was a lot worse than coming home and seeing a note on the door or finding one under the magnet on the refrigerator. It was worse than the note the teacher folded and gave you to take home to have signed by your parents.

For a while she did not pick it up. She just sat on the side of the bed and looked at it. Then she knocked it across the table and into the trash basket on the floor.

It stayed there the rest of the day. Every time she walked in the room she had to work hard not to take it out and read it. The longer the day went on, the harder it became. Soon it was night. Caroline took out the whole basket in which the note, along with the other trash, lay. She took all this out to the yard and dumped it onto the grass and sat beside it and set it on fire.

For a few seconds it was a beautiful sight as the different papers and whatever they were made of burned various colors, greens and blues, along with the yellow and gold of the flames themselves, and the glow of it all shone against Caroline's face, and she looked so beautiful in that light that anybody passing on the road who had looked as the car sped by would never have forgotten what they'd seen, but would have carried the picture of that beautiful woman with them forever.

It would have been hard to tell from that distance and in the brief moment of that vision what she was like, why she was there, and what would become of her. It was a terrible and impossible thing to contemplate for Caroline herself, and she remained there long after the note had burned, and she lay on her back and looked at the stars.

She was like a singer or an actress who had danced her way onto the stage and then forgotten the song, or had come out too soon while everyone else was still getting dressed. There she was alone, trying to dance and trying to sing and no one there, no music playing, no laughter, no applause, an empty house on a summer night and all alone.

PART II

Local Woman Bursts into Flames

Chapter 11

How many times could you make love in a long weekend?

You could make love on the same night in which you take this man from his wife. You could do it more than once. Any time you do it more than once in the same night, it counts as triple because of the effort involved.

You could make love on the same day the man's wife drove through your back door and tore up your Oriental rug. You could do that even if you hadn't felt like it and even if your heart wasn't really in it, and it would still count.

You could make love on the way up to the mountains, even though it's only a four-hour drive, by leaving late in the afternoon and stopping at a motel before you get there.

You could do it over and over again up in the mountains as you look sideways out the window and dream of beautiful things.

In the mountains or at the beach, each time counts for two because the added romantic effects of the surroundings make everything seem more wonderful than it really is.

You could do it every night when you come back, and on the nights when you're having your period, you could keep right on. You could do all the things you never did with your husband but that you found out about from the little book you bought when you were living alone and now keep in the drawer beside the bed.

You could make love once on the kitchen floor or up against the new cabinets or twice on the sofa, and you could do it once in the car on the way back from the movies late at night (any position is all right), and once on a blanket outside on the grass.

You could also do it once in the shower and you could do it one time each with pink, red, and black garter belts and stockings to match but no panties and that's all.

Anything beyond that, such as videos, magazines, hand-held devices, extruded, molded latex or plastic products, leather or metal things, and so forth, could not be included because when you got to the point of needing that stuff it was all over, anyway.

You could, you see, make love that many times in a long and wild weekend. You don't have to, but you could.

Chapter 12

After the note had burned and Richard had gone for good and a few days had passed, Caroline began to remember how much she hated being alone.

There were two things she had hated all her life and being poor was one of them and being alone was the other.

Now I've got both, she thought.

She was down at the creek thinking about all this. The creek divided their property from their neighbor's and had been used to establish the boundary all the way around. It was dark and cool down at the creek and the trees grew like mad down there, forming a natural grotto that Caroline loved and where she imagined all kinds of past lives, where Indians and their families might have camped or lived for years at a time, where people passing through on their way across the forest before there were roads and horses and all the rest made a path that led to this sheltering spot and where she could still imagine a worn and vaguely defined trail that she followed even now as she walked along talking to herself.

I really do hate being poor, she thought. I really do.

From down at this lowest part of their land she could not see the house, even though the house was on the highest part of the land. She could not see the road and could not even hear the traffic unless she listened for it. It was a beautiful spot on a beautiful piece of land. It was the kind of place everyone needed but few had, and that's why people were always going on trips to find places like this, and there it was, an unknown presence she had hardly noticed when they bought the place.

They had bought the land from Edgar's brother. The clearing in which they had built their house was an old, worn-out cotton field. The field fell gradually toward the woods, which made a circle around the house except for the side facing the road. The woods sloped at the same gradual degree as the clearing for a while, then fell steeply to the creek, which meandered around the three sides of their property not bounded by the road.

Caroline walked along the side of the creek. Even in the summer there was some water flowing through it and the path she followed, which she imagined had been followed by Indians and travelers for centuries, was used by the animals coming down to drink.

I thought I had it made, she mumbled. I thought I had beat it.

She ambled along, waving a branch above her head to keep the insects away. She had a dreamy look on her face and if she'd been sitting on a porch lazily waving a paper fan and wearing a long white dress, she'd have looked like a woman from the turn of the century, waiting on that porch for all that was to come in life, waiting and fanning and swinging lazily back and forth, mesmerized by all that might be.

Up ahead she saw a tree that had recently been uprooted and must have fallen over, she thought, slowly, as it tore loose and the roots popped and it fell into the branches of the other trees, which had caught it and lowered it down slowly. Like a child sliding down from its parent's arms and onto the ground, the tree, too, must have come down that gently because its branches on the other side of the creek, where it rested, were bent gracefully under and not snapped off.

Caroline walked out on the trunk, balancing on it quite easily with her arms out like a tightrope walker. Halfway out she stopped where a limb formed a perfect rest to lean against.

As she rested, she mumbled and tried to solve the mysteries of her life. She was animated as she talked, and shook her head to console herself and gestured with her hands.

While she talked, a large brown dog walked along the path looking at her. The dog, a short-haired yellow Lab mixed with something else like a golden retriever, had a bright and intelligent face, and every now and again as it walked toward Caroline it stopped and looked at her with its head cocked to one side, as if trying to figure her out. At one point, the dog looked around, as well, as if to see to whom she was talking.

After a few minutes of watching her while staying out of sight, the dog walked out into the clearing in front of the fallen tree and sat down and looked directly at her.

Caroline was talking and looking up in the sky when she sensed the dog.

'Where'd you come from?' she asked.

The dog cocked its head to one side like the RCA dog.

'Have you been watching me?' she asked. 'Who are you?'

The dog wagged its tail in the leaves.

'You're some kind of spirit, that's what you are,' she said.

The dog lay down then, with its paws out in front and its head up, like an Egyptian statue, and kept looking right at her.

'You can stay there as long as you like,' she said. 'I don't mind. I was just trying to figure out how I was going to make it. I sure would hate to sell this place but I don't think I can make it alone. I just don't, you know what I mean?'

Caroline stood up. When she did, so did the dog.

'I like you,' she said. 'I want to know where you came from,' she said and started down the log toward the dog. The dog, however, moved away from her along the path in the same direction it had been going.

'Wait,' she said and stopped, and the dog stopped and turned its head but kept its body facing down the path. 'I'm not going to do anything to you,' she said. She took one more step and the dog walked off, slowly and deliberately, with its ears back listening for her but not turning around even when she got to the bank and called to it. Soon it was out of sight.

*

It's hard to be as happy as Richard and Cynthia felt and not make some other people uncomfortable by the display of such happiness, holding hands and kissing in public and stuck to each other like life itself would cease if they weren't in constant physical contact, staring at each other across the restaurant table, sitting side by side in the car or in the truck, just about too much for the rest of the world for whom the dreams of such a passionate connection had long ago ended.

But there it was, and who was to say it wasn't real? Who was to say?

Not Cynthia as she looked out the window while Richard waited for a truck to arrive. The truck was bringing materials to do more on the house. There were a lot of things that had been let go, little things that would be easy to fix before the house went on the market.

Not Richard, who could feel her looking at him and who turned around and saw he was right and smiled at her.

It was for other people to say. On this morning, as Richard helped the driver back up to the porch, carefully guiding him around the scalped boxwoods and around the flower beds Caroline had so casually destroyed, on this morning the world for Richard was just right.

'So you're over here now,' the driver said. This same driver had delivered lumber and other materials to Richard's shop for years.

'Yeah, I'm over here.'

'I knew something was wrong when I pulled in your old place and didn't see nobody.'

'You went to my shop?'

'I pulled all the way up the driveway and backed up to the door, all the time waiting to see you slide it open from the inside like you always do, and then when nothing happened I realized your truck wasn't there. I would've unloaded the stuff anyway and left it under the shed if your wife hadn't come out of the woods about that time and told me you didn't live there no more.'

'Oh no,' Richard said.

'I'm sorry if I messed anything up. I just looked on the ticket and saw your name and didn't even look at the address. I'm used to taking things to the other place.'

'What'd she say?'

'Who?' the driver asked.

'My wife.'

'She just said you had moved out. She was real nice about it.'

'She was?'

'Oh yeah.'

The driver slid the stuff to Richard, who stacked it on the porch. The unloading made a good break in the conversation and allowed the driver to gauge how much he could find out about this new arrangement.

'So you've gone, huh?' he asked.

'That's right.'

'You mean you done bought this place?' he asked, looking around at it like it was the most amazing thing he'd ever seen.

'No. I didn't buy it. The woman I'm living with owns it.'

'Well, then, you did all right for yourself.'

'I did all right,' Richard said. 'I guess you could say that for sure.'

'Yeah, you did all right,' he said, looking around again. 'Are you going to marry this woman?' he asked, still unloading and handing out the stuff.

'I guess so.'

'I would. I tell you that. If I could get my hands on a woman what had a place like this, I sure wouldn't let her go. I'd hold onto her until she said yes. That's what I'd do.'

'She's already said it.'

'Well, you got it made, then,' the driver said.

'Yeah, I guess I do,' Richard said.

'Is she good-looking?'

'Real good-looking.'

'Whew,' the driver said. 'A good-looking woman with money. That's a sweet combination.'

'Tell me about it,' Richard said.

'Of course, your other wife was a fine-looking lady, herself.'

'I know.'

'And nice, too. She always made me laugh every time I ever talked to her.'

'She was funny, all right,' Richard said.

'But I guess I'll be meeting this one sooner or later,' the driver said and fastened the tie-down straps and got back into the cab. 'I guess you'll be building a shop over here pretty soon.'

'I don't know. I appreciate it, though.'

'Anytime,' he said and drove off.

Cynthia came out.

'All that?' she asked.

'It's not that much.'

'For just those few little things.'

'It just looks like a lot all piled up here.'

'You're so nice to do this for me,' she said.

'Now listen,' he said and held her with his hands on her shoulders out at arm's length. 'What wouldn't I do for you?'

'I don't know,' she said. 'What?'

'Nothing,' he said. 'Absolutely nothing.'

'You're too good,' she said, and together they carried the materials that did not have to be cut into the rooms and left eveything else on the porch, where he had set up his benches and saws.

Caroline had just come up from the creek when the truck pulled in and drove back to the shop. After putting on a good cheerful act about the mix-up, she ran to the house and tried to calm down. First the dog, the ghost dog, had appeared, and now a load of lumber on its way to Cynthia's had stopped off to let her know about it. It was too much.

She got a stack of magazines and some iced tea and settled into a chair with her feet on the arm of another chair she had pulled in place for that purpose and she began looking through the magazines. It was hard to concentrate.

That dog, she thought, was some kind of Indian dog, some kind of Indian spirit telling me something.

She finished the first magazine and tossed it onto the floor and began the next one.

I should have just followed that dog, she thought, and then I wouldn't have been here when the truck came.

It was a hot morning and the chair in which she sat was vinyl. It was hotter in the chair than it was outside. She pushed her hair out of the way and rubbed the iced-tea glass across her forehead.

Of course, if I had followed that dog, she thought, where would we have gone?

Cynthia was trying to learn how to cut a board with an electric saw. Richard was holding her hand on the saw, with the motor off, and trying to show her how to follow the line drawn on the board. It was a little like tennis or golf lessons.

'You start it here,' he said and pointed to a spot on the base plate of the saw, where there was a mark, 'and then as you start it you look up at the line and follow it.'

'But won't it go straight by itself?' she asked.

'Nope.'

'But it seems like it would.'

'It won't.'

'Okay,' she said. 'I'm going to try it.'

She squeezed the trigger. The saw jumped from the torque of the blade and she let go of the saw and it dropped on the floor.

'You've got to hold onto it,' he said.

'I'm sorry. It just jumped out of my hand. It seemed like it started moving by itself.'

'Why don't you let me do it,' he said.

'I want to learn how. I've always wanted to know how to do things like this.'

She held onto it this time and cut all the way across the board.

'I did it,' she said.

'Now put the square on the cut you just made and see if you did it straight.'

'It's not,' she said, looking at the gap between the square and the end of the board. 'What happened?'

'It just takes time,' he said, and recut it for her after which they went inside and out through the back onto the deck, where they were replacing the top board of the handrail, which had become dry and splintery.

After that they went to town.

'I've got to pick up four more pieces of that chair rail if you still want to replace it in that room,' he said.

'I do.'

'Then let's take the truck and get lunch and then go get the stuff and anything else we can think of and we still ought to have time to finish all that this afternoon.'

About the time they left in the truck, Caroline got out of the tub, dressed and left for town. She parked in the municipal lot. A young man leaned out of the booth to hand her the ticket and looked at her legs where her dress had ridden up above her knees. Then, after she got out and was on her way to get a newspaper, two men in a truck with ladders on racks over the cab yelled something at her and she waved to them.

Hell, she thought, I'll wave to anyone. I don't care.

She was concerned, though, that she might meet someone who knew her and Richard. She was still keeping quiet about the whole thing. She didn't want to go into any elaborate lies to get away from the questions of how Richard was and what he was doing and where he was and so forth, because this whole thing, she thought, this whole damn thing is no one's business but mine.

People loved other people's trouble. They looked at the other person intently as they asked, are you doing all right, is there anything I can do? They looked for the signs of strain, of despair, truly sorry for it but glad at the same time it wasn't they who had gone public with the sordid excesses of their lives. What a relief. Poor girl. I always thought they were so happy. She is a little strange, though. Everyone always thought that.

Anyway, Caroline made it from the car to the drugstore without meeting anyone and bought a paper and a vanilla Coke and set herself up in the booth and began to get back into the world. She hadn't even read a newspaper since it all began.

Events had continued to occur without her participation. There was trouble everywhere. There were murders. There were wars. There were accidents. There were unscrupulous men and women denying their guilt in the most believable way. It was easy to understand going wrong. It was easy to believe that they were innocent. After all, if a man could cut the heart out of his own wife while looking her right in the eye, anything was possible.

Cynthia and Richard stopped at a fish house for lunch. The fish house was a long one-story building with a low-pitched roof. It had a gravel drive with two entrances and a huge parking lot. The parking lot was full. There were three ambulances parked side by side as well as a row of UPS trucks out along the edge and a hundred other cars and trucks.

Inside there was bedlam. There was music coming over the speakers which you could feel more than hear. There was a lot of talking and laughing and at the table just behind Richard and Cynthia the ambulance drivers' radios kept announcing this or that emergency. The drivers had put their radios up on the table and each time there was a call, all the people near the table stopped talking to hear what it was.

The fish had been deep-fried in the same grease everything else had been fried in, so that it was hard to tell without looking closely whether you were eating french fries, fish, shrimp or anything else that might have fallen into the cooker.

It was a popular place to eat. You got a lot of food on the plate and there was a free dessert bar as well. The dessert bar had banana pudding with vanilla wafers, all kinds of Jell-O, chocolate-chip cookies, long low pans of cakes with different-color icings and a soft-serve ice-cream machine.

You could go in the place perfectly healthy and come out immediately ready for the cholesterol and heart-attack unit of the local hospital.

'This place is wild,' she said.

'I thought you'd like it.'

'I don't suppose it would do any good to ask for any red snapper or pompano,' she said, making a little joke.

'You can try.'

'I still have my hammer loop on,' she said, looking down at her belt.

'Then you fit right in,' he said.

'Really?' she said.

'No, baby,' he said. 'Not really. If you rolled around in sawdust and glue and beat your fingers up with a hammer you still wouldn't look like a carpenter.'

'I guess not,' she said.

'But you look good to me,' he said.

'That's what I wanted to hear,' she said and leaned across the table and kissed him, and then she looked around, as if she shouldn't have done it.

'It's all right,' he said. 'It's time for the world to know.'

At just past twelve, as Caroline was finishing the paper, a woman and two children came in and behind them a teenage boy and girl. The woman was dragging the two children by holding on to their hands and walking faster than they could keep up with. Both children looked as if they'd been crying but had stopped, possibly on the promise of getting something to eat.

The teenage couple were also holding hands but were walking in slow motion, as if they were either stoned or so swept away by being together they could barely make it in the real world but had to take it kind of easy, like, wow, what's happening, I mean, hey, it's too much.

The two children slid into the booth facing Caroline. Their mother went to the counter to order their food. Caroline smiled at them. They looked down and then back up again to see if she was still looking at them and then down again. They did it exactly the same way, the eyes with the same expression, and the whole thing exactly timed together. Then they looked toward their mother and then back at Caroline.

Their mother came back with three hot dogs. The hot dogs were wrapped in a paper through which the chili could be seen seeping out all over the bun. After she brought the hot dogs, she went back for three Cokes and a pile of napkins.

Meanwhile, the teenage couple had gotten what looked to Caroline like two orangeades and were sitting side by side, sipping and talking quietly.

The two children had gotten their hot dogs unwrapped and were doing the best they could to eat them while trying to keep the chili and onions and slaw from slopping out all over the place. Their mother handed them some napkins and as they spilled a little here and there, they wiped it up.

Caroline put the paper down and folded it up and took the last sip of her Coke and then began to eat the ice.

The boy and the girl were still talking but had either finished their orangeades or had just stopped drinking them but still held them in their hands, motionless on the table in front of them. While they talked, the boy began tickling his girlfriend's arm with his fingers. She rolled her hand over so that the underside of her arm would be exposed and he trailed his fingers up and down her skin while they talked.

Oh my, Caroline thought, and got the chills as if it were happening to her.

Then the little boy sitting in front of her reached across his hot dog, which was neatly on the wrapper, and picked up his Coke, which slid out of his hand and onto the table, going all over his and his sister's hot dog, as well as down the table and onto their laps.

'I TOLD YOU, I TOLD YOU, I TOLD YOU,' his mother screamed at him. 'Now you don't get anything. Not the rest of the day,' she said, and took his and his sister's wet hot dogs and wrapped them up and threw them into the white paper sack they had come in and tried to wipe up the table with the napkins. The more she wiped, the madder she got.

'I told you if you spilled one more thing today I would beat the tar out of you when we got home,' she said, and the little boy as well as his sister sat there trying not to cry, fighting it back, so humiliated with their quiet stifled sobs, while their mother went on and on.

'And now you're crying, aren't you, you little baby.'

She reached over her daughter and grabbed her son's head and forced him to look at her.

'I knew it,' she said. 'You're a bigger baby than your sister,' she said.

Then the mother looked at Caroline and then around at everyone else close by who was watching.

She quieted down then, and leaned over to her son and squeezed his arm so hard Caroline couldn't stand it, and while the mother was telling her son that he had to stop crying before they could leave, that she would not walk out of there in front of everyone with him crying like such a baby, Caroline walked up beside the woman, who turned around and looked at her.

'It was an accident,' Caroline said. 'It was just a little accident.'

'You mind your own business,' she said.

Caroline looked away from the mother and at the two children and tried to say in her look that she loved them, that they were all right, that they hadn't done anything wrong, but it was hard to say all that with just a look, and in just a short moment, so she walked out, afraid of going too far with the woman who had caused it all, afraid of just knocking her right through the back of the booth.

*

In the truck, Cynthia slid against Richard and put her arm around his shoulders and stayed there while they drove out of the parking lot and to the lumberyard.

The lumberyard had a sawmill at one end and a long triple row of sheds that led from the sawmill to the larger and more modern salesroom. The salesroom had a counter where three men wrote orders. Throughout the rest of the building there were bins of hardware and household supplies.

Richard and Cynthia got in line behind a man who was well dressed and well educated. He could have been either a doctor or a university professor. He was smart about something but he didn't know anything about lumber.

'I want a piece of wood,' he said.

The clerk looked at him a long time without speaking, then asked, 'What kind of a piece of wood.'

'I don't know what you call it, but it's a piece of wood that goes on the floor under the door and it has a little piece of rubber on it.'

'He wants a threshold,' Richard said.

'That's right,' the man said and thanked him. 'A threshold.'

'How wide is your door?' the clerk asked. He wasn't going to be helpful at all.

'It's about this wide,' the man said and held his hands apart.

'It's either a thirty-six or a thirty-two-inch,' Richard said to the man. 'Most entry doors are one of those two, and most all of them are thirty-six. Have you got a saw?'

'Yes.'

'Sell him a thirty-six and he can cut it if it's too long,' Richard told the clerk.

'These guys kill me,' the clerk said after the man had gone and he was writing up Richard's order.

'They can't help it,' Richard said. 'He probably knows more about something else than we do.'

'I don't see how half the people who come in here get through the day,' the clerk said, and handed the ticket to

Richard who went out with Cynthia to load up what he'd bought.

The driver who had delivered to him was sitting on a pile of lumber in the shade. Three other men were sitting with him. They were eating lunch. As Richard and Cynthia walked by, the driver winked at him and motioned with his head toward Cynthia. Richard nodded yes, that was her, and the driver rolled his eyes and whistled silently, as if to say boy, she is something nice.

After they loaded up, Cynthia moved over right against him again and they left to go back to her house.

Caroline leaned against a brick wall that separated two buildings. The front of each of the buildings was mostly glass. The brick section between the glass was in the shade. The brick was coarse-cut and had been laid in a random in-and-out pattern that someone at sometime had thought looked interesting. Because of that, it was uncomfortable, but it was better than sitting inside watching children suffer.

The vision of those two innocent, perfectly wonderful children stayed in Caroline's mind like the spots of a flash camera that had gone off two inches from her eyes. Even when she closed her eyes, she still saw it. It made it worse.

She had her hands in the pockets of her dress. The dress was long and came almost to her ankles. As she leaned against the building, she picked up one foot and rested it against the brick and balanced on the other, so that for a moment, because the long dress hid her leg that was up against the brick, she looked like a beautiful woman who'd had the misfortune to have only one leg.

It might have been that that caused people to stare at her, or it might have been that she occasionally moved her lips as she went over that dreadful incongruous scene, where she had witnessed the sweetest, most innocent expression of love as the boy casually and without effort tickled his girlfriend into dreamland, and witnessed at the same time the violent betrayal of the same love, grown older in the mother, gone sour, gone bad, inaccessible now because of God only knows what.

And that's it, she thought. Because of what.

As she thought about that she watched the cars and saw coming from her left on her side of the street Richard's truck, or one exactly like it.

As it proceeded in the line of cars coming up to the stoplight, she saw it was Richard. She saw that Cynthia was right up against him. She put her foot down to balance better and stared at this from the shadows, stared at this woman who had the unmitigated gall to sit next to her husband in her truck, a truck she had made the payments on when the shop was just getting started.

It had been bad enough when they drove up to her house a few days ago as she had waited for Richard and he had surprised her by bringing this thing along with him. But it seemed even worse now.

What made it worse besides the unexpectedness of it all, as well as everything else happening to her that day, was that Cynthia was sitting right up against him. Sitting right up against him like she was meant that she had to be straddling that long, truck-style gear-shift lever that was in the middle of the floor at the center of the seat. It meant that when he was in second gear, or fourth gear, or in reverse, he had to pull the lever down between her legs.

She knew very well it meant that because she had sat there many a time and laughed with Richard about it, played games about it, had fun about it. It was a private, sweet secret from her past that was not supposed to be a part of anyone else's life.

As the light turned back to green Richard casually turned his head to his right and saw Caroline standing in the middle of the sidewalk with a wild look on her face.

'Holy mackerel,' he said. 'It's Caroline.'

'Where?' Cynthia asked, looking all around.

'There, goddamnit,' he said and nudged her to look in the proper direction.

'Oh no,' she said.

'She's seen us,' he said.

'She sure has,' she said.

'We're done for,' he said, and drove off as fast as the traffic would allow.

'Is she still there?' Cynthia asked, turning around to see.

'How would I know?' he said.'I can't look and drive at the same time.'

'Well, don't yell at me,' she said.

'I didn't yell.'

'You did so.'

'I did not.'

'You yelled at me and you pushed me.'

'I never pushed you.'

'You shoved me with your shoulder and it hurt,' she said.

'Oh, baloney,' he said.

Caroline was sitting on the sidewalk exactly in the spot where she'd been standing, and a small crowd gathered around her to see if she was all right.

'I'm okay,' she said.

'Can you get up?' one of them asked.

She was sitting in the middle of the sidewalk as if it was a perfectly good place to sit.

'Yes, I can get up,' she said, without doing so.

'Are you sick?' someone asked.

'Not really,' she said.

'Would you like me to call someone for you?' a person asked.

'There isn't anyone to call,' she said.

'Would you like some help standing up?'

'Yes, I mean no,' she said.

The two people who had begun to pull her up stopped.

'You do or don't?' one of them said.

'I mean I can get up. There's nothing wrong with me.'

'Are you sure?'

'I'm okay. I just had to sit down for a minute. I'm all right,' she said. 'Really.'

Way to go, Caroline, she told herself. I guess the next thing that's going to happen is I'm going to spontaneously combust on the sidewalk and burst into flames.

She walked off with her head up but avoided looking at anyone directly. She was dreadfully embarrassed and blue. She went looking for a place to get out of sight. She opened the door of a pub-and-restaurant combination. It looked dark and cool and crowded. It was a college-town kind of place, full of students and town people of all kinds. She looked for a table and couldn't find one empty so she went to the bar and sat on a stool and ordered a beer.

'She's going to do something,' Richard said. 'I can tell you that for sure.'

'How do you know?'

'I saw it in her face. We've had it.'

'What do you think she'll do?'

'I don't know,' he said.

'Do you think she'll come over to the house?'

'I just don't know. I just know I saw it in her face.'

'Well, let's not go home, then. Let's go someplace else.'

'Like where?'

'Like out of town for a few days,' Cynthia said.

'She could still come over to the house.'

'But we'd be gone.'

'But the house would still be there.'

'Oh,' she said. 'I see.'

'So it'd actually be better if we were there,' he said.

'Or at least if somebody was there.'

'Like who?'

'Like somebody to house-sit. Maybe we could hire somebody to house-sit the place and tell them, you know, a little something about it so they'd be on the lookout for her and stay there the whole time and not go into town or anything.'

'That might work.'

'Or – I know,' she said. 'We could hire a security agency to watch it. Maybe they have the kind of setup where someone could be there twenty-four hours a day. They must.'

'They might,' he said.

'They must. They do it in buildings and stuff like that all the time.'

'It would cost a hell of a lot,' he said. 'I bet it would cost a fortune.'

'I wonder how much,' she said.

The bartender gave Caroline a beer and a menu. In North Carolina, places that served liquor by the drink had to, by law, make most of their money off of food, and the liquor sales had to be secondary. Because of that there were a lot of expensive sandwiches for sale.

In this place, which had an Irish theme, there were sandwiches with names like the O'Malley Burger and so forth. The O'Malley Burger cost as much as four beers, but you got potato chips and a pickle on the plate along with the great big sandwich, and that's what Caroline ordered.

She was on her second beer when the bartender served her the sandwich. She took a big bite and the blood oozed out, and she put it down just as fast as she had picked it up and turned it around on the plate so she couldn't see the raw bite she'd taken out of it and washed down what she had in her mouth with a long drink of beer.

'Is everything all right?' the bartender asked her after she'd sat there awhile drinking but not eating.

'Oh yeah, it's fine,' she said. She picked up a potato chip and ate it and smiled at him and nodded, yep, just fine.

'I thought I saw you shaking your head like the O'Malley wasn't any good. We can take it back and get you something else if you want.'

'Nope. Everything's all right. I was probably just talking to myself. It's been one of those days.'

The bartender left the bill beside the plate.

While she ate the potato chips she looked around the room. Her eyes had gotten used to the dim light and she kept coming back to a woman sitting alone in a booth with one bottle of beer in front of her and a bowl of onion rings beside it. The woman ate the onion rings and drank her beer deliberately, a little bite at a time, a little sip at a time, as if she was lost in thought and the beer and the onion rings were just the pause or commas between her thoughts.

She looks like she's had the same kind of day I've had, Caroline told herself. Of course, I can't imagine anyone else having such a day, she said and looked around some more.

'Another beer?' the bartender asked her.

'I don't think so,' she said and took a ten-dollar bill from her purse and handed it to him with the check. 'Keep the change,' she said.

I need to talk to that woman, she told herself as she got up to leave. I need to talk to someone or I'm going to scream.

'I don't usually come up to people like this,' Caroline said, standing at the side of the table while the woman looked up at her, 'but are you waiting for someone or would you mind if I sat down here for a minute?'

'I don't mind,' she said. 'Sit down.'

The woman was older than Caroline, or if she wasn't she had a lot of miles on her. She had nice eyes but her skin had gone bad and she had a lot of makeup on to cover it up, so that the color of her face was not the same color as her arms or her neck or anything else.

'Are you going to be here for a while?' Caroline asked. 'I mean, what I mean by that is I've had this really strange, really awful day, and I really need to talk to somebody, because I just saw something that's really made me mad and I'm afraid I'm going to do something crazy if I don't get it out of my system.'

*

'Let's get the truck unloaded before we decide anything,' Richard said.

'I wish I still had the dogs,' Cynthia said. 'I wish I hadn't let the children take them over to their father's.'

'Dogs wouldn't do any good.'

'They could bark. They were always good at barking at strangers.'

'Caroline's not scared of dogs.'

'I guess Caroline's not scared of anything.'

'She probably isn't,' he said. 'She's probably crazy enough not to be scared of anything. You're probably right about that.'

'Well, I hate her,' Cynthia said.

'I know,' he said.

'Here we are again, running from Caroline.'

'We're not exactly doing that.'

'Yes we are.'

'Not exactly. Here, take this,' he said and handed her one of the pieces of lumber off the truck, which she carried over and laid neatly against the wall of the house on the porch.

'Well, what are we doing, then?'

'We're being smart.'

'I don't like it,' she said.

'It's the only way to be. We've got to figure out what to do and we've got to do it soon.'

'Okay,' she said. 'I'm sorry. I trust you. Just tell me what you want and I'll do it.'

'Well, first off, do you want me to try to find her and have a talk with her before she gets here?'

'No, I do not. I do not want you to ever go see her again.'

'Okay, then. The first thing to do is decide whether we're going to stay here and deal with what comes or leave and wait it out.'

'Why don't I call one of those security patrols and ask them how much they charge for a twenty-four-hour guard?'

'Okay,' he said.

'For how long do you think we'd need to be away?'

'It's hard to say. Caroline can hold on to being mad for a long time. I'd say three or four days, at least.'

'See,' Caroline said, 'some people can do things that are wrong and some cannot.'

She'd been talking for a little while and was already in high gear and rolling right along.

'See, it's like this. I'm one of those people who feels bad about everything I ever did wrong. Anything I do that I shouldn't just stays with me forever. You know what I mean?'

The woman nodded, yes.

'It's like one time when I was little I had this friend of mine over. Her name was Leslie and she was one of the best friends I had ever had. We did everything together. All summer long we went around barefoot and did everything we wanted. Well, one time we went to my house to get a Pepsi and see, we had this bottle opener on the wall, you know, the kind you hook the bottle into and pull down and the cap pops off, and anyway, I had both bottles and I opened the first one and I opened it too hard and this little piece of glass broke off and I stood there looking at it for just a second and I knew I couldn't get another one because my mother only allowed us to have one each every day, and she'd count them when she got home, so I just stood there for a second and then I turned around and gave it to Leslie, and I said, here, I opened yours first and she took it and then all night long I was afraid the phone was going to ring and her parents were going to tell me that her insides had been all cut up and it was awful.'

Caroline motioned for the waitress to bring her a beer and then kept on.

'See, that was really the first time I had ever done someone wrong and look what it did to me. I can never forget it, whereas some people do things like that all day long and it never bothers them. I don't know. Maybe I wasn't meant to make it. Maybe somehow I was meant to mess up everything I ever did, but I don't believe that, really, do you? I mean about people. Do you know what I mean?' she asked the woman, who took a sip of her beer and a bite of her onion ring and offered Caroline a whole one that had been sitting on a napkin draining off the grease.

'I know what you mean,' she said, and Caroline looked at her while she ate the onion ring, and thought about what she'd just said and wondered if it was true.

'It's a lot of money,' Cynthia said. 'Don't even ask me how much. I could do it, but while he was looking up how much it would be and whether or not he had anyone who could come out right away, I thought, she can't do this to me. She can't do this to us. And I thought, I'm not going to run from her. If we run from her now, we'll have to do it forever.'

'That's not necessarily so,' he said. 'Sometimes it's a lot better to let things cool off slowly than to try to do anything right away.'

'I knew you'd say that, but for me, I just can't let myself do it.'

'Well, then, it'll be just like before,' he said. 'I told you all last month I had to find the right time to tell things to her, and we pushed it and look what happened.'

'I suppose that's my fault.'

'I'm not saying that. I'm not even thinking that. I'm just saying the slower things are allowed to develop, the easier they are to handle.'

'I know you're right,' she said.

'Then let's go,' he said. 'Either that or let me try to find her and talk to her. At least let me phone her.'

'I don't know,' she said.

'Let me phone her. You can be on the other extension and listen to everything.'

'It's not that,' she said. 'I trust you. I really do, baby,' she said and put her head on his shoulder while they sat on the couch that faced the front window.

'It's just what?' he asked.

'It's just that even phoning her is kind of giving in to her. Even having you phone her is like she's won you back a little.'

'I don't think so.'

'It is. I know what I'm talking about.'

'You mean she'll think that?'

'She won't think it so much as it'll just change things back a little for her. I think we need to stop her now. We need to show her it's over and all this madness on her part is not going to accomplish a thing.'

'Well,' he said, 'I'll stay with you and do whatever you want, but don't say I didn't warn you. It's Caroline we're dealing with, and she doesn't live in the same world as everyone else.'

'I know,' she said, and they stayed on the couch. The house was quiet. From far away, from far across what would have been at one time valleys and streams and pine woods so tall and dense at the top the ground below was clear, uncluttered, dark and cool, from that direction, a car came down the road, clipping along, and passed, unaware that the two people inside the remarkable brick home at the edge of the woods were listening, just flew along coming back from town and going home, oblivious to the intensity and interest of the two people on the couch, listening to it pass, just minding its own business, staying on its side of the road, staying in its lane, staying out of trouble, minding the rules of the road.

'It's just that I hate being alone,' Caroline said. 'I hate being poor, as well, and damnit all, here I go again back where I started. I hate going backwards. It takes so much out of you to get where you want to be. One person can't do it nowadays, you know? It's just too hard. You've got to have someone else. That's what makes me so mad about that thing he's run off with. She doesn't need him any more than we need another hot day this summer. You know? She just doesn't.

'People don't love each other anymore. They don't. They just do things together and when they get bored, they leave. I hate that. I really do.

'See, I have this really beautiful farm, I mean, it's not really a farm, but this little piece of land where we built our house, and I mean, built it, we did it ourselves, and it's really nice, even if it is small, and now, goddamnit all, it looks like I'm going to lose the place. For a while there I'd thought I'd done it. I thought I had gotten away from never having any money and growing up poor and I thought I'd made it. I thought I'd done what my mother tried so hard to do, but I guess I didn't. I guess I'm going to be as poor as she was all her life.

'She just never could break out of it. Even when she saved up a little money for something, mostly by hiding it from my father, who could spend money on cars and things like that faster than anyone could make it, even when she'd saved up a little, she'd just blow it on something stupid, like storm doors or something like that. I mean, not stupid, but she couldn't just let it build up until she had enough to change her life. You know what I mean?

'But that's what happens to you when you never have any money. When you get some, you don't know what to do with it. You don't know how to handle it. You go out of control. I guess money makes people crazy. Having it makes you crazy and not having it makes you crazy. Know what I mean?' she said.

'I think probably she won't do anything until tonight. The night is when she always gets wildest.'

They had gone back to work and had done most of what they had set out to do when they began that morning. Cynthia was holding the end of one long board while Richard cut it when the phone rang.

'Damn,' he said. 'I wonder if that's her.'

'If it's her, I'll just hang up.'

'I don't know if that'll work or not.'

'I told you. I don't want to talk to her and I don't want to see her and I don't want you to, either.'

The phone was still ringing.

'Suit yourself,' he said, and she answered the phone while he propped up the end of the board on the back of a chair and finished his cut.

'It's Clark,' she whispered to him as he walked in the room. Clark was her ex-husband. She held her hand over the mouthpiece and blew Richard a kiss. Then she looked away and went on with the conversation. When she started talking again, her face and her voice got so hard the words were like nails shooting into the receiver.

'I don't care what you say,' she said. 'The children are going to stay with me next week just like we planned and you're not taking them anywhere.'

She went on like this about the children for ten minutes. The conversation went back and forth. Richard sat across the room and watched her pace around the full length of the telephone cord, like an animal tied to a short leash. The conversation went on so long and got so repetitive that Richard finally went out on the porch so he could better hear if Caroline drove up or see her if she parked her car out on the road behind the screen of trees.

'See, I guess you could say this sort of master plan for my life didn't work out,' Caroline said. 'I mean, if you gave me a choice of having a good life, but no money, but being happy and having a good marriage and being rich in all the other ways a person could be, I'd take it and forget about the money and that's the way I always thought he felt, too, but I guess I was wrong.

'I hate being wrong but I guess I've been about as wrong as a person could be. All the time I thought, if I'm just everything he ever wanted in a woman, if I just give him everything I have, he'll love me as much as I love him, and my life will be as rich as I always dreamed, you know what I mean. It's like up until all this I really thought I'd done it. I really did,' she said and then stopped talking for a moment while the woman across from her shifted positions in the booth to be more comfortable.

'And see,' Caroline went on, 'I just want to say one more thing and that is that even though I know I shouldn't be thinking things like this, I'm still mad. Real mad. I'm mad enough to kill that woman. I had a cousin who almost killed someone one time and now I know how mad she must have been and I can see from the look on your face that you don't like what I've just said but I'm telling you the truth about everything, and I'm telling you the truth about that, too.

'I hate that phony whimpering little bitch enough to kill her, and I just want to know, I just really want to know,' she said, seeing that the woman across from her had gotten really uncomfortable, 'before I get up and go do something I probably'll wish I hadn't later on, I just want to know what you think of all this.'

'I don't know where to start,' the woman said.

'Anywhere. Start anywhere.'

'Well, I'm late for work already, but I think the first thing you've got to do is calm down.'

'I can't.'

'The whole time you've been talking to me you've been twirling your hair around your fingers over and over again without stopping, and your hair's all pulled out to one side.'

'It is?' Caroline asked and felt it with her hand and tried to get it back in place using her fingers like a comb.

'Forget about it now,' the woman said. 'I think you need to get some help. I think you need to forget about all this until you get some help and let someone who knows more about these things than I do tell you what to do.'

'The hell with that,' Caroline said. 'You think I'm going to see some counselor and have him or her, whoever it is, tell me that I just have to forgive and forget? You think I'm going to do that?' she said, her voice getting louder now so that the few other people who were still there in the middle of the afternoon turned around and listened.

'I'll be goddamned if I will,' she went on. 'That roll-over-and-play-dead crap is not for me. Is that what you'd really do?' she asked. 'Is it really?'

'I've got to go now,' the woman said.

'Hey wait,' Caroline said. 'I don't want you to think I don't appreciate your letting me talk to you about this, but you don't know this woman like I do. Going to a counselor as if there was something wrong with me and letting her get away with this is just the kind of thing she'd wish to happen. I can't do it, don't you see. I can't let her get away with it.'

The woman nodded and walked out. After a few minutes Caroline did too. The sun was so bright it was like coming out of the theater from an afternoon show. The heat was terrible. Caroline squinted all the way to the parking lot.

The parking lot was large and flat and paved with asphalt. The asphalt shimmered in the heat. At a distance and at just the right angle, the cars wavered like mirages in the desert in old movies. The pavement was so hot Caroline could feel it through her sandals.

She couldn't find her car. She walked through the whole lot and couldn't find it.

'I can't find my car,' she said to the boy in the air-conditioned booth. 'Here's my ticket but I can't find my goddamn car.'

'It's right there,' he said and pointed to it. 'I remember when you came in.'

'Where?' she asked.

'There,' he said and pointed to it again.

'Oh,' she said.

'Are you all right?' he asked.

'I'm fine, buddy,' she said. 'Really fine,' she said and walked off. 'I'm in such good shape you wouldn't believe it,' she said over her shoulder.

The inside of the car was hot enough to kill if a person had been locked inside. She opened all her windows and eased herself onto the seat and then started the old thing up and drove back up to the booth.

'Remember me,' she said.

'What?' the boy asked.

'Just remember my face,' she said. 'I'm going to be famous real soon,' and then she drove off, leaving the poor little seventeen-year-old boy wondering how a woman who looked that good could be that strange. He had no way of knowing yet. He had no way of knowing what lay ahead after the innocence was plucked from those girls in the yearbook who wrote to each other, I will always remember you, I will never forget you, you are the best friend I will ever have in my life, I will love you forever, they wrote, and they meant it, and the boy, living in that world, couldn't have understood Caroline and what had happened to her that day and he watched her drive away and wondered what she had meant.

'I'm sorry about that,' Cynthia said after she joined Richard on the porch.

'It's all right.'

'He gets me mad. He's always trying to find some way to get to me, you know.'

'Not really, but it's all right.'

'I mean, he's, oh, well, it's not important. Not anymore.'

'If you say so,' he said.

'Are we finished with everything we were going to do today?' she asked.

'Yes.'

'Good.'

'Yeah,' he said. 'It went fast.'

'You know what I've been thinking?' she said.

'What?'

'That she's not going to do anything after all. I don't know what made me change, but it just came to me that she's not going to do a thing.'

'I wish you were right, but I'm afraid you're not.'

'I am, though. It's something that just came to me in such a deep way I know it to be true.'

'She may not be coming now, but she'll be here tonight. Like I said, she always gets craziest at night.'

'I think this time you're going to be wrong.'

'I hope so. I would like to be wrong this time,' he said.

Even on a day as hot as that, the front porch of Cynthia's house was cool. Since the house was up on a hill and had the pasture in front of it, and because directly in front of the house were three large oaks that had been planted a hundred years ago when some other dwelling had been there, the house was always in the shade in the afternoon and had a breeze, if there was any to have.

'It's nice here,' he said. 'If it weren't for this afternoon, I do believe, I do believe I would be a happy man sitting here right at this moment.'

'You can be one anyway,' she said. 'I'm going to see to that,' she said, and looked across her field and dreamed a quick little dream of peace and happiness and the simple, good life.

Caroline drove home. She was a little drunk. She wasn't drunk enough to have trouble driving or not to know what she was doing, but she was too drunk to figure out what to do after she got home.

Damn this place, she thought. I'm going to kill her.

She picked up the phone and called Cynthia. She was going to tell her she was on her way over. The line was busy. She dialed it again and again. She dialed it so many times over and over that the circuits between the houses stayed open and as fast as she finished the last number it started the busy signal right where it had left off before. She just kept on, punching the numbers in, dot-dot-dot, dat-dat-dat-dat.

An alarm went off in the substation of the telephone company.

'What've we got?' the supervisor asked. He had been sitting at his desk smoking a cigar and thinking about fishing on a cool morning pulled under the branches of a weeping willow when the alarm went off.

'Crazy person,' the technician said.

'You want to shut it down?' he asked.

'Naw. Let it go. See how long it keeps up.'

The supervisor went back to his office. He relit his cigar. Except for Caroline going crazy on the circuits, it was a good day. He put his feet up on his desk and began dreaming again.

'No one's coming today, are they?' Richard asked.

'What do you mean?'

'I mean, except for the possibility of you-know-who.'

'Not that I know of.'

'Okay,' he said.

'Why?'

'I'm going to block the top of the driveway with the truck.'

'You still don't believe me, do you?'

'I believe you. I just want to do it anyway.'

He drove to the top of the driveway. Just off the pavement he backed the truck into the bushes and then pulled it forward and blocked the whole entrance. A car could still pull off the road onto the shoulder, but it couldn't get past the truck and down the drive.

Richard walked back to the house. It was a nearly perfect site. The driveway was paved and curved toward the house in an arc that Cynthia had laid out with the builder when they first looked at the land. The curve broke toward the field and then gradually came back toward the house. The cedar trees that had been planted along the sides when it had been built were now large enough to define the drive and make the graceful curve look even better.

Just as the curve straightened out, the house came into view. The house was set long ways to the road, facing the field. Someone sometime many years ago had noticed this spot and chosen it from what must have been a nearly unlimited number of good places to build back then.

The oldtimers knew a good place to build when they saw one. They weren't forced to build on the side of a hill or in the wet bottoms between the hills where the sun never shone except at noon and where the dampness from the ground came right through the floor and kept the house rotten and mildewed forever.

It was a charmed and special site and Cynthia had known it when she looked at it the very first day. Richard knew it, too. As he walked down the drive, he could hardly believe his luck.

'I sure wish there was some way you could keep this place,' he said, when he got back.

'But why?'

'It's hard to find a place as nice as this. You can go a long way and not ever find a place as nice as this.'

'I never knew you thought that,' she said.

'I do.'

'But it's part of my past, don't you see. It's part of a kind of life I don't want to live anymore.'

'I know,' he said. 'I was just struck, walking down the driveway, how nice it really is.'

'We'll find a better place. If Clark and I could come up with something like this, then there's no telling what you and I could come up with. There's just no telling,' she said.

'Maybe so,' he said.

'I'm going to take a bath now, anyway. When I get out I'm going to cook a great supper. I'm not going to worry about a thing. Okay?'

It was nearly four o'clock when she went up to take her bath. Richard turned on the television. Cynthia could get every channel on the dial, or so it seemed. She had a dish out back hidden from the road and hidden from the front of the house but facing south with a clear range before it.

On one channel a man was selling something. It was hard to see what he was selling at first, because the camera was way back from the product and had taken a long shot of the man and the product and the woman standing beside him who was modeling the product. Then there was a close-up of the necklace. It was a good-looking necklace. It was some kind of gold and there were only 73,000 left to sell. It looked good on the woman. She had a nice neck and her skin looked real good, smooth and brown and healthy.

The necklace cost $116. The woman wasn't for sale. Some women were for sale and some were not. This woman had already been bought. Sometimes you could look into the face of a woman and you could tell whether or not she was for sale, or whether she had merely been for sale and was already bought. Some women were not for sale. You could tell right off there was nothing that could buy them. But there were just a few of those. Most of them could be bought for something, and some of them could be bought for the price of the necklace, or just the necklace by itself.

The woman on the television cost more than the necklace. She was smiling and holding her chest out and her shoulders back because she knew she cost more than the necklace.

The ones who knew they could be bought for the price of the necklace, or for just the necklace itself, didn't look like that. They couldn't stand up straight very long. The smile withered fast. The price went down. There were only 73,000 left. You had to call quickly or they'd all be gone.

At just past four, Caroline ran in from the shop, where she'd been walking around talking to herself, trying to get calmed down. It was hard. She wasn't going to be able to do it.

Some people just give up, she thought. Some people just say, well, that's life. Well, that's my fate. Some people said, here, here's the knife. Go ahead and kill me. Sometimes you got in a situation where it felt like that was the right thing to do and then later you realized it was not.

Being calm and cooperating in your own destruction had a nice temporary pleasure to it. It felt good for a moment, the way a bad headache would have felt if someone had cut the back of your head off with an ax.

Lying on the floor and pretending you were dead and crossing your hands over your chest while your husband said goodbye felt good in that same weird way, but only for a little while.

It was easy to understand how a man could be fooled. Some women were good at it. They had different faces, different legs, different bodies, different words, for different men. When they put the combination together just right, it was easy to understand how a man could get fooled.

Later, though, they got tangled up in the various parts still lying around from the previous lives, and then what? I thought, well, she looked, I mean, it seemed. The sentence was never completed.

It was the thing lately to forgive. A lot of people talked about forgiveness. People talked about it in restaurants and on the radio and in articles in magazines. The people talking had a lot to forgive themselves for the way they talked about it so much. In a weak moment, you yourself could begin to believe that you had to forgive everything like these people did even though you couldn't remember if you'd done anything wrong or not.

It was like a popular song that was played so much pretty soon people were singing it while they drove along sometimes forgetting the words but humming along anyway, coming in and out of it, smiling, blessing those around them, being good, knowing it was right.

Being good got old, though. It was hard work. Left over, though, the smile remained. It was a seductive sight. Tall, beautiful women appeared in skirts so short you could see there was nothing on under them. Their nipples hardened under the braless slip top that rubbed against them all day, and still the smile remained.

The smile of inner peace and forgiveness denied the

vision of short skirts and hardened nipples and it was all quite confusing.

The smile, Caroline thought, is what I hate most about her. The smile, which seems to always be there, is what I hate so much. That sweet and innocent smile that must have been practiced for hours, just hours and hours before a mirror, is what I hate the most.

It was all going through Caroline while she paced around, imagining the worst, making everything more diabolical than it could be, making everything unbearable.

And so, at a little past four, having made a difficult day unbearable for herself, Caroline got back in the car and went for a ride.

Cynthia served. If she'd been playing tennis, every shot would have been in, every stroke perfect, every ace a breathtaking act of precision and grace. Her footwork could have inspired a dance, a ballet as light and effortless as the flight of a bird soaring on the currents.

Cynthia served. Richard received. At the end of the meal, Cynthia won. Richard hadn't even figured out what to do, or where to stand, or how to hold the racquet. He'd just sat there and watched this woman and wondered at his luck.

A week or so ago, he'd been chased around by this sad and crazy person he'd married. She'd run at him like a duck, armless, and quacking and clumsy.

He ate the food and sat in the chair and leaned on his elbow and smiled and watched this woman dance for him, and he wondered, marveled, at his luck.

'It's the quiet, you know,' he said soon after they finished.

'I know. You've told me.'

'She was always talking. I didn't know. I thought, well, maybe they're all that way. I didn't know.'

'It's always something,' she said. 'It could be talking, it could be not talking. It's always something.'

The house was so quiet that the only sounds were the

refrigerator and the central air-conditioning turning on and off. The refrigerator was frost free. It ran a lot. It had a system that heated up parts of it quickly and melted away the frost. Then the compressor cycled on again and cooled everything off again. After it turned on and the motor and compressor smoothed out, you could hear the water dripping into the pan underneath the unit.

Outside, the heat pump did the same thing. It was like a refrigerator itself. In the winter, the pistons went one way and took whatever heat it could extract from the air and blew it back into the house. In the summer, the pistons reversed direction and somehow took the cool from the air and gave it back to the house.

It was a little bit magical. Technologically speaking. It was the emperor's new clothes of heating and air-conditioning. Everyone believed it would work, so it did.

It was the kind of thing that, if studied real hard, didn't make sense. It had a logic and operating rationale that went beyond the everyday life experience of turning steering wheels, for instance, in which it was easy to understand that turning the thing around moved the wheels and the car followed.

The heat pump which pumped the heat either in or out, had an invisible life, like the insides of any guarded construction. It was fragile behind all that sheet metal. A little shock on the Freon tubes and the whole thing would shut down. It could be damaged easily, but left to its own it would magically continue.

It sat there, like a house sits on a piece of land, like people sit in a house, only as safe as what does not happen, only as safe as what does not go wrong.

Everything had a connection. The quiet had some connection to the violent, the peaceful to the mad, and the smooth to the erratic.

'You're right,' Richard said, having just been thinking about things. 'It is always something.'

Richard, then, was connected to both. He was connected to Caroline and he was connected to Cynthia and he was somewhere in the middle and therefore he could feel the pull between the two in a different way than the two women could feel what they were generating. He could feel the impending snap and collision the way a dog darting loose from its fenced yard feels the car just before it hits him.

'It's nice, though,' he said.

'What?' Cynthia asked. 'What's nice?'

'This,' he said. 'All this.'

Caroline saw the truck parked sideways in the drive.

Well goddamn, she thought. That just makes me all the madder.

She stopped her car on the wide, grassy shoulder and looked around without getting out. Across the road six small houses and four mobile homes were jammed together on an acre and a half of land. On either side of the acre and a half were woods as far as you could see. Someone had at one time gotten that acre and a half away from the person who owned all the rest of the land and had spawned over the years the houses and trailers and outbuildings and hog pens with sagging and uprooted fencing where the hogs had nosed under it or leaned over it trying to get something fresh to eat. They were trying to get out of the filthy pens where they had to live their lives, trying to live a little better than the way they saw life around them being lived.

Someone once had a start in life. There it was. Historically. A clean piece of land and a single house and a new life. It had come down to this. Hog pens and chickens running loose and roosting on the porch and droppings splattered all over the place and two dozen dogs all more or less looking alike, and yet continued on the hill across from the rich doctor's house as these people lived their lives in and out of jail, in and out of jobs, in and out of debt, in and out of each other's bedrooms, shooting each other and knifing each other and getting drunk and falling down the bank and onto the road until the sheriff came and got them up and into the yard.

It had all seemed so sordid, such a public display of decadence, of lust and violence, of embarrassingly primitive behavior, while across the road, life emerged from behind the planted line of trees in starched white hospital jackets and clean long station wagons with beautiful faces bobbing up and down just from the joy of being alive.

The money had to have made a difference. The education had to have made a difference. The color of the skin and the privileges of that color had to have made a difference. There had to be an explanation.

Maybe it was a virus. Maybe a virus out there had gone undetected, and had crept across the road and shattered this beautiful happy life and caused it to go mad so that it had to breach itself in its own public display of confusion.

How else could you explain that car full of happy people leaving a house that most people only dreamed about owning, a house that helping humanity had built, leaving for that vacation in the cool of the Blue Ridge Mountains, while the people across the road sweated into the night and fell asleep drunk in stinking clothes, how else could you explain how one day they all had to live apart, how one day the same words that they had heard screamed across the valley between the houses on the hill across the road and their own had come to be hurled out of their own mouths. How else could you explain the cars leaving that fine house in the middle of the night and then returning and then leaving again, going down the road fast, fleeing something that must have looked horrible the way they drove, trying to get away.

All that money had to make a difference. You could buy so much. You could stack up so much between you and the other person that you couldn't get to one another anymore, and that had to help. You could soundproof your rooms to keep from hearing the other person in the middle of the night. You could take a lot of trips to restful places and come back ready to be the way you had to be. You could leave again when it didn't work out.

It must have been a virus, then, that crept across the road, and you would have imagined a doctor could have detected it. You would have thought all that money and all the learning and all that reading and all the civilized achievement would have immunized the people against that virus. You could understand it across the road, living in houses falling over because they'd been built without diagonal bracing, no one knew how to cut the angle required to set the bracings in, because they'd been built by drunks in a confusion of hope and hopelessness, because somehow it couldn't be that everyone was infected.

Caroline got out. She looked one more time at the panorama above her across the road. She knew those people. Even though they were black, she knew them because they were poor and she came from the same place, the same fear, the same confusion. Not as bad. No one white was ever quite as bad off as bad-off blacks, but she knew them.

I hate being poor, she thought. I just hate it.

She had a set of keys to the truck on her key ring. Just as she got to the truck to move it, a UPS van whizzed up to a stop and parked behind her car.

'Do you live here?' the man asked. He jumped from the truck almost before it stopped and actually ran over to her with two packages in his hands.

'Me? Oh. Yeah. I live here.'

'Are you Cynthia?'

'Yeah. That's me. I sure am.'

'Can you take these, then?'

'Sure. I can take them. I was just going down to the house. We've got the driveway blocked because they're working on it.'

'Sign this line,' the man said.

'Right here?'

'There,' he said and held his finger on the numbered line while she signed Cynthia's name.

'Thanks.'

'Sure. Hey, listen. I get a lot of stuff, you know, and any time I'm not here, just leave it on the porch. The other guy always did, okay?'

'All right,' he said.

Caroline took the packages and started back toward the truck until she was sure he was out of sight and then she pitched them in the back seat of her car and drove off in the opposite direction from the UPS truck. She circled around the long way and drove all the way home before she stopped to see what was in the boxes.

It was early evening. The sun was behind the trees but not yet fully down. A few lightning bugs were out. A lone tree frog let loose for a moment and then abruptly stopped, as if it had realized it had started too soon.

The phone rang again, only the second time that day, the first time having been Cynthia's ex-husband, and this one, they thought as they looked at each other, possibly Caroline, but, as the day had gone on and nothing had happened, also quite possibly not.

'It's Anne,' Cynthia whispered to Richard, who nodded and changed the channel on the million-dollar system, looking for something, although he didn't know what.

Anne was seventeen and would be eighteen a month into her senior year. She was named after her mother, Cynthia Anne, but took after her father. She was mad at her mother for kicking her father out and taking up with other men, but she was trying not to show it, even though at times during the past year she had been forthright about it.

To keep from showing it, she acted nonchalant and slightly depressed whenever she saw or talked with her mother.

'Daddy told me,' she said, in answer to her mother's question if she knew Richard was living with her now.

'What do you think?' Cynthia asked.

'It's up to you, I guess.'

'It's not entirely,' Cynthia said. 'I mean, it is, but you and your brother will be living here off and on during school.'

'Well, Mom, really, if I said I didn't like it, what would you do? Really. It's like Daddy said, it's your life now and it's up to you how you run it.'

'Is that what he said?'

'Yes.'

'What else did he say?'

'Ask him yourself. Don't always ask me to tell you what he said about this or that. Ask him yourself.'

'I know what he said to me. I just wanted to know what he said to you.'

'He said something like, I don't know, I don't know, I don't remember exactly,' Anne said. 'He said something like Richard didn't know what he was in for or something like that.'

'He said that?'

'I don't know. Maybe it wasn't that. I can't remember.'

They talked about the trip their father wanted to take them on and why she wouldn't or maybe she would let them go, and eventually decided to talk about it more tomorrow.

'Let me speak to your brother before you hang up,' Cynthia said after they had finished. She looked over at Richard and waved while she waited for her son to get to the phone.

'He can't come now,' her daughter said about a minute later.

'Is he in the bathroom?'

'No. I don't know what he's doing.'

'Go back and tell him I want to talk to him.'

'Oh, Mom,' she said and set the phone down and went to tell him.

Her son's name was Clark also, but Jr., and he had taken to calling himself C.J. when he made the jump from elementary to junior high. He was fourteen and in the ninth grade but still called Cynthia 'Mommy'.

'Mommy,' he said when he got on the phone, 'didn't she tell you I couldn't come now?'

'But I wanted to talk to you, honey,' she said.

'But I was watching the baseball game,' he said.

'It'll still be there when you get back.'

'It won't either. It's the ninth inning.'

'Well, I wanted to ask you something very serious.'

'What?'

'It's something I haven't told your sister yet. I wanted to talk to you about it first.'

'What is it?'

'I was thinking I might have to sell this house and I wanted to know what you thought about it.'

'Oh Mommy,' he said, 'why would you sell the house?'

'Because I need the money. I'm going to buy us another place, just smaller. I will need the money as time goes on. Do you understand?'

'Can't you just keep it and get a job or something? I love that house. I've got my dirt bike there. What are we going to do with my dirt bike? Where am I going to ride it if you sell the house?'

'You'll be driving soon. You won't miss it after a while.'

'That's two years from now. I can't ride it in town.'

'Well, just think about it. Talk it over with your sister if you want to. I think I'm going to have to do it.'

'He's worried about his dirt bike,' Cynthia said to Richard after she hung up.

'I don't blame him,' he said. 'If I were fourteen and were about to lose my motorcycle, I'd be worried, too.'

'I guess we can find another place that has some land with it.'

'I guess so,' he said.

'If it's not too expensive,' she said.

'Maybe,' he said. 'Maybe we can.'

When Caroline got home she carried the boxes to the house. The first box was from a mail-order food company. It was full of enormous cashews and pistachios and pecans and about a thousand dollars' worth of other nuts. The second box was from a lingerie company that had a name that implied something secret and naughty.

'Goddamn and double goddamn,' she said when she opened the lingerie box.

'THAT DOES IT,' she screamed and tossed the box across the room. *'THAT REALLY DOES IT.'*

She picked up the phone and dialed the number. It rang. Cynthia answered it.

'YOU BITCH,' she screamed. *'I'M ON MY WAY OVER THERE AND I'VE GOT SOMETHING FOR YOU,'* she screamed but Cynthia hung up halfway through the sentence and the phone went dead. She called again. This time Richard answered.

'SHE'S HAD IT,' Caroline screamed, and then she hung up before Richard could say anything.

Caroline ran into the bedroom. She took off her dress and her sandals and laid out her fighting clothes. She had to choose what to wear carefully. It was like the time two guys in high school had been at each other all week one time and had finally agreed to fight it out after school on that Friday. The whole school was electrified.

They were fighting over a popular girl. The two guys were popular as well. One was on the basketball team and the other was on the tennis team.

The fight had been kept from the teachers. Rumors swept the student body all day. One of the guys was supposed to have had a karate lesson one time. The other was supposed to have brought brass knucks. There was a lot of talk about the brass knucks. A couple of guys on the football team said if he pulled the brass knucks out, they were going to take them away from him. Other people said it was only fair to balance out against the karate lesson. Just hearing the words 'brass knucks' made everybody wild.

It had been more or less the social event of the season as everyone tried to find someone else to go to the fight with. All the regular couples went together. A lot of people decided to go in groups. It was an enormous crowd. Nearly everyone who didn't get picked up by their parents after school or had to ride the bus home or usually rode the bus home but had gotten a promise of a ride with someone who had a car was there.

The fight was in the woods at the back of the parking lot. It was less likely to draw attention there, as the teachers would assume everyone was just heading out to the cars on the usual chaotic Friday afternoon.

The two guys squared off. There were no brass knucks. The fight was over in three seconds. It was the most anti-climatic thing anyone could remember. It was the biggest disappointment since the time this guy told everyone he was going to put a rubber with mayonnaise in it in this goody-goody nerd girl's desk and when he did and she saw it with the whole class looking and expecting a lot of screaming and crying and running from the room all she did was look at it and ignore it, without even turning red or anything; the fight was the biggest disappointment since then. It had just been one good punch and the fight was over.

'I knew it,' Richard said. 'I told you.'

Cynthia couldn't believe it.

'What'd she say to you?' she asked.

'I don't even know. She just screamed something.'

'I can't believe it,' she said. 'I really thought, I really had this strong feeling that she wouldn't do anything, that it was over.'

'No way,' he said.

'How long will it take her to get here?'

'Ten minutes,' he said. 'Or twenty minutes if she takes a little time before she leaves. It's only ten minutes to drive if you drive it fast,' he said.

'I'm going upstairs,' she said.

'What for?'

'I want to be alone for a while. For just a few minutes.'

'Don't you think you ought to just leave?'

'No.'

'Don't you think you ought to just leave me here and let me take care of it?'

'No,' she said and went upstairs.

It had been known for years that when you were going to fight someone, what you wore was terribly important. The Indians knew it. The natives in the Tarzan movies knew it. It had been known for a long, long time.

Caroline left just after dark. She drove fast. She was wearing Cynthia's new lingerie on her head. It was arranged so that it looked like some kind of wild and primitive headdress. In Caroline's mind, it looked good. It looked strange and it looked wild and it looked good.

Caroline went the back way. The road went around curves and hills, and alongside a huge lake that had been built to supply water to the town years ago, the road passed through a swamp. The swamp fell off to one side of the road where the road itself had been built up to go through it. On the other side of the road the land rose steadily and was all wooded.

Caroline came around this curve fast. She had her bright lights on. As she came around the curve she drifted into the other lane.

There was a car coming toward her. As she drifted farther into the car's lane, the driver pulled closer to the side of the road and as Caroline slid completely into the other lane, the car left the road and spun onto the shoulder.

Just before the car went into the air, Caroline saw the woman and the little baby in the front seat. She saw them as clearly as if she had taken a snapshot of them with some special kind of night film and had developed it in that instant and saw the look on the woman's face as she had one hand on the steering wheel and the other flung out toward the baby, which was strapped into the baby seat.

Then, as she tried to get herself stopped the other car went into the air. It went into the air quite nicely. The lights of the car shone across the swamp and into the trees and then they, along with the car, fell out of sight. Caroline heard a kind of bump-bump-bump, and then, as she stopped her car, she didn't hear a thing. Not one thing.

Cynthia and Richard stood in a dark room and looked out the window. Something was wrong. Caroline was not there yet. Every car that came down the road kept on, not slowing down, not giving any indication that the people in the car had anything to do but to get where they were going. It had begun to rain again. It was a slow and eerie summer rain. Usually, on a night as hot as that, there should have been thunderstorms, but there was no thunder and no lightning, just a slow, drenching rain that had blown up suddenly and then gone, and now was coming in again.

Rain affected people in different ways. A lot of people who had grew up in the country always talked about how well they had slept under tin roofs when it rained all night when they were children. An especially hard rain or an especially violent storm often made people remember something that happened during a similar storm.

The rain brought people to a stop. They had to consider what it meant. Did it mean they couldn't go out. Did it mean the event was canceled. Did it mean the grass would live, the garden would prosper, the well would survive and would not go dry? Did it mean that now, as they stood quietly for a moment, they were safe, that the house they had built would keep them dry and that their lives that went on inside that house would continue on in the same way, unimpeded and unaffected by the storm.

It was only for a moment that people stopped to consider what the storm meant, and then they went on, doing as they'd always done.

'Well,' Cynthia said.

'I don't know,' he said.

'It's sad, in a way,' she said.

'I know.'

'That's what I thought when I went to be alone upstairs a while ago. That it was sad. For everyone.'

'Yes,' he said.

The rain swept across the field. The spotlights all around the house were on. For a while they could see and hear the rain in the trees across the field before it hit their house. Then, like a wave coming ashore, the rain swept right across the field and against the house, a hard rain but eerily quiet, as if the rain had become separated from the wind and the lightning and the thunder and was out there all on its own, just tearing along out of control.

Caroline ran toward the other car, which she could see in the swamp. It had landed on its tires. Its lights were still on. They were dim. The lenses had mud all over them. Inside the car Caroline could see the woman and the baby. They looked green, from the green and red dash lights illuminating them.

Good God almighty, Caroline thought. What have I done?

She ran right off the bank and fell herself, suddenly, as if she'd dropped through a trap door. When she landed, she fell onto her face but got up and scrambled over to the car.

'Are you all right?' she asked.

The woman's window was down. The baby was sitting in the child restraint seat as if nothing had happened. The woman, however, was trembling and couldn't get the strap loose from the little girl.

About that time other cars stopped. In what seemed like about thirty seconds, a whole crowd was down at the car.

'It was my fault,' Caroline said. 'I did it. I was going too fast.'

'Were you in the car?' someone wanted to know, shining a flashlight in her face and seeing how ragged and covered with mud and slime she was.

'No. I was driving another car. I'm the one that ran her off the road.'

They got the woman and baby out. They had to pull the

doors real hard because they were halfway buried in the muck. When they got them opened, the muck and slime oozed into the bottom of the car.

About that time a reporter came running down and took pictures of everything. He had heard about the wreck on his police radio. The highway patrol got there at the same time.

'This woman ran her off the road,' someone said and pointed to Caroline.

'Yeah,' she said. 'I was going too fast. They're okay, though. Nothing happened. I'm going to pay for everything.'

'They're all right,' someone told him. 'They don't need an ambulance.'

'This is the woman who ran them off the road,' the same person who had told the reporter told the trooper.

'You better go sit in my car,' he told her, and then looked at her and changed his mind. 'Or better yet, just stand beside it.'

An ambulance came anyway. It had heard about the wreck on its radio. They made the woman lie down.

'She's going into shock,' they kept telling each other. 'Get her immobilized.'

They laid her down with her baby in her arms and took her away. The patrolman sat in his seat looking at Caroline's driver's license. He was filling out a form. Most everyone else had left except for a carload of teenage boys who kept talking about how she must have gone off the bank and what could have happened, how she'd just missed that tree, and so forth. It was the best thing that had happened all night.

The trooper kept writing things down. He had the other woman's license as well, and he was quietly filling in the lines while Caroline stood by feeling stupid.

'Tell me what happened,' he finally said.

'I'm not going to sit here all night waiting for her,' Cynthia said. She was cracking from the strain of not knowing.

'Well, let me call her then and just talk to her. It's really as simple as that.'

'No, you're not going to call her, either. She's not going to dictate our lives just because she's crazy. I hate that in people. I've seen it before.'

'Well, then, tell me what you want.'

'I want her to come over,' she said.

'You do?'

'I want her to come and get it over with. I don't care what happens, I just want it to end.'

'I do too,' he said. 'I don't know how to bring it about. I'm sorry, really. It's my fault.'

'It's not your fault. It's not your fault at all. It's just that I've been in these kind of situations before, where someone has got you all tangled up in their own craziness, and I'm not going to let it happen to us. I'm just not.'

'Well, I'm with you,' he said.

'There're good people and there're bad people, and the bad always make life hell for the good people.'

'That's true,' he said.

'I'm ready for her, that's all. I'm ready to do whatever I have to do and get it over with. It's me she's coming after, you understand. Not you. And I'm not going to run from her anymore.'

'Well, I'll tell you what happened,' Caroline said. 'I'll tell you the whole thing. Go ahead and throw the book at me because it was my fault and I admit it.'

'Just tell me which way you were going and where she was and what happened to cause the accident.'

'I was on my way someplace going real fast because I was mad about something,' she said and he started to write it all down, 'and I was really flying. I was probably going about sixty or sixty-five and my steering's no good anyway, I mean, it passes inspection and all that, but it's always been kind of loose, kind of weavy-like, you know, like when you ride up on one of those seams in the road where they joined one piece of asphalt to another,' she said, and he looked up at her and stopped writing, 'and when your tire gets on the seam the car kind of whips around a little, kind of like it's on a track, and anyway, I was coming around this curve and the car just started going over the line and I couldn't pull it back.

'I mean I tried to slow down but she was coming around the curve from the other direction and all I could think of was to try to hold it in the road and not go over any farther, but then she kind of swerved toward me like she was trying to get in my lane to go around me and then like we both swerved back and messed each other up, you know, like if you've ever met anyone in a hall and you try to go one way and the other person moves the same way, you know, and you just kind of go back and forth, well, that's what happened.

'And then she just kind of went off the bank and into the air and I thought, well, I've killed them. My life is over. I've killed them all.'

While she'd been talking he had been rummaging around in a bag on the seat, and when she finished he said, 'Would you mind taking a few tests, please.'

'Oh. You think I'm drunk. I'm not. I'll take them, but I'm not drunk. I'm not on drugs either. I'm just a little worked up, that's all.'

After she tested clear, he finished his report and wrote out two tickets.

'I'm going to charge you with speeding and with reckless driving. You won't lose your license, but it'll be bad on your insurance rates.'

'That's all right,' she said. 'It was all my fault and I believe, I firmly and really and truly believe that people should be responsible for their actions and that one of the things wrong with the world nowadays is that people think they can do things to other people and not have to pay for it. It's this new thing that's started up in the world that people think they can get away with anything and that's why I owned up to it being my fault right away.'

'Here,' he said. He looked at her carefully and then said, 'Is your car all right?'

'Oh, I'm sure it is,' she said.

'I'm just wondering whether or not you should drive. You seem awful upset.'

'I'm all right. I really am. I won't speed again.'

'Still,' he said and looked down at the form he'd been filling out, 'you are married. Are you sure you don't want me to have the station call your husband and have him pick you up?'

'Oh no,' she said. 'That's not necessary. I mean, it would just get him upset, you know. He'd be so scared just hearing the police on the phone asking about me that it wouldn't be worth it. He worries about me all the time, you know how husbands are, and it'd be better if I just went on back and told him myself.'

'He's going to know something when he sees you,' the trooper said and waited while she started her car and got it off the shoulder. Then he drove off in the opposite direction.

'Move the truck,' Cynthia said. 'I don't want her to think that we were worried about her having seen us.'

'All right,' he said.

'Just park it beside my car. And then leave the porch light on like would be usual and come on in and let's watch a movie or something.'

'Sure,' he said.

He was back in the house sitting beside Cynthia when Caroline parked her car and stepped out. She looked like a painted member of a night terrorist unit, only she smelled bad enough to be discovered long before she could be seen. The rotting organic slime and mud from the swamp smelled like a combination of sour milk and manure.

'She's here,' Richard said when he heard the car drive up and the door slam.

'Just sit where you are,' Cynthia said. 'Let her ring the bell if she wants us.'

'I'm not going to sit here,' he said. 'I'm going out there and tell her to go home.'

Caroline had paused only long enough to better wrap Cynthia's lingerie around her head like a war bonnet. In her mind it looked so good. To Richard it looked pathetic.

'What in the hell are you doing?' he asked, meeting her halfway between the car and the porch, in the illumination of the corner spotlights aimed that way as well as at the front porch.

'I want to see Cynthia,' she said.

'There's nothing for you to see her about,' he said. 'Just go on back home and leave us alone.'

'Leave us alone?' she asked.

'That's right.'

Just then Cynthia walked down the steps to where they stood. She walked carefully and slowly. Caroline saw her and all the fight that had left her came back, even more so.

'You bitch,' she said.

'Caroline,' Cynthia said in a calm voice. 'What has happened to you?'

'Don't worry about what's happened to me,' she said. 'think about what's going to happen to you.'

'Damn you, Caroline,' Richard said. 'That tough talk from high school just doesn't get it.'

'I DON'T CARE WHAT GETS IT,' she screamed. *'I'M GOING TO KILL THAT WOMAN STANDING RIGHT THERE AND THEN I'M GOING TO KILL EVERYTHING.'*

Cynthia looked at her sympathetically and then smiled at her, gently and with understanding.

'FUCKING SMILING AT ME,' Caroline screamed. *'I'M GOING TO HIT YOU SO HARD YOU'LL NEVER GET UP. I HATE YOU. I HATE EVERYTHING ABOUT YOU.'*

'Let's go, Caroline,' Richard said and started toward her.

'Let her talk,' Cynthia said. 'It has to be gotten out.'

'Let her talk,' Caroline mimicked. 'It has to be gotten out. *GODDAMN YOU.* Where'd you get that fucking voice? It makes me want to puke. That fucking phony voice. Everything about you is phony. Everything,' she said and then went off into a list of everything she ever hated about everybody. She included everything and anything she could think of.

'That goddamn car you drive. I hate women who drive cars like that. You know why? They're whores. They're goddamn whores like you. Who bought you that car? Who? You all ride around in your fancy cars looking so good and you're rotten inside, all of you. Just absolutely stinking rotten.

'Everything you have is because you're a whore. You've been a whore all your life. *HOW THE HELL ELSE DID YOU GET THIS HOUSE, YOU GODDAMN WHORE?'* she screamed.

About that time, the people across the road and up on the hill came out of their houses and gathered where they could see what was happening. They peered through an opening in the trees to see the white people in their front yard lit up like actors in an outdoor drama.

'There they go again,' one of them said.

'I thought that woman had done got through with all that. I thought the doctor done left long ago.'

'That look like a new one,' another said. 'I been seeing him driving in and out in that truck these last few weeks.'

'I swear,' one of them said. 'A person would've thought white folks with that much money wouldn't have nothing to worry about.'

'That's right.'

'But they sure do have their trouble.'

'Look now,' one of them said as Caroline pulled her headdress off and slung it at Cynthia.

'YOU AND YOUR GODDAMN BEAUTIFUL LIFE,' she screamed. 'Riding around in your beautiful car with your beautiful children and everything just a goddamn phony act. *YOU GODDAMN WHORE,'* she screamed, and the sound of her voice bounced around the valley as if it were amplified.

'Oh my lord,' one of them said up on the hill.

'She got another woman mad at her, that's what she gone and done.'

Caroline continued on, running up one side and down the other of the list of everything she had always hated.

'And the way you walk, *YOU FUCKING BITCH,'* she screamed, 'like you have to be so careful how each foot hits the ground, like you're just too precious, too fragile, *YOU PRINCESS-AND-THE-PEA PIECE OF SHIT,'* she screamed, *'TO WALK LIKE A NORMAL PERSON.'*

Caroline paused. She was momentarily out of things to say.

'Are you through?' Cynthia asked. Her voice was so soft it barely carried ten feet, but somehow its diaphanous texture settled around Caroline like a noose.

'SHIT,' she screamed.

'All right, Caroline,' Richard said. 'That's it. This is going nowhere.'

'I'LL KILL HER,' she screamed and charged Cynthia, who put her hands behind her and stood quietly, as if her calmness would stop Caroline.

It didn't, of course. Nothing could've stopped Caroline then. She saw herself moving so fast and going so hard she could have gone through a wall like a cartoon character, leaving a silhouette of herself in the wall as she passed through it. She hit Cynthia then, going that hard, and knocked her back five feet and onto the ground. Cynthia never got her hands out from behind her back and lay there like she was tied up while Caroline hit her in the face twice before Richard pulled her off and held her down.

Cynthia didn't move. She couldn't even feel what had happened to her. She'd never been hit in her life. Never. She didn't even know her lips were bleeding.

'Now you've done it,' Richard said, trying to hold on to Caroline. He had her arms pinned but couldn't get hold of her legs. She kicked and tried to get loose.

'JUST LET ME GO,' she screamed.

'You take it easy,' he said, holding her actually as tight as he could and still barely containing her. 'You just take it easy,' he said again. It was hard to come up with the right thing to say when you were flailing on the ground.

Then Caroline did stop. She lay still in her husband's arms on the lawn of this dreaded woman's house while the woman, who had been knocked silly, finally moved, rolled over, and held her mouth and began to moan.

'Oh damn,' Caroline said. 'Let me go.'

'Are you going to leave?' Richard asked, still holding on.

'Just let me go,' she said. 'I've pissed myself. I've pissed all over myself. Oh, damnit,' she said and got up after Richard let her go. 'I'm sorry, Richard.'

She looked down at herself. It was hard to see anything because she was so filthy anyway, but she could feel it.

'I hate you,' she said to Cynthia, who was on her stomach, holding her mouth. 'I hope I hurt you. I'm leaving, but I'm glad I did it.'

'I quit,' she said, walking away. 'But I hope you go to hell, Cynthia. I really do. You don't deserve Richard. You're a whore,' she said again, only quietly this time, 'just a whore, and someday you're going to be fifty years old and what does a fifty-year-old whore do with herself?' she said and stood almost out of the light, looking back at her husband and the woman on the ground.

'I love you, Richard,' she said. 'I won't bother you again. I won't ever bother either one of you. Have a good life,' she said. 'I love you, baby. I wish I'd done better,' she told him and got in her car and drove away.

The people on the hill watched her coming toward them up Cynthia's drive. They were above the drive, so Caroline's lights never did shine on them. Caroline turned down the road. They watched her until the lights of her car were out of sight.

'Something bad going on over there,' an old woman said.

The group broke up and walked back to their little houses. The houses leaned this way and that. Between two of the oldest houses was a new double-wide mobile home set up on a foundation. It looked good. It was the nicest place up there. The government had helped pay for it. They were proud of that house. It was another start. They could stand in the yard and be proud of that fine new home. It had come completely furnished. It was aluminum on the outside. It was air-conditioned and had electric heat. They weren't going to ever have to tear their own siding off their house to burn in the wood stove on a cold winter night. Those days were over. They could drive up and look at that fine new home and be proud.

The old woman who'd said something bad was going on over there stayed by herself on the hill overlooking the road and watched the man lean over the woman in the yard. She saw the man holding the woman as if the woman needed help, and then she saw them go into the house and turn off the outside lights.

The woman on the hill was short and stocky. She did not look like people had learned they were supposed to look. Her face lacked the expressiveness and the excitement of the twentieth centrury. Whatever was going on inside of her stayed inside, and so, while nothing showed on her face that night, she was still deeply disturbed.

It made her sad to have witnessed such a thing, black or white. It made her feel bad. She prayed a little by herself, and made a sign in the dark above the road, asking God to help all the poor souls in this world who were hurting at that moment, and after she prayed, she went back into her old house and closed the door.

Cynthia washed her face and held a cold washcloth to her mouth. She was trying to talk and hold it on her lips so she could explain to Richard what she had thought was going to happen.

'You see, when I went upstairs by myself earlier, I made myself get very peaceful. I made myself understand that the fear that I was feeling had no power over me. I made myself understand that and then it came to me that she could not harm me,' she said and put the cloth back to her lips and held it there and then took it away and looked at it to see if the bleeding had stopped.

'And when I walked out there tonight I knew that somehow if I could just keep in my mind and in my heart this goodwill toward Caroline, that she would not harm us, and I tried, and for a while it worked, but then I got scared or something, and I let it go.

'Still,' she said. 'I guess it did work. Because really, she didn't do a thing. Not like we expected. And now, I'm sure, aren't you, that she will never bother us again.'

'Yes,' he said.

'Somehow I can tell this time that it really is over. That we've made it.'

'I hope.'

'You have to say yes. You have to. It will help to believe it. Okay.'

'I believe it,' he said. 'And I'm sorry. When all this started between us, I never thought it would get this rough. I'm sorry.'

'Don't be sorry. All things lead to something good.'

'If I could just believe it. If somehow we could just spend a whole month, maybe, with nothing to bother us and every day could be as good as they have been so far, then I guess I could believe it.'

'It will happen,' she said.

'Life with you is good,' he said. 'Finally, after all these years, things seem right.'

'They are,' she said.

It was quiet again. It was the quiet and the stillness that Richard loved, and Cynthia gave it to him and it made them both content.

Caroline took a shower. She threw her clothes out in the yard and left her shoes and socks outside. The water coming off her skin was filthy. She still stank a little after she finished, so she washed again. She scrubbed herself hard enough to hurt.

I ought to die, she thought. This whole thing, this whole

day, this whole act, telling that boy in the booth I was going to be famous, telling Cynthia all that stuff, acting tough like some little high-school fool, and I can't stand it, she thought. I can't stand being a fool. I just hate it.

She fell asleep on the couch. She had on her heavy robe. Though the night was still hot, she had been cold when she got out. It was after midnight. She turned on the television. She didn't even know what she was watching when she fell asleep. She had a lot of nightmares. Everything was happening. She was falling and getting lost and the brakes wouldn't work. Just everything. The television was still on. The scenes changed rapidly on the screen. The light from the screen flickered through her eyelids. The flickering made her nightmares worse.

She found an old prescription bottle of tranquilizers she'd gotten once from a teacher who had told her they made her crazy and wanted rid of them. She took two and put on her pajamas and got into her own bed.

Then the long day, the endless night where she played tough and had had her heart broken in the drugstore, and where she had seen the vision of herself once in love and the long day and night where she had almost killed a woman and a little baby and later made a fool of herself once more, but the last time trying to act out some fantasy of rescuing her husband out of the hands of that evil woman, the long night was over and she slept.

The pills that had made the other woman crazy barely affected Caroline. The whole bottle would have probably just gone into her system and gotten lost, trying to chart the path through the system the way it'd been taught in the laboratory, using the connections and neurons of a normal person. In Caroline, however, the pills just spun around like bumper cars, going backward and then frontward, until, after a while, they didn't know which way to go.

It had been that bad for Caroline. Had a surgeon opened up her head that night, he would have jumped back in surprise. 'What's this,' he would have called out to the crew standing around. 'This thing,' he would have said, 'why, this thing is supposed to be over here, and this thing here, it's supposed to be over there, and where's the such-and-such, and good God, what's that?' he would have asked, and everyone would have looked down into Caroline's opened skull and wondered how this woman had made it as long as she had.

PART III

Jeep, the Wonder Dog

Chapter 13

It was early July. Richard had moved out the second week of June. Caroline had driven the tractor through the door a couple of days later. Less than a week after that, she had burst into flames in Cynthia's front yard just like she had feared she would.

People called on the phone. Lucille called. Caroline told her anything that came to mind, but she did not tell her she was now living alone. People called wanting to talk to Richard about this or that, a job or a past job or for advice about something. She gave them Cynthia's number as if it were a work number, as if it were a place they might reach him during the day.

At night, she unplugged the telephone. When a telephone was unplugged, it rang in the ear of the person making the call but was silent on the receiving end. Sometimes in the night she could imagine she could still hear it ringing, far off, as if the call were still getting through. Once she picked it up, but there was nothing. Not even the dial tone. After all, it was unplugged.

The house was empty, quiet, and strange. The grass grew. The garden came along. The tomatoes were coming in. The corn was tasseling and the silks were ready to catch the seeds when they dropped. The old tractor sat in the shed waiting for something to do. It had no muffler. The front end was slightly dented and scratched. It would always be a reminder.

The farmers in the area had harvested their wheat, their barley and their oats and had planted back in the same field milo or sorghum grass or soybeans. Most of it had been sod-planted in the stubble of the small grain. Through the rows of stalks cut uniformly short, like a field of dead sticks, the green plants emerged within their own rows, and it began again.

There had to be rain. The rain had to come at the right times. Then it had to stop for a while to let the milo or the soybeans dry. All this usually happened. Somehow, year after year, it usually happened all right.

To the west of Caroline's house, all this work with the land went on. The trucks came and went. The tractors and the wagons and the combines and the silage cutters and the harrows so wide they had to be manufactured to fold up like the wings of a bird just to get down the road or go through a gate, all these serious working machines came and went.

To the east of Caroline's house, the traffic flowed, going into town, going to work at the universities, at the hospitals, at the insurance companies, at the coldly sculptured research buildings of the corporate dreams, at the little shops that catered to the beautiful men and women with so much money, at the grocery stores where everyone joined in and fought it out in the sensory overload of the luminescent aisles which were electrical in their confusion.

And, in the middle, Caroline waited, living halfway between these two worlds, not far from either one, but not a part of them, either. She waited. She waited quietly. She knew something would happen. She knew that something was finished and that something new was going to happen. Quietly now, for the first time in so long, she waited to see what it would be.

Chapter 14

At the same time in this same week, early in July, Cynthia's children came to stay with their mother. They had taken the trip with their father that their mother had originally objected to, and now were home to spend a week with her. After that, they were going to spend the rest of the summer back at their father's.

Their father had moved into town. He had bought a small four-bedroomed house in a new subdivision that had been built on ten acres of land right in the heart of town. The ten acres had been part of someone's property from long ago and had stayed empty of development for all the years the old couple who owned it lived. When they died, their children sold it for a million dollars.

On the ten acres were now thirty-two houses. The houses were modest but nice, and all had different floor plans and none looked the same from the outside. These houses had paved driveways with two-car garages and basketball courts beside the garages and were in no particular way especially pretentious or rich-looking or anything other than just average small two-story houses on quarter-acre lots with concrete driveways and a small front yard and lots of bushes and flower beds and a number of hardwood trees here and there that had been saved during the development.

Yet these houses cost over $300,000, nearly the worth of Cynthia's larger, grander house on its ten acres. Such was the change in the area from the time that the doctor had built the fine house in the country for his wife and their two children.

So, although the houses were just as nice as they could be, there was, as the son C.J. had said, no place to ride his dirt bike. The bike was kept, then, in Cynthia's barn, where the horses had once been kept. It was usually on its side, because it fell over when its stand slowly sunk into the soft straw-covered earth inside the barn. C.J. could've prevented this by putting a board under the stand and spreading out the weight, or by leaning the bike against the wall, but riding it was such a charged-up experience it was too hard to think and do it at the same time.

For a fourteen-year-old boy, it was a little like having an out-of-body experience, a kind of mystical coming of age, where the flying piston of the engine and the force of air drawn through the air cleaner as C.J. held the throttle wide open, where the deafening noise of the high-rpm two-cycle engine, something like the engine of a chain saw, where it all suddenly fit with the way he felt inside, wide open and flying blindly with the sound of his own blood loud as the engine itself.

It was, riding through the field and across the homemade ramp that sent him a foot into the air, though it felt like ten feet or more, it was a peculiar and accidental manifestation of his own psychic drama, and C.J., back home for fifteen minutes, had to rush out to relive it, over and over again, right away, having missed it more than Cynthia could ever know, could ever imagine.

'He's on it already,' she said to her daughter as they watched him spin out of the barn and take off across the field as if he would never have to stop, as if the field were infinity itself and he were going to find the end of it.

'It's like he just waits for it,' her daughter said. 'Back at Daddy's, he just watches television.'

'Doesn't he go out with his friends?'

'I guess so. I guess he does. But mostly he just watches television.'

'I guess he's upset about the divorce,' Cynthia said.

'Oh Mom, give me a break. He'd be that way if nothing had happened. He's always been that way. He's quiet around the house, but when he gets with his friends, he's wild.'

'He's wild?'

'I don't mean bad wild,' she said, seeing her mother was alarmed. 'I mean he acts the clown. He cuts up. He's real popular. The girls like him.'

'Well, I'm glad of that. I really 'n truly am.'

Out in the field, C.J. held the throttle open and sped toward the trees at the end of the field. The field was about four acres. It was 200 feet wide and 750 feet long. When he began at one end from a standing start he could get up to forty-five miles an hour before he had to slam on brakes at the other end. The forty-five miles an hour over the rough pasture felt like a hundred miles an hour. Still, he was trying to push it so he could get up over fifty before he had to stop.

'Look at his hair, sticking out the back of his helmet,' his sister said, and laughed.

Cynthia put her arm around her. They waited at the window until C.J. had put on his brakes and turned around, then they went back into the kitchen, where they kept on talking while Anne made a deep-dish peach pie, which she had just a few days earlier made for her father, and was now showing off for her mother.

'Richard'll love that,' Cynthia said.

'Uh huh,' Anne said.

'We all will.'

'When's he going to be finished upstairs?' Anne asked.

'Soon. I wanted to replace the rotten French doors before anyone saw the house.'

'I like those French doors.'

'I don't mean rotten that way. I mean, rotting, as in coming apart.'

'Oh,' her daughter said.

Cynthia peeled the fresh peaches and Anne lined the pan with dough. It was four o'clock. They would put it in just before they sat down for supper so that it would be cooking while they ate, and just slightly warm when it was time for dessert.

*

Caroline's car ran badly. It took a long time to start and it misfired off and on while she was driving. When she turned it off with the motor hot, it was even harder to start. She called the mechanic she and Richard had always used and asked him if she could bring it by and wait for it while he worked on it.

'But there ain't nowhere to wait,' he said.

'I'll sit in the shade and read,' she said. She didn't want to tell him that, unlike times in the past, she could not have Richard pick her up and bring her back at the end of the day.

When Roy had told her that there was nowhere to wait, he hadn't been just making up an excuse to keep a woman from hanging around the shop. The shop was a cartoon of junk and old parts and broken-down trucks and cars. It was the main repair shop for the pulpwood cutters, and their trucks were always broken from going into the woods and running over stumps and getting stuck in mud and sliding into trees.

The trucks were strange-looking vehicles with battered cabs but no actual beds on the back. In place of the bed there was merely a frame with a rack at each end and one in the middle, a little like firewood racks that were sold to homeowners to keep wood stacked on their porch. From the middle rack on the truck a winch-powered crane swung around, and this was what was used to pull up the five-foot sections of logs used for pulpwood.

Cutting pulpwood was one of the hardest and hottest jobs known to man. A chain saw running on a hot day in the middle of a pine forest was like an above-ground version of hell, and the men who worked these jobs were sullen, usually hard-drinking and mostly black.

Roy was talking to a group of these men when Caroline drove up. Roy had never been anywhere but was an expert on world affairs and read the local paper every day when he got home. He always had an opinion on world events, though he often had things mixed up. When Nixon opened up the door to China, Roy told everyone that it was the least we could do after dropping the A-bomb on them during the war.

They were talking about the A-bomb again when Caroline got out of her car and came up to them. For a moment they got quiet, but when Roy nodded to her and started talking again, no one paid any attention to her for a while.

'I tell you what I'd do,' Roy said.

'What would you do, Roy?' one of the men said.

'I'd bomb them damn Libyans off the face of this earth, that's what I'd do.'

'How would you do that, Roy?' someone asked.

'I'd take me one of them A-bombs and put it in the back of my pickup if I had to and drive it over there and blow the hell out of them, that's what I'd do.'

A few of the men laughed at that, and one of them felt obliged to correct Roy of a major flaw in his argument.

'I hate to tell you this, Roy,' he said, 'but you ain't going to be able to fit no A-bomb in the back of no short-bed pickup.'

Everybody laughed at that because Roy obviously didn't know enough to figure out you need a long-bed pickup to haul an A-bomb.

'Well, hell, I'd get it over there some way,' he said and walked off and approached Caroline.

'How're you today?' he said.

'Just fine.'

'Where's Richard?'

'He's working.'

'Well, I'll get right on it, but I can't promise how long it'll be.'

Roy's sons were working in the back sheds, which had been built onto the original building. Roy was short and he had had five sons, all one right after the other and all of them were shorter than he was and each was shorter than the other, as they were all somewhere from the ages of eleven or twelve up to about nineteen or twenty years old. When they were standing together they looked like a series of wooden Russian dolls that fit into one another.

'I'll get Junior on it,' he said and called his oldest son, who came around and awkwardly spoke to Caroline and then drove her car around back. It was hard to talk to women. What was there to say?

Caroline went out under a tree and sat on the hood of an old car. She tried to read but there was too much to watch to be able to really get into the book, so she shifted around and just killed the hour looking at everything going on.

I could be a mechanic, she thought. If I were a mechanic I could turn Richard's shop into a garage and always have a bunch of people coming in and out and I could fix their cars for them.

For a little while it was a nice thought, always having someone about and doing good for people, but as she thought about it, she had the feeling that it wouldn't work, that it would be filthy and tedious and people would get mad at you and they wouldn't pay you and you'd get your knuckles busted up like she'd just seen Junior do when his wrench slipped off something and he slammed his hand into the hinge on the side of her hood, and like all the other dreams of change she was trying to come up with, it faded and she went back to her book, still waiting for whatever it was she was now supposed to do with her life.

'Your car's ready,' Roy said.

'Oh. Okay. What was it?'

'I don't know. Ask Junior when you get it. Here's the bill.'

She paid it and asked Junior. He looked at her sideways when he talked.

'Everything. I mean, just a lot of stuff. Your air cleaner was all clogged up and your points was pitted and there was a crack in the coil wire and a couple of other things.'

'Well, thank you very much for fixing it,' she said.

'It's all right,' he said. 'It was nothing.'

She drove home. The car ran better. If there was anywhere she needed to go now, she could go. She wouldn't break down. A dependable car was an important part of a new life.

Chapter 15

Cynthia and Richard and the two children prepared for supper.

'Anne made the pie,' Cynthia told the two men.

'I bet it'll be good,' Richard said.

'Maybe,' C.J. said. 'The one she made at Dad's the other day had all the skin with it.'

'I was trying to do that,' Anne said, 'because that's where all the vitamins are.'

'I like it better the other way,' he said.

'I peeled them,' Cynthia said.

'Good,' her son said.

They were having spaghetti with meat sauce and French bread and a salad. The spaghetti was green and was a new kind of spinach pasta.

'Mommy, what's that?' C.J. asked.

'Spaghetti,' his mother said.

'I never saw green spaghetti,' he said. His face was beginning to turn the same color.

'It's all right. It's still spaghetti,' she said.

'I can't eat it,' he said. 'Just give me some bread.'

'It tastes the same,' his mother said.

'It's better for you, too,' Richard said.

'It looks weird,' he said. 'I don't want any.'

C.J. took the meat sauce and pushed it around with his bread and ate it that way. The new pasta actually wasn't as good. It was heavy and had a taste that didn't really go along with what you had in mind when you ate spaghetti. Richard thought that C.J. had used good judgment. He told him. He was trying to connect with him in some way. It was hard. When he told him, he then got on the wrong side of Cynthia.

'Well, I like it,' she said.

'I just didn't like the color,' C.J. said.

'I like it, too,' Richard said. 'I just mean I think the regular thin stuff is better.'

'I was trying to do something different,' Cynthia said.

Anne cleared the table. She brought in the pie. It was warm. It was good. C.J. had ice cream along with it. Everyone else was too full. After supper, Richard and Cynthia went to town to a movie.

There was an awkward moment at the ticket window. Richard didn't have enough money. They had to get out of line.

'What's wrong?' Cynthia asked.

'I'm sorry,' he said. 'I'm out of money.'

'Oh,' she said, truly surprised.

'Well, I mean,' he said, embarrassed but trying to explain, 'I haven't worked, I mean, you know, almost the whole time. Except for you. It's just that I've got to get back into things pretty soon.'

'It's my fault,' she said. 'I should've thought of it. Here,' she said and gave him two twenties. 'Just tell me next time. All you have to do is ask,' she said. 'I don't mind at all.'

He took it and they got back in line.

'Let me just give you a signed blank check when we get back and you draw out as much as you think you'll need. Okay, baby?' she asked and put her arm around him and kissed him.

'I guess so,' he said.

Back at Cynthia's house, Anne walked through her mother's room looking at her new clothes and at Richard's things. She picked up Richard's jeans and smelled them and put them back. She looked in the dresser that used to be downstairs but had been brought up sometime while they were away and saw a few drawers half full of Richard's clothes.

Her mother had two closets full of clothes. She wasn't tall enough to wear the clothes, but she wished she were. She had quit growing and would never be as tall as her mother.

She took after her father and had short wide feet and was more like his sisters than she was like her mother.

She lay on her mother's bed and picked up a fashion magazine. She was reading it when C.J. came in.

'What are you doing?' he asked.

'Nothing. Why?'

'I want to go somewhere.'

'Well, we can't. We didn't ask. You should have said something beforehand.'

'I didn't think of it until now.'

'Well, I'm not going to drive that truck,' she said, and they both laughed.

'Well, I'm not going to ride in that truck,' he said.

'They've got to get me a car,' she said. 'This is the year they've got to.'

'They always said we have to wait until college.'

'I know, but I can work on both of them now, about having to drive back and forth between the two houses.'

'Yeah,' he said. 'It's different.'

'I bet I'll have one before school,' she said.

'I wish you had one now.'

Cynthia and Richard left the movie early. It was no good. They went to get ice cream. The ice cream was good and was better than you could get in the stores. It had a lot of different things in it, and seemed to be especially creamy. It was expensive, though.

'We might as well go back,' he said while they wandered around eating the dripping ice cream.

'I can't finish mine, anyway,' she said.

'It's too hot for ice cream,' he said.

'I know. That doesn't sound right, but it is. Unless you're in the air-conditioning.'

'I'm going to throw this away. It's good, it's just too rich.'

'Let me have a taste before you do,' she said. She licked it.

They started back. Once out of town, there was little traffic. It was nine-thirty. Some of the houses were already dark. The people had gone to bed. Some of them were all lit up, and you could see the people sitting or standing or moving across the room in a captured moment in their lives. Mostly they were just going to get something to eat, or to change the channel. Rarely was anything going on like the drama of Cynthia and Richard's own recent lives.

Richard made a right turn onto another paved secondary road. He continued on for a mile or so before Cynthia spoke.

'Why are you going this way?'

'Oh hell,' he said.

'What did you do?'

'I forgot where I was going.'

'Go on and ride by there if you want to,' she said.

'I don't want to,' he said. 'I'll find a place to turn around.'

'No. Go ahead. We might as well now that we're this far along.'

'I'm not going to look,' he said as they prepared to pass Caroline's house.

'A person can't tell what kind of car is going by on the road at night,' she said.

'Caroline could tell it was you,' he said. 'If she were deaf, dumb and blind she could tell the minute you got anywhere near her.'

'You're always ascribing all these outlandish characteristics to her,' she said. 'It hurts my feelings.'

'I'm not trying to do that at all,' he said, and let it go. They were almost there. He had to concentrate on the road.

'There's the house,' Cynthia said.

'Is that right?' he said and still didn't look.

'I saw her,' she said. 'I really did. She was sitting in a chair in the kitchen at the table. I saw her. She was just sitting there, looking across the room.'

'Well, good,' he said.

'I didn't see anyone else, though. There could've been. Maybe she was talking to someone.'

'Maybe she was,' he said. He wasn't going to get drawn into it.

'I wonder if she was,' she said. 'Sooner or later there's

going to be someone else, you know. I wonder what you'll think of it, then.'

'I don't know,' he said. 'I'm just the driver. I'm just here driving the car. I don't know anything.'

The road was dark but Cynthia's house was all lit up. It looked like every light in every room was on. The children were watching television. C.J. was downstairs watching on one set and his sister was upstairs watching on another. The air-conditioning was running. The stove was still on, heating up the room, trying to make the 425-degree setting on its dial come true, but having a hard time because C.J. had left the door open after heating up a frozen pizza. The harder it worked, the harder the cooling system had to work. Cynthia shut the oven door. Later they all slept.

Chapter 16

One morning Caroline went back down the hill to the cool bottomland where the creek flowed. She wandered along the path. She stopped beside the uprooted stump of the tree that had fallen over the creek and watched the ants crawling around the soft dirt the roots had thrown up. The ants were following an invisible trail to something and, a couple of inches away, were following another one back into their nest. They must have been carrying something in their little hands on their way back, but she couldn't see anything.

Caroline was feeling blue and when she felt blue she could feel desperately blue. The other day she'd been wildly happy as she had come up with the idea to hold a local children's Olympics, only not in the usual sports and games, but with crazy, wild and funny games. She got excited about this for a while, but then everything fizzled as she tried to make the ideas into something actual, tried to figure out how she would actually cause it to happen, and what the crazy, wild and funny games would actually be.

She had days like that, when she was consumed with a great idea only to have it fade away the further along with it she got. Then she'd be blue, and when she was blue she would think about money and how she was going to make the house payments and what she could do and whether or not to quit her job and sell the place and disappear for a while. Thinking about that really got her down because the land and the house were what she loved most in life, now that Richard and the dream of the beautiful life together was over.

She knelt beside the ants and watched them run back and forth. The earth where she knelt was black and cool and soft, and she took off her shoes and sat against a nearby tree and pushed her feet into the dirt and wiggled her toes and felt better in the dark and cool and secret place, below the road, and out of sight.

While she rested and buried her feet in the dirt as she used to do at the beach, she began to feel that she was being watched and she looked around her and down the path and saw the dog, the ghost dog, the Indian dog, that she had seen before.

'Well I'll be,' she said out loud. 'It's you.'

The dog was sitting politely about a hundred feet away from her. It wagged its tail when she spoke, sweeping the leaves and dirt behind it as it wagged. Its face was so expressive that as it sat there with its tongue lolled out and panted quietly, it looked as if it were smiling, maybe even laughing. As it panted, its head slightly nodded back and forth, as if it were saying yes, it's me.

'I guess it is the same time of morning,' she said. 'I guess maybe you come through here every day on your rounds. Is that it?' she asked.

After she spoke this second time, the dog lay down in the path, but kept its head up and its eyes on Caroline.

'I guess you're going to stay there until I move out of your path, aren't you?' she asked. 'Well, I'll move. Just let me get my shoes on.'

She brushed the dirt off her feet and put her socks and shoes back on. She was wearing thick white cotton athletic socks with her tennis shoes, along with a pair of loose khaki shorts and a kind of 1950s-looking Mexican Indian blouse, something like the women had worn in the old cowboy, Indian, and Mexican bandit movies of the time.

'Are you going to let me pet you?' she said, and stood back out of the way so the dog could keep on coming if it wanted. 'I promise you I'll be your friend.'

The dog left the path and took a drink of water from the creek. Then he trotted up the bank right over to Caroline and sat in front of her.

'You must remember me,' she said. 'I sure remember you.'

She patted him on his side and on his shoulders and then rubbed him under his chest and tickled him with her fingertips under his chin.

'You're nice,' she said. 'You've got a pretty face.'

While she talked to him, the dog looked up in the air and sniffed, moving his head around as if trying to locate the direction of the smell. Then he stood up and shook himself and glanced back at Caroline and yawned, looking embarrassed when he did, as if he'd had a thought about something and he'd had to yawn it out of his system.

'I don't know,' Caroline said. 'What was it?'

The dog walked off a little ways and then stopped and looked back at her.

'I'm going to follow you,' she said. 'I want to see where you go.'

Up ahead, the creek made a turn and formed one of the corners of Caroline's land. The path went straight. They crossed the creek at a ford where the rocks had tumbled together and caught the silt and dirt washing down and made a high spot in part of the creek that the dog, and then Caroline, jumped to from the bank. Once on the little ford, or island, they walked a few steps and then jumped on the other bank. Up the bank, the old path continued on.

This is very strange, Caroline thought. The dog kept walking with its ears slanted back toward Caroline and only every now and again, when she made a noise or spoke out loud, actually looked back. As the dog walked, it stopped here and there and marked a tree or a bush, after which it sometimes kicked up a little dirt toward the marked spot.

As they walked, they got deeper into the woods. She knew they were leaving Edgar's brother's land, or imagined they were, anyway, having in mind they were heading somehow a little west and a little south. She knew from the plat of the lands around her that the brother's land stopped over this way and there were a couple of large unbroken tracts of land ahead, one owned by a paper company and one or two owned by some people from up north.

It would have been surprising to many people in Chapel Hill and Durham, especially those who had moved there recently, that there existed these great tracts of unbroken land so close to these cities. It hadn't been long, though, as any oldtimer could tell you, since rich men from up north with famous family names came down to their great tracts of land and hired local white men to be their guides, and hired some local blacks to do the cooking and cleaning, and spent their vacations hunting turkey or deer or raccoons or running rabbits.

That went on until some time around the Second World War, when it began to come to a stop, and by the middle of the fifties, no one from the old rich legendary families ever visited anymore. Some of the land was sold off, some of it to the paper companies, some of it cut up in smaller pieces as the heirs divided up their property, and only a few of the tracts stayed whole and untouched.

It must have been this part of what Caroline remembered from the plat that she and the dog now entered, going off the brother's land, which had been cut over some time about fifteen years ago, or just before they bought their piece off of him when he was trying to get some money. It must have been those two large tracts of the paper-company land that she and the dog stepped into, as they left the thin new growth of the cut-over land and went into a dark and tall forest of old-growth pines.

It was so sudden it was remarkable. Of course it had to be sudden. It had to be as sudden as a line drawn on a map. It either had to be that sudden or someone was in trouble for cutting someone else's timber.

But it still amazed Caroline, and she thought, I have never walked this far not knowing where I was going, and she called out to the dog, 'Wait a minute, okay?' and the dog stopped and waited while she looked back to remember how it was she had come. The path was still clear. It had to be a path all the animals moving along the bottom used, she thought. Otherwise, it wouldn't be so well worn.

As long as she could see where she was coming from, she felt a little better.

'The only thing I want to ask you, dog,' she said, 'is whether you're following me or I'm following you?'

She had a feeling the dog was just walking along with her and that she had taken it away from wherever it usually went.

'Because what I'm doing is trying to follow you. I want to know where you live and whose you are, you get me?' she said.

They walked a long way. The old pines were huge. She had never seen pines like these. They looked like the pictures of the giant redwoods or the enormous old cedars she had seen in photographs about the West. The floor of the forest was nearly clear of undergrowth, due to the carpet of pine needles and the density of the branches at the top of the trees, which shut out most of the light.

These trees would make beautiful lumber. There was no explaining how this place had escaped the timber merchant and the logger, except that the people from up north who owned the land either had forgotten about it or were actually preserving it in its original state.

The lumber from these trees would have been a rare find. It would have brought almost any price. The trees were so large in diameter they could have been quartersawed. They would mill up flat and perfect and straight-grained. The color of the boards would age to a rich blend of yellow and red and gold. A room paneled with this lumber would be like a shrine. Flooring made from this lumber would lie flat and would wear forever. It would glow with its color beyond anything that stains or mixtures could ever imitate.

'This is a special place you've taken me,' she said to the dog as she stopped and the dog sniffed around some more. 'I wish Richard could've seen this place. I don't know how we missed it.'

She and Richard always walked their property line every winter, usually on Thanksgiving Day. The leaves were down by then and the woods were clear and you could see where you were going. They explored in different directions each year, but they had never gone this far.

That made her sad. To think they had missed this. There it was though, that whole life that had to be reckoned with.

The forest just went on and on. Every now and again the dog stopped ahead of her and looked back and smiled, that same smile as before.

'I hope you're about there,' she said. 'A little adventure is one thing, but I don't want to get lost,' she said and then thought, gulp, if I'm not already.

Soon the path led up a long hill away from the creek. The light was brighter. It was either a clearing or the end of the old pines. The dog walked toward the light and Caroline followed.

Chapter 17

The next morning after Cynthia and Richard had been up late watching television with C.J. and Anne, the children left in Cynthia's car to go shopping and mess around. Richard was finished with everything on the list that Cynthia had thought about doing before the house went on the market and he spent most of the morning getting his tools back into the box on his truck and cleaning up the rooms where he had worked. Cynthia hadn't had a maid since she decided she had to live a simpler life, and there was a fine film of sawdust in the rooms.

After Richard cleaned up as best he could, he went to find Cynthia, whom he hadn't seen or heard from the whole time he was straightening up. He found her in the little corner room at the end of the house that she called her Navajo room.

She and Clark and the children had taken a trip out West years ago and visited Indian reservations and the national parks. Cynthia had gone into an altered state when she came in contact with the Indians and their blankets and pottery and icons and feathers and skirts and jackets and she'd nearly bought out two or three entire trading posts.

She bought so much that everything except a few long fringed skirts and blouses had to be shipped back to her house. The shipping had to be arranged carefully so that it would not arrive back before they did. For the rest of the trip she wore her Indian clothes whenever she felt the occasion was right.

Then, when she got back, she emptied the corner room that had been her office and turned it into her Navajo room. She covered the walls with blankets and put rugs on the floors and hung the ornaments of war, religion, peace and fertility all over the walls. The room changed then, more than just in looks. Whenever she went into this room, she was overcome by the spirit of the objects.

She was on a daybed, propped up against the wall on some pillows. The pillows were covered in Navajo designs, and she herself was wrapped in a blanket.

'Are you cold?' he asked.

'No. Why?'

'You're wrapped up in that wool blanket.'

'Oh. No, I was just thinking. I like to feel this blanket. It's wool, but it's soft. It was an old blanket I bought off a woman. She said it had been her mother's.'

'Must be old,' he said.

She didn't say anything for a little while, and when he looked at her, she seemed to be pouting.

'What is it?' he asked.

'I don't want to sell the house.'

'Then don't. That's what I said a long time ago. Don't.'

'But I have to.'

'Why?'

'Because I can't afford it. Because I'll soon run out of money. Because of so many things.'

'It's paid for, isn't it?'

'Yes.'

'Then what's to afford? I can keep it up. That won't be a problem.'

'The taxes, for one thing. The property taxes on the house and the ten acres are almost $5,000 a year.'

'No kidding.'

'No kidding. They've got the whole place valued at almost a half a million dollars, but I asked a real-estate person about it and she said it was unlikely I could get that, and I told the county about it after Clark left and I started to see the bills I'd never seen before, but the person at the county offices said the only thing I could do would be to appeal it and hardly any appeal was ever successful.'

'There must be something we can do.'

'I don't know what.'

'Let me think on it,' he said.

'Don't worry about it. I'll get used to it. This is how I get used to things that are hard on me. I just get quiet and think about them a long time. Don't worry about me, okay?'

'All right.'

'Just think about what we might do after we sell it. Be thinking about that. What kind of house we can build, or where we can find another place.'

'It costs a lot to build nowadays,' he said.

'I know it does,' she said. 'I can't spend too much. We will just have to build a simple house with a room for each of the children and one for us and then not much else. I've got to have a room for my Indian stuff, though,' she said. 'I just have to have this room.'

'We can do that,' he said.

'Why don't you draw something and let's start thinking about it, okay?'

'Sure.'

Later that afternoon C.J. and Anne returned. C.J. had a five-gallon can of gas he had taken to get filled up. He had filled it up this time with super-high-test. He poured about a gallon of it into his tank and while his sister unloaded a bag of groceries her mother had asked her to get on the way home and carried that and a couple of other things she had bought at the mall, C.J. tried out the new gas.

The gas didn't do anything the first run across the field, but as it got down into the carburetor and replaced what little of the old had been there, it seemed to make the bike faster. C.J. watched the speedometer as he blasted across the field. The speedometer only went to fifty. The needle for the first time got above forty-five. It was hard to see and keep his eyes on where he was going at the same time, but it had done it. He kept on then, wide open, trying to bury the needle.

Upstairs, his sister tried on her new clothes. She liked the new clothes fine, but they didn't look the same in the house. She wasn't sure anymore she'd bought the right thing. She called one of her friends to consult about it.

'I don't know,' she said. 'You know those lights, they make everything look different.'

'I know,' the friend said.

'I saw those colors in *Vogue* and they looked, like, I don't know, really great, but I don't know anymore.'

'I know. I do that all the time,' she said.

'Wait a minute,' Anne said and peeked out the door.

'What was that?' the friend asked.

'Mom's got a new boyfriend. I forgot he was in the house and I was standing here almost naked and forgot to lock the door.'

'Ugh, that's creepy.'

'He's all right. I just forget sometimes.'

'How many is that now?' the friend asked.

'How many what?'

'Boyfriends.'

'Oh. I don't know. Three. Or four. Three, I think.'

'My mom had so many I lost count. They didn't move in, though.'

'This one's all right. He's quieter than the others. The others were always trying to be my friend, you know. My friend,' she said again, as if it was absurd.

'Yeah.'

'But anyway, why don't you come over?'

'Okay.'

'I'll call you when I work everything out. I'm trying to find the right time to get either my mom or dad to think about buying me a car.'

'Oh, that'd be great. What kind?'

'I don't know. Anything, I guess.'

'You'll probably end up like me, getting their old car.'

'That'd be okay,' Anne said. 'Just so I could get around.'

'What's that noise?'

'C.J. He's on his bike.'

Downstairs, Cynthia leaned up and looked at her son, going back and forth as fast as he could go. Upstairs, Anne talked and looked out the window and watched as well. Richard sat on the porch, out of sight behind a bush that had grown up higher than it was supposed to when it was planted. From there he could see the boy twisting the throttle and kicking the shift up through the gears. The noise was so loud it was all anyone could do to not look, and across the road the old woman who'd put the sign on them that night stopped to see what it was.

She'd been draping the wet clothes over tree limbs and bushes to let them dry. The whole yard was covered with clothes laying all over the trees and shrubs. The old woman had something working in her, something from Africa. She could've just come up from the river after scrubbing clothes against the rocks and hung them out on the bushes. There was something lingering in her from the tribe and the jungle, and the little mosquito buzzing across the field day and night across the road made her uneasy.

C.J. zoomed. The dirt bike jumped and flew across the grass. He was fourteen years old. His heart beat like the piston inside the hot motor. He was trying to outrun something. He was trying to go faster than something. He didn't know what it was.

Cynthia went back to the daybed. Anne hung up the phone and looked at herself in the mirror. Richard scratched his head and went back inside. The old woman laid some more clothes out. It was a summer day. There wasn't anything special about it. It was just another day.

Chapter 18

The dog went out of sight over the hill and Caroline walked ahead until she could see the clearing. The clearing was less than an acre. An acre is a big piece of land in a city, but in the country it doesn't look like much. An acre is a little more than two hundred feet by two hundred feet square. In the city, this acre could have numerous buildings on it. In the buildings there could be fifty thousand people, all stacked on top of each other, working feverishly, answering the phone, moving pieces of paper from one place to another, looking or not looking at each other, while in the country, on any given acre of land, there could be nothing, or nearly nothing, happening. Just the trees and the bugs and this or that walking or flying through.

So the acre of land which came into view to Caroline could have been just the clearing made when a couple of huge trees had toppled over or died of disease or old age or broken in half. It could have been just a poor spot in the soil where not much grew. She couldn't tell exactly what it was she was coming to, but no matter what she was thinking, she had not once imagined she would come upon a picture-perfect log cabin with a rusty tin roof and a brick chimney up one side and a porch facing her with an old dug well in front of it. She would never have imagined such a thing out here in the middle of nowhere. It was such a shock to her that she stopped dead in the woods out of sight and reached over to a tree and touched it, as if to steady herself.

She had to steady herself not only from the sight of this little house in the middle of nowhere, but because, as the dog walked across the yard covered with pine needles just like the forest around it, a woman came out the door and spoke to the dog on her way over to the dug well. She was carrying a bucket. She looked like someone Caroline knew or had known. She looked a bit like Caroline herself. She had on work pants and a man's cotton shirt and she had long blond hair done up in a braid that went down to her belt.

The old well had a simple roof over it. The roof was supported by two poles that went in the ground beside the well. The well itself was round and lined with flat stones. The stones had been built up three feet above the ground. On top of the stones was a wooden cover. The cover was hinged in the middle and the woman opened one half of it and folded it back onto the stationary half. Then she lowered a bucket down into it by hand. There was no winch or windlass over the well. She just leaned over and lowered the bucket and then pulled it up. After she pulled it up, she dumped the water into another bucket and went back toward the cabin.

The dog walked beside her. When she looked at the dog, the dog looked at Caroline. Then the woman stopped and looked in that direction, too. Though she was looking directly at her, Caroline did not think she saw her, due to the fact she was still in the shadows of the forest.

For a moment the woman was still. She looked at the dog, who wagged his tail and looked again at Caroline. Then the woman went inside and the dog drank some water out of his own pan on the ground under the overhang of the roof where it could catch the drips when it rained, and after he finished drinking, he lay on the porch with his paws placed over the edge of the boards so that they rested downward, the way a person's hands would do if he let his wrists hang over the end of the arms of a chair.

Good gracious, Caroline thought. Where in the world did this place come from?

Her heart was beating fast. She knelt down right where she was. She wanted to go up and meet this person who had this dog who had, it seemed, as she thought about it, come and gotten her, but she just couldn't decide how to enter this peaceful and absolutely one-hundred-percent-o private world.

Then, as if Caroline's heart wasn't beating fast enough as it was, a man, a positively gorgeous, healthy, beautiful-looking man, came out with the woman and looked toward Caroline. The man looked a little like the woman. They were both tanned and both had light-colored hair, a bit sun-bleached, and since she was obviously wearing his clothes, they looked even more alike.

It was a sight that shook Caroline up about as bad as she could remember. Everything in her that was telling her to go out and see who these people were was also telling her not to move.

The dog stood up when the man came out. All three of them stood on the porch looking at her. Then the man waved his hand and motioned for Caroline to come. Caroline did. She smiled. She felt crazy, happy crazy, and the closer she got the better things looked, the way a picture slightly out of focus would look so much better if it were gotten perfectly into focus.

The cabin was low to the ground. It had been built on rocks set at each corner and in the middle of each side as well. The porch was even lower to the ground, so that the people were less than a foot above her as she approached. The dog came out and nuzzled his head under her hand and followed along.

'Hello,' the man said. The woman smiled.

'Hi,' Caroline said.

'Are you alone?' the woman asked, looking behind her.

'Yes. I followed your dog here.'

'You did?' the woman said.

'I did. It's really strange. I saw your dog a few weeks ago in the woods behind my house. And then today I saw him again and, I don't know, I just got this idea to follow him and see where he was going.'

'Oh,' the woman said.

'Was it far?' the man asked. 'Do you live far from here?'

'It seemed like a long way but I can't really tell. We just kind of wandered and wandered until we got here.'

The man and the woman looked at each other briefly and

made some contact Caroline couldn't figure out. They held hands as they stood together in front of Caroline and their fingers were interwined. After they looked at each other for that brief moment, they looked back at Caroline and she thought they must be worried about something.

'Well, I didn't mean to come here like this and bother you. I can go back now if you want. I love your dog, though. He's really special.'

'You don't have to leave,' the man said.

'Stay and have lunch with us if you like,' the woman said, 'I was just getting some water to wash off the vegetables when the dog walked up.'

The inside of the cabin was one big room. The logs were exposed inside as well as out and looked as if they had recently been rechinked. The floor was laid with wide boards and both the floor and the logs were the color of light brown dust, though the cabin itself was clean and neat. In a corner was a double bed and between the bed and the dry sink at the other corner were two stuffed chairs covered with cotton spreads.

There was a small bookshelf along one wall, filled with books. Beside the dry sink was another bookshelf with a few books on the top shelf and cooking utensils on the rest. It was cool inside the building, even though it only had three small windows. The windows were on each side of the cabin except the side where the door was, and on that side there was only the door, which they left open as they entered.

'This is beautiful,' Caroline said. 'These logs are huge.'

'It's an old place,' the man said.

'Sit down,' the woman said and pointed to a chair. 'I'll make lunch.'

'I can help if you want,' Caroline said.

'It's all right. It's not going to be much.'

'My name's Caroline, by the way.'

'I'm Walker and that's Ellen.'

'This is real nice of you to ask me in,' Caroline said. 'You've got to come see me sometime so I can reciprocate.'

'We don't go too many places,' Walker said. 'But thank you anyway.'

'That must be why I've never seen you around,' Caroline said.

'We mostly just stay out here,' Ellen said.

'I like that,' Caroline said. 'I like that kind of life.'

'What does your husband do?' Walker asked, looking down at Caroline's ring.

'Oh. My husband,' Caroline said. 'Oh yeah. Well, he,' she said and began to fumble her words, 'he just does a lot of different things, I guess, I mean, I haven't, you know, really seen him in a while,' she said and then it was out. It was finally out. She had finally told somebody.

'Oh, I'm sorry,' Ellen said. She could tell by Caroline's face she didn't mean her husband traveled a lot, or was gone temporarily on business.

'It's all right. It's about all over, anyway. I'm not going to start crying or anything. Actually, I feel really great now. Really. Just sitting here in this beautiful house is making me feel really, really good.'

Across the room was an old wood stove. The wood stove was rusty and looked as if it had been in the cabin forever. It was the type of stove known as a laundry heater, and it was attached to the brick chimney with a long run of pipe. At the place where it entered the chimney, shiny creosote surrounded the pipe.

On top of the stove was an arrangement of dried flowers. There was also an arrangement of dried flowers and grasses on a table near the stove. Beside the arrangement were pictures, and some of the pictures were old and looked like family snapshots from long ago, and some of them were of Ellen and Walker. They were younger in the only picture Caroline could make out from where she sat, but looked nearly the same.

'This house has made a lot of people feel good over the years,' Walker said. 'It's an old place that's seen a lot.'

'I can tell,' Caroline said. 'I can feel it.'

Besides that, there were two other things Caroline could

feel in the air while she watched Walker helping Ellen with the lunch. She could feel the awkwardness of what she'd said about her husband being gone a long time, and she could feel the effects of the look that had passed between the two people out on the porch.

After a few minutes they went to the table to eat. There were two chairs at the table and another one just like them against the wall. Walker carried it over and they all sat.

'This lettuce had gone by a little,' Ellen said.

'It was starting to bolt,' Walker said. 'So we're trying to eat it up now.'

'Mine's the same way. I've just been letting it go, though. I always do.'

'Listen,' Walker said, as they served themselves, 'out on the porch we looked at each other like we were worried, and you saw us.'

'I did? Oh yeah,' Caroline said. 'I remember now.'

'The reason we looked at each other was not that we didn't want to have you, but that we've lived here a long time, a really long time, and no one's ever come up before, except one old man looking for some coon dogs and that was a long time ago and he just passed through apologizing and telling us he wasn't actually hunting on the land, just looking for the dogs.'

'It's all posted,' Ellen said.

'I saw the signs,' Caroline said.

'And after he left, we thought, well, I guess that's it. He's going to tell some people and pretty soon we're going to be out of here.'

'You see,' Ellen said, 'we don't own this place.'

'We don't even know who does,' Walker said.

'We just found it a long time ago and moved in.'

'And the whole time that we've been here, we've been expecting someone to come tell us to leave, or someone to come up, and now, after all this time, you have appeared.'

'Wow,' Caroline said.

'And so, out on the porch, we looked at each other and thought, well, I guess it's going to happen.'

'What he means,' Ellen said, 'is that we are afraid that you won't be able to keep the place a secret.'

'And we won't blame you. We don't really have any right to the place except that no one else lives here.'

'You mean you don't want me to tell anyone about finding this place?'

'That's what we're hoping.'

'If it's possible,' Walker said.

'I won't then.'

'You have to understand we've been real careful here,' Ellen said. 'We have given as much to the place, or more, than we've taken.'

'If we ever have to leave, it'll just be the better for us having been here.'

'Oh you don't have to explain,' Caroline said. 'I understand everything better than you could imagine. If you had to pick someone to come walking out of the woods and discover this place, you couldn't have picked a better person than me. I won't say a word to anyone. I can see you have some kind of really special thing going here and I would be the last person in the world to want to mess it up.'

They looked relieved.

'I believe you,' Walker said.

'I do, too.'

Besides the lettuce, they had tomatoes cut up in quarters and some crackers that were almost stale.

'Excuse the crackers,' Ellen said when Caroline took some. 'We try not to do any cooking or baking during the summer. We can things outside on the stove in the yard, but we don't make biscuits or anything like that except in the winter.'

'They're fine,' Caroline said. 'And this water is really unbelievable. It's the best-tasting water I've ever had and I thought we had good water.'

'It's because there's nothing here. Nothing but thousands of acres of woods around.'

'Who owns this place, anyway?' Caroline asked.

'We don't know. The name on the posted signs is all faded out. It looks like Jones, or something, but we just don't know.'

'You really don't know?' Caroline asked.

'We don't.'

'Good gracious,' Caroline said. 'If it weren't rude, I'd ask you to tell me all about how you found it and how you live here. I'm just about crazy to know, it's such a dreamy thing for me.'

'It's not rude,' Walker said, 'but what do you mean?'

'What do I mean what?'

'It's such a dreamy thing, you said,' Ellen told her.

'Oh. It's just I've been thinking of a life like this lately. It's kind of what I started out to want, and kind of what we started out to have, but then it changed. That's what I mean.'

After lunch they went out back. The old stove where they canned was set up with the pipe just sticking out the back and was rusted badly.

'We're afraid to use it in the house. It was out here when we came. We just use it like they did, we guess.'

'Whoever they were,' Caroline said.

The dog came around the side of the house and joined them. They all went to the shade that was at that moment behind three large old pear trees. The pear trees and dogwood and what looked to Caroline like a couple of old peach trees with no fruit on them were the only trees in the area different from the huge old pines that surrounded the clearing like a fence.

Walker sat in the pine needles and Ellen lay down in front of him and put her head on the pillow created by the fold of his legs. Caroline sat down opposite them and then lay down on her side and propped her head up with her hand with her elbow on the ground.

'Tell us where you live and all first,' Walker said. 'Tell us what's going on out there in the world and all that, and then we'll tell you how we found this place.'

And so Caroline started in. The two people who had

innocently asked Caroline to talk had no idea they were getting ready to receive a verbal overload the likes of which they hadn't known in years.

Chapter 19

Richard visited some builders he had done cabinets for in the past. There was a lot of construction going on and plenty of work. Northern companies had moved into the area and brought with them executives making so much money that, whereas before only doctors and a few other people could afford houses that cost three or four hundred thousand to build, they were commonplace now.

The kitchen cabinets in a house like that cost from fifteen to thirty thousand dollars, and often the people wanted built-in bookshelves, breakfast nooks, window-seat toy boxes and all kinds of other things. Two builders told Richard he could have their cabinet jobs right then and there. Richard then told Cynthia about this when he got back.

'I can't sit around here and just draw up our house plans. I don't feel right about it.'

'But, baby,' she said, 'I want to be with you all the time. When the children leave next week, why don't we just go back to the mountains for a little while.'

'That's all well and good, but still, I've got to get some money coming in.'

'I told you not to worry about it.'

'But I do.'

Cynthia had come out of the Navajo room and was in the great room attached to the kitchen. The children were upstairs and the house was relatively quiet.

'But drawing us a house plan is something that's really important that we need, and I can't do it. Only you could.'

'I know. I'll do that. I just need to do the other, too.'

'Well, all right,' she said. 'But take on a small job. Don't take on too much. What if we sell the place and have to get started on the other house right away.'

'I'll work it out. Those things always take a long time to get going.'

'Sit beside me,' she said. 'Tell me about what you're going to be doing.'

'Well, the first thing is that we've got to figure out a way to either work something out with Caroline so I can work in the shop or temporarily move the shop over here, which would be a huge job and almost impossible, because we'd have to convert the barn and all that, and wire it for the machines and all.'

'Well, then it's out,' she said. 'I do not, absolutely do not want you working over there.'

'You could come with me. You could help.'

'I want to help you, but not over there. I forgot about that when I said yes. That won't work.'

'It might.'

'It won't.'

'It might.'

'Don't keep saying that. It won't.'

'Well, honey,' he said, 'I can't just sit around here doing nothing. I feel rotten doing that.'

'Let's think of something else, then. How about painting the outside. The trim. The children could help you. You could do the high parts and me and the children could do the low parts. How about that?'

'I guess,' he said.

'You don't sound enthusiastic.'

'I don't like to paint.'

'Well, then, don't do it. We can think of something else.'

'Going back to work is the easiest thing.'

'Except for the situation with the shop.'

'Right.'

'How much would it cost to fix up the barn to use as the shop.'

'Well, some, but not much, but if you're going to sell the place, then it wouldn't be worthwhile.'

'Would it make the whole place worth more?'

'I don't know. You'd have to ask a realtor.'

'Come here and sit beside me. You're always standing up and pacing around when we talk about things like this and it makes me nervous.'

'All right. I know I do that.'

'I want to tell you something. I want to tell you what's important to me and what isn't. Okay?'

'Sure.'

'Rub me while we talk like we did the other night. That makes me feel so good.'

She put her bare feet on his lap and he rubbed her toes and the tops of her feet and her arches while she began once more to go over how she wanted to spend the rest of her life. She was dreaming it, over and over. She talked about it and she dreamed it because she was so close. It came out of her all the time. It welled up. It overcame her. She had lived half a life in the wrong way. Now she could see where she was supposed to be.

'Art's important, see,' she said, 'and good food. You have to have beautiful things in your life and you have to keep yourself healthy, but more than that, you have to have love. You have to be loved and you have to give love, and when you do that, all the rest of the good follows. I've thought a lot about it.

'There's nothing richer than a man and a woman, nothing richer than both of them thinking the same thoughts, living the same life, and sharing it all in this kind of bonded way. It's a kind of sexual thing. It feels sexual, if you know what I mean.

'I don't mean to say that money is not important. I'm practical enough to know it is, but with money, you just want to be able to pay your bills and have enough left over to make life comfortable, but not lavish and self-indulgent. I've been there. It only works for a little while.

'That's why I want to sell this house. It will give us the nest egg we need. It will just be so wonderful. You don't know yet how much I love you. I haven't been able to make you know it yet. I guess that's a hard thing to do. I never made Clark feel anything because there wasn't anything to feel, and he knew that, but it didn't matter. Other things mattered to him. His idea of the good life was not my idea of the good life, although he was a good man, more or less, relatively, I guess you could say, but we were different people.

'I feel like I've been waiting for you all my life,' she said, and he nodded. She closed her eyes then while he tickled her feet and her ankles. She just couldn't imagine anything nicer at that moment even if C.J. did come stomping through the room on his way to the kitchen.

He wore huge high-top tennis shoes and never tied them, and when he walked he thumped and clumped along as though his feet were too heavy for him to pick up and set down properly.

'That's his second lunch,' she said.

'He's growing.'

'I don't even think I ate,' she said. 'Did you?'

'No.'

'I don't want to eat, though. I haven't had much of an appetite lately. I'm getting too thin, aren't I?'

'You look great.'

'I don't know why I'm not hungry. I ought to be. I always have had a good appetite.'

'Let me make you something, then,' he said.

'I can't. I pulled the ham out and got ready to slice some, but it made me feel sick and I put it back. I'll just wait until supper.'

Chapter 20

They were still lying on the ground in back of the cabin a half hour later and Caroline was still telling them about a half a million things that had happened in her life. She was remembering a vacation at the beach she hadn't thought of for a while.

'And we were down there having this great time and one day there was a storm way out in the ocean somewhere and you know how after there's a storm all kinds of things wash in on the shore. Well, I hadn't thought about it really, and I went in, even though there were all kinds of things floating on the surf, and then, bam, I got stung by this jellyfish.

'It hurt real bad, but anyway, that's not the point of why I'm telling you all this. See, after I came out of the water I felt like I was going to be paralyzed and my arms were stinging real bad and hurting and I got cramps and Richard helped me inside and I lay down on a towel in my bathing suit and tried to be still and he called the emergency room and they told him it would go away by itself and so he sat with me and after about an hour, he was reading to me some kind of magazine article or something, he got in bed with me and wanted to make love.

'I know it sounds weird, but he told me later that me just lying there all flushed and still and hurting had just kind of made him crazy for me and I wouldn't let him, and the reason I'm telling you is that in all the years we were married that is the only time, the absolutely only time he ever wanted to make love that I said no. Now isn't that something. You ought to hear the stories other people tell me. Well, damnit all, if our life was that good, and it was, I'm telling you, then why is it over? I mean, I never made love to him out of some kind of charity crap or anything like that. I wanted to. I always wanted to. And except for that jellyfish time, we always did.

'It's just hard to figure it out,' she said. 'But I'm getting there. Boy, my throat is dry. Can I go over and draw up some water?'

'Sure,' Walker said. 'We've got to go in now anyway and take our nap.'

'We always take a nap around this time of day,' Ellen said. 'It's just something that we always do.'

'But you stay, all right, and when we get up we'll celebrate with a bottle of wine we've been saving for a long time,' he said.

'Oh that'll be great,' Ellen said. 'I had almost forgotten about that bottle.'

They went inside. Caroline drew some water from the well. It was cool and tasted good and it felt like some sort of special elixir just to drink it, the way you might feel after walking across a two-acre burning-hot parking lot and into an air-conditioned building. It just refreshed her that much.

I love this place, she thought. She wondered if they were inside making love. I'd do it, she thought. I'd make love to that guy in a second. She was terribly attracted to both of them. Hell, she thought, I'm so desperate I'd make love to her.

She sat on the porch. The front door was still open. She could hear them inside. They were talking quietly. The dog came around from the shade and through the sunny part of the yard and dropped beside her in the cool of the porch as if his legs had been cut out from under him. He just flopped over and ended up lying on her feet.

'I like you, boy,' she whispered. 'I forgot to ask them what your name was.'

Caroline had a blissful rest herself. She felt the way a person working in a laboratory all her life and staring down the necks of microscopes until her eyes fell out might feel when suddenly one day there it is, the little organism, the little life force she'd been looking for all that time. It was there. For a while she might have thought, well, no, I guess it's not there. For a while she must have felt like quitting, that she had gone completely wrong, that she had been mistaken and that her premise was going to make a fool of her in the end.

That's the way Caroline felt. She knew that somewhere someone was living the sweet charmed life away from all the terminal madness of the world and she had stumbled into it. Here it was.

The way that Walker and Ellen moved together was like the way two dancers on a stage moved in perfect alignment and rhythm. The way they talked, the way he said half of the thought and she finished it, just touched Caroline to her soul, as if their minds were lined up and cleared out of anything but what both of them were thinking at the same time. And she was wearing his clothes. That killed her. She always loved the way a woman looked in men's clothes, kind of casually putting the lie to the necessity of strutting your stuff, but knowing he knew it was there and that was all that mattered. That killed her.

She wished she'd done it. She wished she could still do it.

'The dog's name is Jeep.'

'How'd you know I was just thinking about his name?' she asked Walker, who was standing behind her in the doorway.

'I didn't. I just thought we hadn't told you. We had an old Jeep when we got him. Years ago. Before we found this place. That's how he got his name.'

'I like it.'

'He's a good dog.'

'I know it. Did you get rested?'

'Oh sure.'

'I'd hate to think I messed up anything.'

'You didn't. Come on in. Ellen's out back. When she returns, let's open that wine.'

Ellen was on her way to the outhouse. The outhouse had been reconstructed and was far away from the dwelling. It had a real, actual toilet seat in it, and the hole below it was deep and far away and dark. It had been constructed so that there was a ventilation pipe coming out the back of the building, which made the place more acceptable.

Caroline went there after Ellen returned. Sitting there for a moment, she realized that beside having no indoor plumbing they didn't have electricity. She hadn't thought about it until just then.

'Well, I'll tell you how we live,' Walker said after she got back and they opened the wine.

'It's really easier than you might think,' Ellen said.

'We do go to town, see,' Walker said.

'But only rarely.'

'We go at night,' he said.

'We use the same path Jeep uses. We just go before it gets light and then wait near the road until morning.'

'We use our backpacks so that it looks like we're just two hikers walking into town.'

'We only go about three or four times a year,' she said, 'and we buy a whole bunch of stuff we need then, stuff we can't grow or even stuff we've just been missing.'

'Like a Coke or something,' he said.

'I have to tell you it's hard to give everything up.'

'We don't think about what we don't have that everyone else has, but when we go in we kind of buy a couple of Cokes and something like some fresh fruit we can't grow.'

'Like melons, or oranges,' she said, 'and then we bring the stuff back and have a party.'

'We get a can of dog food for Jeep.'

'That's the hardest thing,' she said, 'is getting enough dog food for him.'

'That's why he hunts a lot, I guess. He's never looked or seemed hungry, though.'

'Anyway,' she said, 'we get the newspaper then and go through it and all it does is make us glad we're away from everything.'

'We go by the used-book store and get a bunch of books and then we load up and start back.'

'It's usually a heck of a load,' she said. 'We start back toward night but while it's still light enough to be safe on the road, and then we wait in the edge of the woods.'

'We start off,' he said, 'just sitting on the bank like we're resting.'

'Then we slip back little by little until we're out of sight and then we wait until night. Jeep leads us back.'

'That's how he brought you here. He knows the way. He seems to know it's his job.'

'And how long have you been doing this?' Caroline asked.

'A long time.'

'I don't even know,' Walker said.

'But we wouldn't leave.'

'Not unless we had to.'

'We hope the people never come back to this place.'

'It's ours now. If we had the money, we'd buy it.'

'But then it would all change,' she said, 'like we've talked about. Once you own something, it changes everything.'

They talked a long time. They were so mellow to start with the wine hardly affected them. Caroline went woozy almost right away. The wine went straight to her legs and also to part of her that hadn't had much attention lately. They kept filling her glass up. She was much drunker than they were when the bottle was empty.

'I swear,' she said, 'I'm nearly smashed. I can't believe it. I ought to drink more often. Except I know it's bad for me. Every now and again's all right, though. It's one of those things that moderation has to govern, you know what I mean. It's like what I was reading about what the Pope said the other day. He said everybody was too materialistic. Well, I know that. You know that. We both know it. That's why you live like this and that's why I want to live like this and that's why it's so amazing I found you because I've been thinking about it ever since Richard left and fell for what whore, I'm sorry, I guess I shouldn't say that, but you don't know her like I do, but anyway, she's just the person whose life wouldn't exist if she didn't own a bunch of stuff. She'd just be nothing.

'But anyway, I didn't mean to get into that. What the Pope also said in this article I read in the newspaper was that sex and materialism were the new scourge of the world. New? I was thinking, baby, you only got half of that right. I wouldn't give up sex for anything. I mean, he's wrong about that. Don't you think?'

'I'd say so.'

'Way off,' Walker said.

'I know. Way off. I love sex,' Caroline said, 'and I always have. They say a person who likes sex that much might be neurotic or something, I read that in a magazine one time, but I love it anyway. I don't care if I'm neurotic that way. I don't mean I want it all the time, you know, but when I love someone, I love to have sex with them. It's just like the whole thing is hanging on the edge of something or stuck just below the top of a hill, you know what I mean, unless the sex is there with it. It just kind of rolls everything over. Life's so much easier when it's there and it's good,' she said and then caught a glimpse of herself talking about sex so much when she was obviously not having any, that she embarrassed herself and then tried to get out of it.

'I mean, you know, it's not like life's all over and done with when you don't have sex, but, oh well, I wish I hadn't gotten started on that. I didn't even mean to. What was I talking about in the first place? Does anyone remember?'

'I think it started out with drinking,' he said.

'And moderation,' Ellen said.

'Oh yeah. That's right. Well, I'm too drunk to talk good sense for a while. I'm just going to sit here and be quiet.'

Caroline fell asleep in the chair facing west. She woke up when the sun was going down behind the trees.

'Uh oh,' she said and looked around. She was alone in the cabin. She found them in the garden. The garden was in the shade by then. They decided it was too late for her to try to get back before night even if they followed her and let Jeep find the way, since Jeep, although he always knew the way in and out, sometimes wandered off on tangents and couldn't always be relied upon to go directly where he was supposed to.

She spent the night there, then. They took the cushions off the stuffed chairs and laid them on the floor and made her a bed. Then she thought about it and asked them if she could sleep outside on the ground.

'It's so quiet and so really special out there I'd just like to sleep in the yard.'

They took the pillows and a spread out there and she made her bed in the yard about halfway between the woods and the house.

'There are deer and stuff that come around at night,' Walker said. 'They won't bother you, though.'

'I know. We have them around our house. I see them every now and again around the edge of the field.'

The night was darker than usual. It was cloudy. There was no moon. It was so absolutely quiet in the dark that when Caroline lay as still as she could she almost lost the sense of her self, of her body. It was a little like being lowered into a tank where the water is the same temperature as your body, and the only sound you can hear is the blood in your ears and your heartbeat.

She lay a long time without falling asleep. The dog was in the house and the door to the house was closed. They said he barked too much if they left him out. They had to be careful. They had a dream of a place and it was understandable that they needed to be careful about anything that might lead to its demise.

She fell asleep and then woke up soon afterwards. She had this feeling that she ought to go inside and get in bed with them. That if she did, they would let her. That if she did, she would make love with both of them. Somehow, even though she knew she ought to feel strange about wanting to make love to both of them, out there, with just the three of them, it seemed okay.

She thought about it a long time. She really wanted to go inside and be with them. She wondered if they had talked about it. She had made it stupidly obvious how lonely she was. If they had talked about it and thought it was all right, and she was out here all alone even in this beautiful paradise of silence and thought, and she didn't go and let the night slip away, then what a waste it would have been.

She couldn't do it, of course. She would have been humiliated nearly to death if she'd been the only one thinking that and had come in and made a fool of herself. She let it go, then, and tried to sleep.

During the night she had many dreams. She woke up and opened her eyes every now and then. The absence of light was remarkable. It was nothing like being in a city. It was not even like being in a house in the country, where there was always something on somewhere, a night-light in the bathroom or a car coming down the road or the red glow of the wood stove or just the green illuminated dial of the clock.

Here there was nothing. When she opened her eyes she couldn't even tell her eyes were open. It was just as dark as before. She couldn't see the cabin. She couldn't see the trees, but she could, she thought, feel them. Their presence was there. They had stood there for hundreds of years and she could feel they were there.

She slept. The sun came up at that time of year around five-thirty. She opened her eyes when the first light appeared. She did not move. She lay as still as death. All around her in the yard and at the edge of the woods were deer.

The deer had come on her during the night. For hours they had watched her. They sniffed her and watched her and when she never, not once, moved, they came closer. Now, as she lay with her head to one side and her eyes open, she saw them. They were pawing at the pine needles and sniffing the ground, looking for something to eat, she supposed. They moved slowly. They never kept their heads down long. All of them looked up and around quickly and repeatedly. The deer were all does and most of them had fawns with them. The fawns did not look like Bambi. They looked like smaller versions of their fat brown antlerless mothers.

They looked a little like goats but they were much prettier, more graceful and wild. Caroline lay still. It was something that had never happened to her before. She had seen wild animals plenty of times but had never been this close to them.

It made her heart beat fast. It made her tremble. One of the deer looked right at her, right in her eyes. She shivered, she hoped without moving, all the way down her spine. Something connected. Something elemental in her had made contact with the same thing in the deer.

The deer walked around her slowly. She faced the same way. Her neck began to crick. New deer passed in front of her. She never saw a buck. There were, it seemed, about three females and three or four or five fawns. They sniffed the air. They grew still. The deer moved this way and that. One of them jumped suddenly, and then all of them jumped, and when they did, Caroline jumped with them.

She heard the dog then, scratching on the door and whining. Someone let him out. The deer leaped into the woods. In a matter of seconds they were gone. They were completely out of sight. The dog came tearing past Caroline and right after them. He didn't have a chance.

Later in the morning Caroline and the dog and Walker and Ellen went back down the trail toward Caroline's house. They were only going to walk so far to make sure she could find her way back. At the edge of the old forest, they turned back, and Caroline was on her own.

They took the dog with them. Caroline followed the trail along the creek and to the spot where she had met Jeep and then back up to her house. Her house was still there. It was the same. Nothing had happened the whole time she had left it. Maybe some things had happened, but she didn't know about it. Maybe the phone had rung. Maybe someone had come to visit. Maybe the television silently broadcast messages to itself, waiting to be turned on and release them into the air. Maybe a lot had happened, but none of what might have happened could matter much to Caroline.

She had seen something. She had seen these two people and she had seen this cabin in the middle of that primeval forest and she had made contact with the deer. It was an amazing day. It was a miraculous day. She thought, I will never be the same again. She thought about it as she climbed up the hill to her house and went in.

She had seen something. She had slept in the midst of the deer. They had protected her in the night. They had come around her and stayed with her. They had remained with her as she awoke. Something had passed between them.

The communion with the deer, though, had taken Caroline somewhere new. She felt it in her, like a physical presence. It made her want to be quiet and still. She climbed the hill then, and went across the little field, and sat in her house and she was amazed.

Chapter 21

Cynthia and the children and Richard were watching television. The children were still awkward around Richard, and Cynthia was trying to discover a way to get everyone relaxed. That meant Richard, too, who talked even less than usual when the children were around.

She was also trying to bring up the idea of the sale of the house and figure out a way to include them in on it and let them work up some enthusiasm for the move and the new life. She was thinking they ought to take a trip together and then when they came back organize a giant yard sale and get rid of all the things they didn't really want or wouldn't have room for.

'We could go to the mountains,' she said. 'Wouldn't you like that, Richard?'

'Yes.'

'I thought you already went,' C.J. said.

'But I mean all of us.'

'All of us?' Anne said.

'Sure,' her mother said.

'I don't know. I never get to see my friends as it is,' she said. 'How long would we have to stay up there.'

'A week,' her mother suggested.

'A week?' Anne said.

'A week?' C.J. said. 'What would we do for a whole week? Where would we go?'

'We could go to Tweetsie Railroad. You haven't been there in a long time,' his mother said.

He looked at his mother as if she were positively, totally, and permanently insane.

'Tweetsie Railroad?' he asked. 'Mommy, how old do you think I am? Just tell me. Take a wild guess.'

'I know how old you are.'

'I think we've outgrown the Tweetsie Railroad,' Anne said.

'Well, what then? We could find someplace else.'

'Could I take a friend with me. Could I take Bobbie?' her daughter asked.

'I guess so,' she said. 'Would that be okay with you?' she asked Richard.

'Sure.'

'Well, then I get to take someone also,' C.J. said.

'Where would we all sit?' Anne asked. 'How many would that be?'

'It'd be,' her mother said, 'let me see, it'd be, one-two-three-four-five-six. It'd be six.'

'You sit in the front with them,' Anne said. 'I get the back.'

'No you don't. You sit in the front.'

'You can have the back seat,' her mother said to Anne, 'along with Bobbie, and you can make a place in the way back with pillows and the like, along with whoever you take.'

'What about the luggage?' Richard asked.

'We can use the rack on top.'

'I don't want to do it, anyway,' C.J. said. 'Maybe for a day or something, but not for a week.'

'Me neither,' his sister said. 'A week's too long.'

'We got to go to Dad's next week, anyway,' C.J. said.

'That's right,' Anne said.

'Well, I want to go somewhere with you,' their mother said. 'You've already been on a trip with your father. I want to take you somewhere.'

'We will,' her daughter said. 'We will, but let's think about it for a while. Maybe the beach.'

'The beach would be better,' C.J. said.

'Would that be all right with you?' Cynthia asked Richard.

'The beach is hot this time of year, but it'd be all right, anyway.'

C.J. had the remote-control television device and he changed the channels while they talked. He went through about 165 channels in less than a minute and couldn't find anything he wanted to see. He came all the way around to where he had started and began flipping through them again. They were all seized by the activity on the screen and the effort to actually come out of the experience having found something to watch, but when he started around again, his sister blew up at him.

'You do that all day. I hear it going even when I'm in my room. Can't you just be still for once,' she said, but before he could answer she turned to her mother and said, having found a good place to bring it into the conversation, 'See what I mean, Mom. If I had my own car I wouldn't have to sit around here enslaved to my brother's habits. I need a car. If I had a car you wouldn't have to take me everywhere. I wouldn't always have to ask to use yours. You wouldn't be stuck here while I had it.'

'You wouldn't have to ride in the truck,' C.J. said, hoping it would be funny, though no one laughed.

'I could come visit you whenever I wanted to. Daddy said he'd pay for half of it if you would pay for the other half.'

'If she gets a car, then I get to have a bigger bike,' he said. 'The one I have isn't fast enough. It isn't big enough. I need one that's bigger. This one isn't safe. It's too small. A bigger one would ride better. This little one bounces all around too much. I could get killed and thrown off it bounces so much. A bigger one would be much safer and they have larger brakes and all that. And anyway,' he said, 'if she gets to have a car, and you pay for the whole thing, the least I ought to be able to do is trade mine in and you could pay for the rest, and that way I'd be paying for half of it myself, where she wouldn't be paying for any of hers.'

That was the longest speech C.J. had ever given in his life and he could still hear the sound of his own voice coming back at him when he finished, so he started flipping the channels again, trying to drown it out.

'What do you think?' Cynthia asked Richard.

'Well, it's, you know, kind of up to you. Whatever you think.'

'I tell you what we'll do,' she said. 'You know I have to sell the place and when we move there won't be room for everything, so we'll have a yard sale and split the money.'

'What kind of yard sale?' C.J. asked.

'What are we going to get rid of?' her daughter asked.

'We're going to make a list of the things we just don't want anymore and have a gigantic yard sale and if you two will help me organize it and get the stuff ready and price it and be there to help all day long, I'll split the money with you three ways.'

That pleased C.J. just fine. He was ready to sell everything in the house. They all talked about what they had to keep and then worked around from room to room in their minds, getting rid of this and that, and while they talked, Richard sat there watching television, and watching them, and nodding and smiling at the three while they whirled around him.

After a while he and Cynthia went outside. It was a clear night. There were more stars in the sky than a person could count. Above the horizon to the east, they could see the lights from the city of Durham glowing into the sky. If you didn't know that the city was in that direction and that the amber glow against the black sky was merely the lights of the cars and buildings and houses and signs in the city, you would have wondered at what kind of beautiful natural phenomenon it was.

It was the same thing Caroline could see from her porch as she sat alone and ate a Popsicle and watched the world glowing from a distance, still beautiful at that distance, but sadly betraying that beauty at close range, the amber glow, which seemed as warm and quiet as love and life itself, dissolved into chaos and paranoia and the blinding force of cold personal desire once you got close, and it was better to stay away. Beauty was so much easier to believe in from a distance.

It was just as lovely from Cynthia's yard. She and Richard

held hands and walked up the driveway. The trees along the driveway were dark. The driveway was warm on their bare feet. It retained the heat of the day like a stone warmed in the fire and taken to bed by the people who had lived on the land years earlier.

After they got to the end, they walked back toward the house. A hundred miles away a pilot in a jet fighter flying low began to live out the dream of C.J. and so many others. He opened up the throttle and roared ahead. His eyes rolled back. His lips trembled and distorted. He roared onward, covering the earth with his sound and his speed like a god.

Cynthia and Richard sensed his approach. Something made them stop and look up. He came over the trees. He wasn't making a sound. For a second, he just came silently. Then his sound caught up with him and hit the earth like a bomb and Cynthia and Richard dropped where they stood, just as if they had been afraid the jet would've struck them if they hadn't ducked down.

The sound reverberated and shook their bones. It turned Cynthia's stomach inside out. The old woman across the road picked herself up off the ground and made a sign in the sky. The jet departed. The noise diminished and then was gone. It was quiet again.

The animals in the woods which had hidden or found shelter began to move again. Cynthia and Richard went inside. Caroline stayed on her porch. Though she was miles away, she felt the tremor from the jet, as well. For a long time she listened as the plane flew away. Then there was nothing but the orange glow of the lights coming over the horizon and the slow, rhythmic creak of her chair as she rocked slowly back and forth.

PART IV

Don't Wear My Flip-flops

Chapter 22

Caroline had learned to drive when she was fifteen. Her mother took her out in the car to a parking lot. Her father was at work. It was a Saturday afternoon and the mill was running seven days a week. When it ran seven days a week, everyone worked because it was possible that the next month or the next year it would only be running four days a week, or three, or not at all.

Two of Caroline's friends went with her. They were in the back seat. The car was a 1956 Ford. It had automatic transmission that only shifted twice, and you had to give it a lot of gas to get going. It had a brake pedal ten inches wide and a visor extending out over the windshield. It had an AM radio and the radio was on the only station that played music teenagers would listen to.

The car was old and had been bought used but was in good shape.

Her mother drove to the side of the parking lot. She switched places with Caroline, and Caroline started the car. She knew how because she had been allowed to practice starting it at home. Then she shifted into drive. Her mother told her to aim in a straight line and take it easy and get the feel of a car in motion and how the steering affected it and how much pressure to put on the gas pedal.

After she drove about seventy-five feet, or about the width of a small front yard in town, her mother told her to stop. Caroline mashed the brake pedal hard. Everyone in the back ended up in the front. There were no seat belts back then. Her mother ended up against the dash and the two friends ended up against her. Caroline hit her face against the steering wheel and cut her chin.

The car had power brakes. Normally the brake pedal

would only move about two or three inches at the most. Caroline had mashed it all the way to the floor. The car had never stopped that fast before. No car had ever stopped that fast before. The laws of physics had to be revised after that.

She was thinking about that on her way to Lucille's because a squirrel had run out of the woods and onto the road in front of her. The squirrel froze when it realized a car was coming, and Caroline cut to the right to avoid it and it went to the right, and when she cut back to the left, it went left, so that they both weaved and darted back and forth until she finally slammed on the brakes and gave the squirrel time to figure out which way to go.

The squirrel darting back and forth was like the way she felt in her mind now as she tried to decide whether or not to tell Lucille, or anyone for that matter, that she was going to have a baby.

She had been to the doctor two days earlier and had confirmed the next day what she had thought. Too many things had said yes, even though just as many had said it was not possible.

It had all really begun to form far back in her that day in the woods with the deer, when she had by accident connected with the clear, penetrating eye of the fertile doe, but of course it had not been until much later that she began to notice all the usual signs that things inside of her were not the same.

With Caroline, it might have been an immaculate conception, or it might have been a hysterical pregnancy, or it might have been the visit from the alien life force that left her with child.

So, as she drove along in her old car to see Lucille, she was happy, but at the same time, and equally in degree, confused and worried. The fact of being with child made everything, absolutely everything, different.

She didn't know what to do. She wanted to tell Richard, but hadn't yet, not knowing how or what to expect or whether or not she really wanted to let him know after what he did to her. Of course just as soon as she thought about denying him this wonderful news she couldn't stand not knowing how he would react, and she would then decide that she would have to tell him, in person, actually, to see his face. Then, a little later, she'd decide not to again, and it went around and around.

She turned into Lucille and Edgar's driveway. Edgar was home. The pig had outgrown riding in the front seat. Sometimes he took the pig in the back in the truck bed, but it was about over. The joke had run its course.

'Well, we haven't seen you in ages,' Lucille said as she met her at the door. 'Edgar was just saying the other day he wondered how you all were doing.'

'Just fine,' she said.

'You sure are looking good,' Lucille said.

'You sure are,' Edgar said.

'I never saw you look so good.'

'Yeah, she don't look tired, neither.'

'No, she doesn't,' Lucille said. 'I told Edgar when you got out of the car that you looked a little tired, but I take it back.'

The way they talked and the way they were looking at her meant they had heard Richard had left her. The next question clinched it.

'How's Richard?' Lucille asked.

'Well, just fine,' Caroline said.

'Uh huh,' she said, and Edgar said the same thing, uh huh, and then they all stood there for a long second and then went inside.

'So what you all been doing?' Edgar asked.

'Just messing around, I guess,' Caroline said.

'Well, that's good. That's the best thing to do, just mess around,' Lucille said. 'That's what we do, too. Just mess around.'

'Actually I haven't seen Richard in a long time,' Caroline said.

'Is that right?' Edgar asked.

'Well, now, Edgar, we have to be honest with her. We did hear something about that, Caroline. But we weren't going to say anything if you didn't want to talk about it.'

'It's none of our business, really,' he said. 'You don't have to tell us a thing.'

'But I don't mind, you see,' she said. 'I minded at first, but now so much else is going on it's like something that happened long ago. Real long ago.'

'Uh huh,' they both said again. Every time she told a lie, they said uh huh, the same way the old-timers up in Maine breathed in when they said yup, or yep, giving the word the extra dimension that showed they knew something was wrong with what had been said, but were willing to let it go.

'Well, it is,' she said. 'Really.'

'Uh huh.'

'I'm glad to hear you're all right,' Lucille said. 'We've actually been worried about you. We've driven by I don't know how many times thinking to stop in, but Edgar just kept saying to leave you be, that when the time came for things to be known, they would be known.'

'Oh well, you could've come in any time you wanted. I wouldn't have cared.'

'Well, where did that boy go?' Lucille asked. 'I have to tell you, sugar, if what I heard was true and he left you for another woman, I think he ought to have his head examined.'

'Well, he did leave me, and he did move in with this other woman, but I swear, to this day, I don't think he knows what he's doing.'

'That's for sure. Any man that'd leave you'd have to be crazy,' Edgar said. 'I always said that, didn't I, Lucille?'

'You did. You've said that I don't know how many times.'

'It doesn't matter, though, because I've got really good news. It's just something that I'm so happy about I just have to tell someone.'

'Well, what is it?' Lucille asked.

'I'm going to have a baby,' she said and just smiled so big she almost cried from the happiness of it, while Lucille and

Edgar said, uh huh, almost before she'd finished the sentence.

'Uh, huh,' she said.

'Uh, huh,' he said.

'That's amazing news,' she said.

'It sure is,' he said.

'Well, it *is* Richard's,' Caroline said.

'Uh huh.'

'It is. And it's wonderful. I've always wanted a baby.'

'Well, of course you have,' Lucille said.

'I know it's a little strange, but I've thought about it a lot and I can't make myself be any way but just wildly happy about it.'

'Well, sure,' Edgar said.

'But sugar, does he know?'

'Not yet. I'm going to tell him tonight. Or tomorrow. Don't you say anything for a few days, maybe a week or so, all right.'

'We won't say a word.'

'Not until you tell us to,' Edgar said.

'But, Caroline honey,' Lucille said, 'as long as I've known you and as much as I like you I feel I have to ask just how in the world you're going to handle all this by yourself.'

'I've got a whole plan,' she said. 'I don't want to go into it now. But I've got it all worked out.'

'Uh huh,' Edgar said.

'Well, we're happy for you,' Lucille said and hugged her. The people in her church had started hugging each other in the past few years and she tried it out as often as she could. Edgar hadn't hugged anybody in years and didn't intend to.

They spent another hour having lunch and talking about everything but the baby and Richard and then Caroline left and Edgar and Lucille spent another hour trying to make sense of these two incongruous pieces of news.

Things had to make sense. People like Edgar and Lucille had to believe in the predictability of life, in the proper and traditional structure of things. There was a little room for doing different things. For thinking different things. But there wasn't much. A man could leave a woman and a woman could leave a man. A woman could get pregnant, and many a woman had, and raise the child by herself, but by God, she wasn't supposed to be happy about it. There were things that people could do within the bounds of what had always been done, but there were right ways to act when you did them, and for a single woman to happily announce that she is pregnant with the child of a husband who has run off with a rich woman down the road and for that woman to seem happy about the prospect of living some sort of impossibly romantic life, just her and the child, well, it was too much.

A man might ride around with a pig in his truck. He might name the pig after his wife. He might tell his wife she looks like a pig. He might tell her she smells like a pig. He might tell his friends he'd just as soon have intercourse with the pig as with his wife. They could laugh at that and most of them could understand it. There were a lot of things a man could do, but one thing he couldn't do was to get his wife pregnant and then run out on her.

A woman could let her husband call her a pig and could let the pig ride in her seat and she could let him tell jokes about her, but, by God, if he got her pregnant, or pignant, whichever it would be under the circumstances, she sure as heck couldn't be happy about it.

It didn't make sense. Some things were allowed. Others were not. Caroline had gone too far.

'Well, she's in for a big surprise,' Lucille said.

'She don't know what she's in for,' he said.

'I believe you're right,' she said.

'She's about to get a dose of that stuff they call reality,' he said.

'I hope the poor girl will come out all right. She sure is a sweet thing.'

'Crazy, though.'

'But sweet. I do love her, I swear I do,' Lucille said, and she went to her room feeling sad and wishing there was something she could do besides pray and think good thoughts.

Edgar left in the truck.

Caroline had been home an hour when she saw Edgar pass. He turned his head casually toward the house, but his gaze was intense.

She thought about what she'd done and realized she had let herself tell them so she'd be forced to tell Richard. It was a stupid way to go about things, a stupid way to make a decision, but it had come about and there it was and she resolved to tell him that night, like she said, or the next day.

Chapter 23

The children were back at their father's and on Tuesday morning Cynthia came downstairs feeling rotten and saw Richard standing at the stove cooking breakfast and wearing her flip-flops.

'Don't wear my flip-flops,' she said.

'What?'

'I said, please don't wear my thongs, my flip-flops,' she told him again and nodded toward them with her head.

'Oh. Sorry.'

'Your feet are bigger than mine. If you wear my flip-flops, you'll stretch them out.'

'Okay,' he said and slipped them off and stood at the stove barefoot. 'You want any sausage this morning?' he asked.

'No,' she said. 'I don't want to even smell it.'

He switched on the exhaust fan over the stove. Cynthia picked up her shoes and looked at them and put them on her feet and then took them off again.

'Look, baby, I want to show you something,' she said. 'See how these are made? Your heel has been in a different spot. See?' she asked him and pointed to an indentation in the foam rubber toward the end of the shoe.

'Oh yes,' he said. 'I see.'

'Now when I put them on, they don't feel right.'

'I'm sorry,' he said. 'They were just there beside the bed and I slipped them on.'

'But that's the point. When I got up to slip them on, they weren't there.'

'Okay.'

She put them back on her feet and flopped across the room to a chair. Richard turned over one of the sausages and sliced into it with the spatula to see if it was done. Then he turned the rest of the patties over while Cynthia studied the spot where the thongs went through the sole.

'I can't wear these anymore,' she said.

'I'll get you some more. They were worn out anyway.'

'No, they weren't. They were fine. But your foot is so thick it's pulled this little button thing on the underside nearly all the way through.'

'Well, I told you I'm sorry. What else do you want me to do?'

'Nothing.'

She pouted while he folded up four sections of paper towel and drained the sausage. Then he took a pan of frozen biscuits out of the oven and made himself three sausage-and-biscuit sandwiches, which he began to eat with a glass of milk.

'These are good,' he said.

'There are certain things people do that are like body language,' she said, ignoring his comment. 'You understand? Like things people do that show respect for other people and things people do in the way they look at another person or in their voice that shows they feel a certain way toward that person or the way they stand when they talk to you. You know what I'm taking about?'

'I guess so.'

The biscuits were still good, but he stopped eating so he could pay better attention to her.

'It's like using someone's comb or toothbrush. Putting on their shoes without asking them is the same thing. It says, without saying it out loud, that I don't respect you. It gives the other person the signal that they're being used, that they're only there for what the person can get out of them.'

'Are you kidding?' he asked. He was truly dumbfounded by what she was suggesting. 'I can't believe I'm hearing what I think I'm hearing coming from you.'

'It's just that you get up, you come down here, you start making breakfast, you get out the sausage and those frozen biscuits I bought for C.J. . . . '

'I didn't know you bought them for C.J.,' he said. 'I thought you liked them. I made them for us, not just for me.'

'And you don't even ask me what I want. You just get up, put on my flip-flops and come down and start cooking my breakfast. That's body language, Richard. That's clear body language.'

'Well, I couldn't be sorrier I've done something wrong. I had no idea. I didn't think it mattered. If I'd known how important your flip-flops were to you, I would've rather died than wear them. I swear. That's the truth.'

'Oh, forget it,' she said. She saw on his face how bewildered he was. 'I just woke up feeling bad. I don't know. I just feel so crabby I think I'll go back to bed.'

'It's okay,' he said. 'You're probably right, anyway. I probably do things without thinking to ask you. I'm glad you said it.'

'You're fine, sweetheart,' she said. 'You're not only fine, you're the finest I've ever known. You do everything just right. Just forget I ever came down. I'm going back upstairs and when I come down later I'll act like I just woke up. Okay?'

'Sure,' he said, and she kissed him on the back of his neck and then she went up and he heard the door to the bedroom close.

He picked up the sausage biscuit he'd been eating. It didn't taste the same. It had gotten cold and the grease around the edges had turned white. The biscuit had lost its taste as well, and he put the whole thing, the plate and all, into the toaster oven, and heated it back up for a few minutes. When he took it out, he still couldn't eat it. The little patties of sausage tasted as if they'd been made out of rubber from someone's old flip-flops. They even looked like it, dirty-looking brown circles. It was amazing how fast a really great meal like hot sausage biscuits could go cold and tasteless like that. It was truly amazing.

He left Cynthia a note telling her he'd be back for lunch. He went to get her a new pair of shoes and also a new mantelpiece for her downstairs fireplace. She hated the one that was there now. It was made from old railroad crossties. Her husband had designed it and had it built when the house was under construction. It was heavy and splintery and awkward. She had seen one in a restoration magazine she liked. He knew where a friend of his had torn some out of a house before it was demolished. He went to buy one.

After he left, the phone rang. It didn't ring upstairs because the ring had been turned off. It rang downstairs, though. It rang and it rang and it rang. The little clapper inside the phone vibrated between the two bells, shimmering on its thin wire holder like the delicate stalk of a tiny flower shivering in the wind. The beater on the end of the wire pounded on the bells. It was possible if a person let a phone ring long enough, the clapper could snap in half. Then the phone would still be ringing, the call would still be going through, the little stalk would still be shimmering and trembling, fulfilling its electronic mandate to alarm the occupant of the incoming call, but the signal would be in vain.

The phone continued to ring. The clapper held. The two bells inside the phone called out. They said, answer the phone, Cynthia, Caroline is calling. We have important news for you. Answer the phone. Please.

Chapter 24

Caroline heard Richard's truck even before it pulled into the driveway. She knew the sound of that truck as well as she knew his voice. She watched it stop beside the house and she waited to see what he would do. She was shaking all over. He didn't come in, though. He just tapped lightly on the horn and leaned out the window when she appeared at the door.

'I need to do something in the shop. Just for a little while,' he said.

She looked toward the back of the truck and saw the mantelpiece.

'Who's it for?' she asked.

'It's just a job. I've got to make a couple of new pieces of molding to replace some that were torn up when that thing was taken out.'

'Go ahead,' she said.

'How've you been?' he asked.

'Oh, just fine. How about you?'

'All right.'

'You look good,' she said.

'So do you,' he said.

That was as far as either of them could go, so Richard drove on. Caroline went inside and stayed in the room in a place where he couldn't see her and watched him out the window. She'd just been calling him on the phone and there was no answer and now he'd arrived. That was a sign if there ever was one, and she then began to work up courage once more to tell him what she had been ready to tell him earlier that morning.

It was going to be much harder face-to-face, though, and she didn't think she'd be able to do it, so she called him on the extension that was in the shop. It was on the same line as the one in the house and rang to the same number, so all she did was to dial her own number and then hang up fast. When the ringing stopped, she could pick the receiver back up and the call would be complete.

The shop also had a light overhead that was hooked up to the phone so that if the machinery was on, the light blinked to indicate a call. While Richard was setting up the shaper, a machine with various bits that could cut different kinds of molding patterns, the phone rang and the light blinked.

At first he didn't answer it, thinking it was someone calling Caroline, but when it went on and on, he went to where the phone rested on a board supported by an angle bracket, and he picked it up.

'Hello,' he said.

'It's me.'

'Oh.'

'I wanted to talk to you.'

'All right. For a little while.'

'Does Cynthia know you're here?'

'No.'

'She won't like it.'

'It'll be all right. I've got to figure something out about getting my machinery out of here.'

'I suppose you do.'

'What did you want?' he asked.

'Well, I've got a whole bunch of things to tell you.'

'Why don't you wait until I finish and tell me on the way out.'

'I don't want to do that, because I might not be able to tell you everything if I see you too close. See, I'm real scared right now because of all the things I need to say. I'm so scared I feel like I have to go to the bathroom, you know what I mean?'

'Well go ahead then, and just talk to me later.'

'No. I can't stop or I won't be able to start again. See, like, a little while ago I followed this dog.'

'What dog?'

'Well, it doesn't matter, but I followed this dog through the woods along the path, you know, the one that we used to walk on near the creek, and this dog led me to where he lived, and where he lived was this really wonderful old cabin with these two people who lived there and I met them and I spent the night and in the middle of the night when I woke up there were all these deer around me and one of them looked at me a long time, really looked at me, really deep into me, and I felt something happen to me.'

'Just wait a second, Caroline,' he said. He had been trying to let her just run on but he had gotten too lost to let it go any further. 'First off, what cabin and where was it and who were they?'

'Well, their names were Walker and Ellen and the cabin was in the middle of this great big tract of virgin-growth pine timber.'

'I never knew about any place up that way.'

'Well, it doesn't matter. Just forget about that part of the story for a minute. Let me just go on and tell you what I'm really trying to get to. Okay?'

'Go ahead.'

'All right, then. So, a little while later I began to suspect something and a couple of days ago I went to the doctor and, well, the most amazing thing in the world has happened, and guess what it is?'

He couldn't guess. He couldn't even get close because it would have been the last thing he would have ever thought.

'Just tell me,' he said.

'I'm going to have a baby.'

'Oh my,' he said.

'Oh my is right. Isn't that fabulous?'

'Are you sure?'

'How could I not be sure. Of course I'm sure.'

'Well, Caroline, I hardly know what to say. I guess I'm sorry for you, in a way. I mean, what are you going to do? I mean does the father know or do you even know who the father is?' he asked.

'Damn you, Richard, you stupid creep. What do you think I've been doing all this time, sleeping around or something? You stupid fool. You're the father. It's your baby. I'm going to have your baby.'

If Richard had been hit in the side of the head with a shovel, and hit hard, or if he'd run full speed into a brick wall and bounced off it without falling, if either of those two things had happened to him they wouldn't have caused any more of a look of total shock, surprise, disbelief and bewilderment than crossed his face just then.

'I am?'

'Of course you are,' she said. She suddenly felt so good she had to run up to see him. 'Wait. I feel better now. I'm going to come up and tell you about the whole thing.'

He was sitting on the worktable when she came in. The worktable was higher than a normal table and his feet dangled off without touching the floor. There was sawdust on the floor and the top of the table was covered with it as well.

'It's really mine?' he asked.

'It is. Isn't that amazing? I mean, you'd think I'd be worried to death or something, I mean, I guess you would, I guess that's what most people would be doing in my situation but it's just made me so happy I don't know what to do. Of course I wish it could have happened under better circumstances and I wish, I really do, baby, that you were still with me, but as far as taking the second best thing that could come, this is it. You know I've always wanted to have a baby. You know that.'

'But Caroline, I'm not trying to be crude about this or accuse you of something or anything like that, but we didn't even make love for the whole month before I left. Don't you remember?'

'I remember, but I remember something else, too.'

'And on top of that,' he said, still trying to construct the events in his mind, 'I thought you were taking the pills.'

'Well, let me just tell you, then,' she said. 'You just sit there.'

She loved him so much then and he got to her as much as she'd thought he would when she decided to tell him over the phone, but one thing had happened she hadn't expected and that was the bewilderment and the softness that was showing, the tenderness and the confusion that appeared on his face, in his eyes, in the way he sat on the table and swung his feet back and forth while he looked down and then back at her and then down again.

'You remember that night when I got mad at you and threw my pills at you across the kitchen table? Well I never took them after that. I don't know why I did it, but I just threw them away. I guess I figured you were never going to make love to me or maybe I just did it in one of those fateful unconscious moments that people do that determine the rest of their lives of something like that, but anyway, I just threw the whole pack away and never thought about it again. I was upset about other things at the time, if you remember.'

'But what about . . . ' he started to say.

'And it's true we hadn't made love in such a long time during all that, but we did once. We really did. Don't you remember?'

'I'm trying to,' he said.

'It was the day I drove the tractor through the door and you brought me home and we made love and I fell asleep, remember, like this incredibly deep sleep and when I woke up I thought you were still here but you'd gone and you left me that note. Now do you remember?'

'Oh hell,' he said.

'And that must have been it, you see, because I assure you I have not gotten near another man since then. Not once. I mean, I've looked at a few, but I hadn't worked up to it yet.'

'Well, I'll be,' he said.

'But I'm not going to bother you about it,' she said. 'You don't have to do anything. You don't have to support me or support the baby or anything. You can just stay with Cynthia. You don't even have to tell her. You can just stay with her and marry her or do whatever you want. I'm not going to bother either one of you. I've gotten this understanding, see, about the whole thing and while I love you and will always love you and while she doesn't and will never, I've decided to let life take me wherever it will. I've decided to quit fighting so much.'

'But it won't work,' he said. 'She'll find out sooner or later and you'll have to quit your job and then how will you live and damnit, Caroline, there's just a million things you're not even thinking about in your typical fashion of making everything that happens into some kind of romantic adventure.'

'Oh, no,' she said. 'That's where you're wrong. I mean, not about romantic adventures. I will always do that. But about the other million things. See, I'm going to, with your permission, sell this place and move away.'

'Really?' he asked.

'Really.'

'But where will you go?'

'Up to the mountains, maybe. I'm not sure. Somewhere I can be alone and have my baby.'

'But we owe so much on the place. There won't be that much left over after the mortgage is paid off.'

'There'll be enough. I'll give you your half and the way I've figured it, my half will be enough for me for a couple of years of really basic and simple living.'

'I don't want my half. That's not the point. You can have it all. The point is,' he said and then got lost, 'the point is, well, I just don't know. I don't know what I was going to say and I don't know what to think.'

His weakness and confusion turned her on about as much as he had been turned on while she lay in the bed red and flushed and weak from the jellyfish. She understood it now. She'd never seen him so weak and lost.

'I'm sorry, honey,' she said. 'I didn't mean to shake you up so bad. I really thought you'd be annoyed at me a little. I didn't know it'd hit you like this,' she said and stood between his legs and hugged him and laid her head on his chest.

'Yes,' he said. 'I am shook up.'

'It's all right. You'll get over it. It'll be okay.'

'I don't know what to do.'

'Just take it easy. It'll be all right,' she said and kissed him on the cheek, and then again. 'Let's go on down to the house and get something to drink and we'll talk about it some more.'

She filled up a glass with ice and poured him some apple juice and did the same for herself.

'Thanks.'

'You're probably not used to this heat and all, living over in that air-conditioning.'

'I'm not thinking about the heat at this moment,' he said.

'I suppose not.'

'And you're really pregnant?' he asked, as if it was still dawning on him. 'When is it due?'

'March.'

'Oh. Is it a boy or girl?'

'They don't know yet, dopey,' she said and rubbed his scalp with her fingernails. She had a way of using her fingernails in his scalp and on his forehead like acupuncture that just cut loose all the nerves in his system. He always liked it and she started in on it then.

'Don't do it,' he said, but didn't move.

'Why?'

'Just don't.'

'But I want to.'

'I can't,' he said. 'We've got to talk, and that's all.'

'Okay,' she said and sat across from him. They talked for about an hour. He went back to the shop then and finished the molding and glued and nailed it onto the mantelpiece. Then he carefully tied the mantel to the sides of the truck so that it rode upright and drove back to Cynthia's.

Cynthia ran out of the house when he arrived. She saw the mantel. She recognized it as the one she'd commented on. She climbed up in the back of the truck and looked at it closely. He climbed up with her. She hugged him and kissed him and said she was sorry for the way she acted that morning. He said he was sorry, too, and had bought her the mantelpiece to make up for being a little too self-centered, which she had rightly pointed out. She protested that she'd been wrong, but he allowed it had been true.

'Anyway,' she said, 'I've been waiting and waiting for you.'

'I guess it's our first real fight,' he said.

'Except when you yelled at me in the truck when we saw Caroline on the street.'

'Oh yes. That's right.'

'Well, it just proves we're not perfect.'

'Nope,' he said.

'Maybe close, but not perfect.'

'Yep.'

'Where have you been for so long, anyway?'

'At the shop.'

'Oh.'

'I had to make some pieces to fix this here,' he said and pointed to it. She couldn't see what he was pointing out due to being temporarily blinded by the thought of where he'd been.

'But I thought you wouldn't be going there, except, I mean to say, except when I was with you.'

'Well, I was trying to surprise you. I wasn't planning on going, but I had to.'

'You could've come home and gotten me.'

'I just didn't think it was that big a deal.'

'It is. Did you talk to her?'

'Yes.'

'And what else?'

'What else what?'

'What else did you do?'

'Just talked.'

'About what?'

'Things.'

'What things?' she asked.

'Anything. Nothing. Everything. What do you want me to say?'

'You don't have to say anything. You don't even have to talk to me. And what's more,' she said, 'you don't even have to give that to me. I don't want it now. Give it to her. That's probably who you want to give it to anyway.'

'This is turning into just like this morning,' he said.

'That's because you've hurt my feelings again. I hate for you to hurt my feelings. I just hate it. It shouldn't happen. You should know better. You know everything about me. You should know better.'

'Well, I can't win,' he said, meaning a lot more than she knew at the time.

He unloaded the mantel while she went in the back room. He took his tools in with him and carefully and quietly as possible tore out the old mantel. It was a hard job. It had been lag-bolted to the brick. The lag bolts had rusted in their lead anchors and some of them were hard to turn. Some of them had been stripped and pulled right out but some of them were stuck.

After he got the old thing down he set the new one in place but did not attach it. He propped it there temporarily and got Cynthia.

'It's beautiful, I'm sorry,' she said.

'It does look good. You were right. The other one was just plain brutal.'

'It always reminded me of a stockade, or whatever that thing was where they put you if you did wrong,' she said.

'A pillory,' he said. 'Yeah, it looked a little like that.'

'I told Clark when I saw it that he was trying to give us all a message with that thing, but he didn't get it. He didn't get a lot.'

'I'm glad it worked out, anyway,' he said.

'It's lovely. It's graceful and charming and, I don't know, just right.'

'When it's painted you won't even see where I repaired it.'

'You're so smart,' she said.

'Listen,' he said.
'What?'
'There's something I've got to tell you.'
'Okay.'
'I've been trying to figure out whether I should or not since I left Caroline's. I think, in order for things to stay honest, I should. But it's weird, I have to warn you of that.'
'Well, just say it. Go on.'
'Will you let me explain how I feel about it after I tell you, before you have any kind of reaction.'
'Sure.'
'Caroline's going to have a baby.'
'She is not.'
'She is.'
'Whose is it?'
'Mine.'
'Yours?'
'I'm afraid so,' he said.
'Well, that's too much. That's really just too much for me to have to live with right now.'
'I know. The day started out weird and now look where it's gone.'
'You don't know the half of it,' she said.
'What do you mean?'
'I just found out I'm pregnant, too.'
For a few moments there, after hearing that, Richard thought he might have fallen down, that he was no longer standing up, that he had come off the floor and turned over in slow motion and landed on his head. It was perfectly understandable for a man who's just found out he's gotten two women pregnant at the same time to no longer be able to tell if he was standing up or not, or where his legs were in relation to his head, or whether his heart would ever be able to supply enough blood to his brain to be able even to think how to cross the street by himself again.
You couldn't really fault a man who's enjoyed the passions of beautiful women and never found himself in trouble who suddenly finds himself nailed down on his

back like a catfish on a board getting ready to be skinned and thrown into the coals. You couldn't fault that man for having a moment of dizziness.

There was no reason to blame Richard or make light of him for not being able to say anything at that moment, and there was, of course, every reason to understand how he couldn't even find the right nerves to go with his tongue or find the right set of signals to allow him to close his mouth, which had fallen wide open and in such a slack-jawed manner that he no longer even looked like himself.

He looked, instead, exactly the way he felt. It had been one thing to have taken in Caroline's news so abruptly that he had staggered and reeled like the dynamite man. To have this second piece added on just blew him up completely, the same way the dynamite man might have looked if the promoters had talked him into actually swallowing the dynamite, or holding it in his hands as it went off, explaining to the poor fellow, who had literally, one would have to imagine, taken the last and only job he could get, which was blowing himself up directly, and repeatedly and on purpose, after having been blown up by the world in surprise fashion all his life, so that by the time the promoters got to him, he was ready to do it to himself.

It was a little like that for Richard, a little like he had gone from a bunch of near misses all his life to a direct hit, a little like he had nearly beaten the odds, but not quite, and now, like a daily double that had been ready to pay off with a lifetime reward, it collapsed around him as these two sleek, high-strung thoroughbred women presented him with their news.

'I just found out I'm pregnant, too,' she seemed to say again as he heard the words coming at him a second time, not that she had said them again, but just that they had that much in them, enough to stay in the air as long as it took to make him understand, and he nodded and finally closed his mouth and took a seat next to this other woman, who was now a different woman, an unmistakably different woman, from just a few minutes ago.

The mantelpiece across the room no longer seemed so important. It really no longer seemed to be anything at all, just another mantelpiece in another house and nothing more.

It stayed there, propped up by the chair on one side and the stick wedged against it on the other, as the two people who had come together to admire it and bless it and discuss its fine lines and its grace, as they settled down beside each other and wondered at how fast things could change, and pondered the events of this astonishing day.

Chapter 25

During the next few days there was a lot of activity. There was a lot of talking as well, and in between the talking and the activity, there was a lot of heavy contemplation.

New lessons were learned. Whole new ways of acting appeared. What once might have been all right might now no longer be all right. It was a bit awkward. One never knew what to expect. Richard reached over one night just before Cynthia fell asleep and lightly touched her on her arm.

'Don't touch me,' she said.

This was a new phrase. It was like a set of words that had never been used in that sequence before. Don't — me, with anything you might think of to go in between, began to be taught. It was like learning a new language.

At Caroline's, the two women from the real-estate company came and looked around and left. They later told her she could get a lot of money for the place. It seemed that in the years since they had built it land values had gone up even more than she had known. She believed what they said. A sign went up on the lawn. The telephone began to ring. Edgar and Lucille were upset. They waited and then they came by to see her. She explained the plan. It made them uncomfortable. People were not supposed to leave other people. Husbands didn't leave wives. Friends did not leave friends. Neighbors were supposed to be neighbors for life. That was the way they had grown up. It was the way it should have been, even if there was evidence it was no longer that way.

It was all out in the open, then. People looked a lot better in beautiful clothes than they did naked. In clothes, you saw what they wanted you to see. It's best just to see that.

Naked, you didn't want to look. Scars suddenly appeared, distortions in the picture. Without the clothes, it was much harder to believe in each other. It was often thought it was the other way around. That was clearly not true.

So the sign went up. The sign said FOR SALE. It listed the name of the company. Above the name of the company, on a separate add-on to the sign, was the name of the woman who should be called should anyone be interested in buying what was left of this life, the land, the house, the broken spirit.

The sign did not mention the broken spirit. It did not mention the baby. It did not mention what Caroline's cousin Marlene had done to that man. It forgot to list not only the horrors that had occurred but the sweet days and nights of love and tenderness that had once been there.

It was just a sign. It didn't say much. It didn't say enough for anyone to be able to think beyond the phone number and the name of the woman who was in charge of the sale of the place. Mostly, you might say, that was enough. All the rest was best left out of sight.

The little sign on the post pushed into the ground so that it was not quite plumb, but leaned over a bit in the direction of the force of the wind, was really the strangest part of the whole business for Caroline, who was still, until that time, quite happy and relaxed. The sight of the sign in the yard, though, the thing there where nothing had ever been before, was unsettling. It said to her, this is over. You are leaving. You will never return again.

It made her sad, and for the first time since she so joyfully began to follow through on this new plan for her life, she stopped. Like the woman with the fixed smile on her face, the smile of inner peace that said to the world, God is with me, like that woman who smiles bravely and blindly as she pulls into the traffic, and cars skid and twist and bend like rubber to avoid her, like that woman who had once thought that, if only she kept on smiling and thinking good thoughts, nothing could harm her, nothing else could befall her, like that woman who is hit from all sides by a half dozen cars at once, she ceased to smile, as she was hit from all sides by the thoughts of what lay ahead for her and this child and Richard, who somehow must be made to know how much he belonged with her now, and with his child.

While Richard was the recipient of this change of heart by Caroline, he of course had no way of knowing it, as he struggled to deal with Cynthia and to figure out what best to do, himself, trapped with her in the middle of this amazing and disturbing situation.

He could understand, when he thought about it, Caroline's explanation for getting pregnant. It was like her. It fit. It did not fit for Cynthia, however, and so, when she explained it, even after she explained it and he thought about it, he still couldn't quite accept it.

'It was to do with chemicals,' she had said. 'It was to do with a kind of purification. It's very silly now, but how many things look bad in retrospect? Lots,' she admitted, and he agreed.

'It was to do with getting the chemicals out of my body, out of my system. I stopped taking any medication. No aspirin, no pill, no anything. I thought I could handle it with other means. I kept up with my days. I used things that were temporary. I never told you because I didn't want to worry you. It was a very difficult time for me. I'd never given over to a man as I had to you. I'd never made love so much or gone so far. I was swept away. I let myself go. I tried to keep up with it, but I guess I failed. It was all part of the same thing, of the new life, but I didn't make it through the way I planned.

'You made love to me too much. I couldn't get into any kind of pattern. You made love to me morning and noon and night sometimes. I loved it but it was too much. I wanted you to, but it was just too much. I should have known. I should have stopped you. I should have gotten us back to reality sooner. You were just too strong on me. You were just too much for me. I was believing in a lot of things and a lot of things I was believing in were new to me.

'In a way, you should have known that I wasn't able to handle what you were doing to me. Instead, as I think back on it, you took advantage of it and made it worse. I know I loved it as much as you, but you should have known. You shouldn't have taken me so far and not let me come back when I needed to. I was trying for so much and I guess you could say I was trying for too much. And now,' she said, 'here we are.'

Other people were there beside Richard and Cynthia and the new person. C.J. and Anne were there that next week. Cynthia stared at them like she hardly knew them, trying to figure out what they would think of their new baby sister or brother, trying to imagine it, trying to imagine this family that began to look to her like one of those strange families one often saw in the news, where the loving mother and father had adopted one child from each part of the world and brought them all together, and had thrown in, for a little extra work, just to see if they could make it or not, a few disturbed and confused children as well.

'What's the matter, Mommy,' C.J. said.

'Are you sick?' Anne asked.

She couldn't answer. She didn't know the answer. Richard kept quiet. There were times to talk and times to keep quiet, and when the children and their mother were in the room together, it was time for the latter.

Anne got a car. It was easier that way. C.J. got a faster bike. He could hit fifty without too much trouble before he had to brake. It was good to finally go as fast as he'd always wanted to go. It was good to see how it felt. People were trying it all the time. People were speeding and going out of control all the time. It was good to do it in the field in front of Mommy's house where if you wrecked no one would see you, or if you wrecked and got hurt, Mommy could come help you. Some people were trying to speed and were wrecking out there in front of everyone. Fifty miles an hour didn't seem like much when you just talked about it, but with the wind rushing by and the sound of the motor reducing everything else to oblivion, it was right where you always wanted to be, about to fly, but still on the ground, about to crash, but not going to, about to go too far, but able to stop. It was good for a child to learn these things.

Richard hadn't learned them yet. He had gone past Caroline's house on the day the children were to go back to their father's at the end of the week and had seen the sign for the first time and had stopped in. There had been a lot to talk about. Caroline's face had glowed like there was a light somewhere behind it and it was shining through her skin, through the strands of her hair, through her eyes. She was so warm anyone, not only Richard, but anyone four feet away from her, could have felt her presence.

Cynthia didn't like it when Richard got home from Caroline's. She could see Caroline in his face. It made her mad. She was mad anyway. She'd been sick all week. She was always sick in the early months of her pregnancies. She was sicker than ever this time. She kept feeling like she was going to lose the baby. She kept thinking she was going to miscarry. She was in a foul mood when he came in.

'You were there again,' she said. 'You don't even have to tell me. I can see. It's all over you. If I got up and came over and smelled you, I bet I could smell her on you. Goddamnit. I'm sick of this. Is it her or is it me? Who is it? You can't go back and forth. It isn't fair. It sucks, if you want to know the truth. All that I've done for you. All that I've given to you. I never knew. It's all changed now. I just never knew how much a person could take from another person and still be ungrateful. You even bought my presents for me with my own money. Isn't that something? You bought me the mantelpiece with my own money. Some present,' she said and looked like she was going to spit.

'It's so different when you really get down to it. I don't know why I didn't see it all in the beginning. I had this stupid fantasy that I don't even know where it came from. I wish I'd found out before it was too late how wrong a person could be.'

Richard stood in the room where he'd been when she started. He was so used to these outbursts now that he went dead while she went on and on until she exhausted herself. It had happened a lot recently. It was happening again.

'I always thought that a man taking care of a woman was a nice thing, but I never knew until now how nice it really was. A woman taking care of a man just doesn't feel right. It doesn't look right and it doesn't feel right. It's right when a man takes care of a woman. It's right for me. Now I know. I never knew until I didn't have it. I guess that's the way it is. Men have always taken care of me and that's why I guess I never knew how important it was to me. I like it when a man does things for me. When a man gives me money. When a man provides for me. It's almost a sexual thing. Being taken care of is what makes the whole sexual thing real and true and what makes it work.'

She went on and on like this. She either didn't know what she was saying and was so screwed up by the chemical madness inside her that Richard excused it and tried not to listen, or she did know, and if that was so, he thought, well, I'm still in trouble, but even worse than before.

PART V

Modern Times

Chapter 26

They were all in trouble. Someone had to do something. Richard was stuck. He couldn't move. He was like a person caught between two tracks with trains coming from opposite directions. There was just room enough between the trains for him to stand while they whizzed by. If he fell either way, he'd be cut in half.

It was the first time in his life he hadn't known what to do. It was the first time he had not known how to fix what had broken.

Cynthia barely slept. Because she barely slept, she kept him awake, as well. She roamed the house, and when the children were there, she did the same, but more quietly. In the middle of the night, she tried to think. When she couldn't be still enough to think, she tried to read. There were books open to the first page all over the house. A dozen of them lay on the tables and on couches and chairs and all of them were face down, open to the first page, a trail of distraction.

Then, out of the sleepless nights and out of the long, rambling tirades and out of the haggard looks and the new way of putting words together so they said things they'd never said before, Cynthia saved the day. She became a hero, of sorts, and saved everyone. She saved C.J. and Anne and she even saved Clark, and though it was entirely accidental, she saved Caroline as well.

She made it so she was not going to have a baby after all. She did it on her own. She did it without telling a soul. She made the decision quickly one day, and had it done before she could change her mind.

In some places in the world, in some cultures, in different times, the decision would have been condemned.

Silas, the old Quaker farmer, would never have understood it. Every year as the seasons changed and brought that day around again, he grieved for his lost son. He could never have understood it. It was a good thing Silas had stayed on his isolated farm and had died before the world he had known had completely disappeared. It would have been too hard on him. Had he not remained hidden back off the road on his farm, his innocence and his goodness would have been slammed back in his face.

Times had changed. People had changed. What was once wrong might no longer be wrong. Things had been lost. Reasons for acting or thinking in a certain way had been lost. The sense of absolute right and wrong had failed. People tried to do their best, but no one was sure anymore.

After something this cataclysmic had been decided, other things demanded to be decided as well. What was left needed to be decided. What had been lost needed to be decided. What things could be forgiven and what things could not be, but at least could be forgotten, needed to be decided.

Cynthia, however, had difficulty coming up with the right answers and Richard, a little late, began to wonder if he, too, would have made the same decision Cynthia had. Like a man coming up for air for just a second and getting a glimpse across the surface of the water of what was going on all around him while he was struggling just to stay afloat, he gasped for a moment at what he saw and then went under again.

Even before Cynthia told Richard he had to leave, that it would be better that way, he knew it, but like the person who stands in the clear now that the tracks are free and he can cross, he remained motionless, the blur and the speed and the noise and the rush of it all still with him.

Cynthia cried a lot. He sat beside her and held her hand and tried to understand what was right.

'I did love you,' she said. 'I might still love you. I don't know anything anymore.'

He held onto her and tried to say something, tried to say the right thing, whenever she paused. After a moment of silence, though, she spoke again.

'You were so important to me. You were so right. You were the richest thing that ever happened to me.'

'And you were to me,' he said.

'But I can't go on with it. Something is wrong or we wouldn't be where we are right now. Something is not right. I am just so tired. I am just so very worn out. I don't know what else to say or do.'

'I don't either,' he said.

'Didn't it seem right?' she asked. 'Didn't it?'

'Yes.'

'I know. I know it did. I don't know what happened,' she said.

'I don't either. These last few weeks have been like a bad dream for me.'

'And dreams like that are not supposed to come true,' she said. 'You understand?'

'I do and I don't understand.'

'It hardly matters, anyway. I've got a lot to live with now. I've got a lot to settle within myself. It's clear, at least, that it's not going to work anymore. I'm an old woman. I feel like I'm a hundred years older than I was just a while ago. I can see things now I couldn't before. I did wrong. Something got into me and I did wrong.'

'It didn't seem wrong at the time.'

'I know,' she said. 'That's the maddening part of it all.'

'Maybe we shouldn't be so hard on ourselves.'

'I know I did wrong. That's all I can say.'

'What'll we do, then?' he asked.

'I'm going to do nothing. For a long, long time. Just nothing. And I feel so awkward right now, so really messed up, I want to be alone.'

'You want me to leave?' he asked.

'I don't want you to, but I do. I have to put myself back together.'

'You mean just leave. Like that?'

'It's probably the best way. Staying on will make everything harder.'

'And never come back?'

'Don't say things like that. You can see me anytime. Anytime at all. But wait a while. Wait a month. Wait a couple of months. Let me get sorted out. I'm scattered all over the map. I don't know who I am anymore.'

'I just don't know what to say. It's all happened so fast.'

'Too fast.'

'Maybe that was it.'

'What?'

'Too fast.'

'I don't know. I don't even want to talk about it anymore. I just want to be alone. That's all I really want right now.'

Chapter 27

'I thought you might come back,' Caroline said. 'I wasn't sure, but I thought it was a real possibility. I thought that all along and tried to keep it all in perspective, but the last time you were here, I knew you would. When you left, I said to myself, something's changed. He'll be back. I just knew it then.'

'You did?' he asked.

'Sure I did. And I thought, if he does do the right thing, I have to figure out what the right thing would be. I thought and I thought about it and decided that the best thing I could do was not get mad. See, I could be real mad right now, and I could be thinking about all those nights you spent with the great and grand Mrs. X – I can't even say her name – while I was home alone, but I'm not going to let myself get that way. I'm really not.'

Caroline was putting on the most determined act of her life. When she had helped him unload the truck, she made herself pretend he had just been off doing a job somewhere and had returned. He had once gone to the coast and carried a load of cabinets down to a restaurant and installed them and was gone a week and then came back in the truck and she'd helped him unload it, and so, for a little while, for as long as she could, she was pretending this was just like that.

'Of course, there'll always be things I think about that I shouldn't, that will get in the way, I know that. I know that's going to happen, but I'm not going to let it bother me. I have to stay real calm now. I have to keep my system, my whole being, you know, in this really sweet and wonderful and like super-positive frame of mind. I have to, you see, because the little baby can feel everything I'm thinking.'

'You think so?' he asked.

'I'm sure of it. I've been reading everything I could get my hands on ever since I found out. That's practially all I've done. There are so many things I want to show you. I've been saving articles like mad. I've got a whole pile of them in that drawer. I'm going to put them in order someday real soon, and then I'll be able to find out what I need to know if I get scared or worried about something, not that I think I will, but just in case.'

'Sounds good,' he said.

'I'm glad that sign's gone. I guess everyone's going to think the place is sold. It's so weird. Now, after all the time I spent not telling anyone you'd left, I'll have to go around and tell them you're back. I should have waited. I should have waited just a little longer.'

They sat on the porch in their usual chairs at the rail, the same places they had often sat in the evening when they were winding down from the day, and though she went on and on about everything and anything, and though he felt like a jigsaw puzzle that'd been dropped and only partially put back together, something about being back home and being with her began to connect.

'Lucille and Edgar and all them are just going to freak when they find out everything's back the way it should be again. They hated it. They always want things to be the same, you know, day in and day out. It was hard on a lot of people. I don't know what I'd have done if your dad had called, and what I was going to tell him and when I thought about that I wondered what your mom would have thought about it if she'd been alive and I was glad, all in all, that nobody did call except all those people who kept calling you to see about jobs until I started unplugging the phone at night. Did you tell your father?' she asked.

'I told him. A little anyway.'

'What'd he say?'

'He just hung up the phone.'

'That's all?'

'That's it.'

'You should've called him back.'

'I shouldn't have called him in the first place.'

'Was he drunk?'

'I think so. He doesn't care what happens to me. He doesn't care what happens to anyone.'

'I know he acts that way,' she said, 'but still, the few times we've visited him, I noticed something in his eyes. Something that gave him away.'

'It's not there. It's just your imagination.'

'I saw it.'

'It doesn't matter.'

The lights were all on. They were on in every room of the house and in the shop and in the shed for the tractor and the corner floodlights around the outside of the house were on, too. All the outside lights and the ones in the shop and the shed could be controlled from the house as well as from out there.

All the physical components of life of these two people were illuminated. Had a team of scientists examined this twentieth-century couple, how much could they possibly have discovered about them? They would probably have gotten it all wrong. They couldn't have known what Caroline sounded like, how she talked, how the words ran on and on and rarely settled on what was really on her mind. They would have been lucky if they could have discovered much about her mostly silent husband. Had they all been frozen right then and there on the porch like Pompeii, few if any of the truths of their life would have been evident. Only a large tractor with no exhaust and what did that mean? A spot in the yard where once some papers had been burned and what did that mean and why were they burned and what was written on them?

So, for a moment, like the moment when the people in the stands realized that the women in the mud weren't going to make it and the whole scene froze in that brief cartoon in the Looney-Tunes of life, Richard and Caroline stopped, too. They were covered with the dust of their own passionate and mistaken eruptions. It made them want to cough.

'I need some water,' Caroline said.

'Get me some, too.'

When she brought the water out, she said, 'I hate her, you know. I still hate her. I'm not going to ask you what it was like to live with her. I'm not going to ask you what other things that I will not allow myself to think about were like with her. I just want you to know I don't blame you as much as I blame her and though I still and will always hate that woman, I still and will always love you, even though I probably shouldn't.'

Chapter 28

Parents can choose to talk about things with their children or they can choose not to. They can talk about only certain things that occur in the adult world or they can talk about anything and everything. Cynthia hadn't been able to figure out how much to tell C.J. and Anne about why Richard had left, so C.J. and Anne were discussing it themselves while their mother rested quietly in the Navajo room.

'This one was different, though,' Anne said.

'Why?' C.J. asked. 'Why was this one different?'

'He got to her in some way,' she said. 'The other men were like, I don't know, more like just dates or something.'

'You mean they were in love?'

'I think so, but I can't tell. It's complicated. It's hard to explain.'

'I could understand why she liked the other ones. At least they were doctors like Daddy. I could see that.'

'There's more to it,' Anne said. 'I might be wrong, though.'

'Is she still going to sell this place?'

'She said she didn't know. She said she wasn't sure of anything.'

'Maybe she'll go back to Dad. It's only a little more than a year. Neil's mother and father were separated for about like three years or something and they went back together.'

'I don't think so. I just don't see it.'

'He sure left fast, I'll say that,' C.J. said. 'If he'd have stayed a little longer, we could've hauled my new bike back here in the truck.'

'You say some of the stupidest things sometimes,' his sister said. 'Who cares about your bike at a time like this.'

'Well, I do because we had to lay it down on its side to haul it and you're not supposed to do that.'

'You fall over with it all the time.'

'I know, but I pick it up right away.'

'Look, let's not talk about motorcycles, okay.'

'Let's go somewhere.'

'Where?'

'I don't know. I just feel like going somewhere.'

'We ought to stay home. We ought to figure out some way to make Mom feel better,' Anne said.

'Shhhh,' he said.

'What?'

'Here she comes.'

Cynthia had on a lot of clothes, as if it were cold weather. Over her long skirt and blouse she had on a hand-knitted white wool sweater that came from Scotland. She was barefoot, though, and maybe that was why she was cold.

'Hi, Mom,' Anne said.

'Hi, Mommy.'

'What are you two planning in here?'

'We're going to take you out to dinner tonight, aren't we, C.J.?'

'Yeah. That's what we were talking about.'

'We'll go in my car,' Anne said.

'We'll pay for it.'

'You can go anywhere you want.'

'I'll even wear a coat and tie if you want to go somewhere expensive,' C.J. said.

'Don't you want to do that, Mom?' her daughter asked.

'I don't know.'

'Come on. It'll be fun.'

'You really want to?' she asked.

'Of course we do. We want to make you feel better,' C.J. said.

They all changed clothes. There were enough separate bathrooms for everyone to take a shower at one time. There was plenty of hot water. The house had three fifty-gallon hot-water heaters. There was one just for the master suite by itself. There was another for the two other upstairs bathrooms. The third was for the downstairs baths and the kitchen and laundry room.

They dressed up. They looked good. They were a handsome family. They were healty. They had grown up well, with plenty of food and all the vitamins and so on that they would ever need for the rest of their lives.

Cynthia looked at her family as they passed in front of the darkened plate-glass window. A woman came from the other direction. In her arms she carried a baby. As she passed Cynthia, the baby in the reflection passed through Cynthia. It scared her.

'What's the matter, Mommy?' C.J. said.

'Nothing,' she said.

They were seated. Cynthia sat in the middle. C.J. was on her right and Anne was on her left. Across the table from Cynthia was an empty chair. The children didn't notice the empty chair but Cynthia did. It seemed as if it were up to her to put someone in that chair. It should have been an easy thing to do. There certainly were lots of men around.

An agreement was made between men and women. The agreement said that you do certain things and I will do certain things. I will give you these things and you will give me those things. In exchange for completing that simple agreement, the chair will never go empty. It seemed such an easy thing.

You do this and I'll do that. Then, the agreement said, when we go out to dinner, there won't be the empty chair to make everything look out of balance.

It should have been easier than it was. Cynthia looked at the menu. The waiter took away the extra place setting once he discovered the missing person wasn't coming. The children ordered. Cynthia ordered. The waiter served them. The food was good. There was plenty of it.

Maybe that was the problem. There was so much of everything. It was easy to want it all. After you got one thing, you wanted the next. It was hard to control. You knew you shouldn't have dessert and just as you decided not to, here came the table on wheels rolling up to you. Good gracious. Look at all that. You really shouldn't. Oh well.

Cynthia declined the dessert. The children ate huge slices of double-fudge this or that and ice cream on the side. Life couldn't be rich enough for childen. They would take it. As you got older, it began to show on you.

Cynthia felt better. She'd had a good meal. Her daughter drove them home. She was a good driver. C.J. was quiet in the car. He seemed to know his mother needed it. Once home, they all went to their rooms. It was a nice house. It was a nice family. Clark had been a good husband. It should have been enough. Anyone could see, it should have been enough.

Chapter 29

'I want to take you somewhere,' Caroline said. 'I've been saving this for the right day.'

It was a cool morning. It had been a dry night. A front had passed through and the weather had changed. By ten, the dew was off the leaves and the grass was dry.

'Just follow me to the creek. I've got to show you this place. It's a little bit like what we always used to want, like the place we used to dream about, you know, when we first got together.'

'How do you mean?' he asked. For the time being, he was hers. He'd go anywhere or do anything she wanted. It was the least he could do.

'You know, the little cabin in the middle of nowhere. You remember how we used to talk about that, even before we got married, how we used to talk about finding some really sweet little cabin to buy, out in the middle of the woods, and just living there, away from everyone, away from everything.'

'Oh yeah,' he said.

'You know, sweetheart, you were the only person in that whole school or in the whole town who ever thought the same way I did. You know what? I wonder how we got born into that place, fitting in as badly as we did?'

'I don't know.'

'Well, anyway, I've found the cabin.'

'You have?'

'Over that way.'

They walked along the path beside the creek. It was about the time of morning when the dog should have been there. The dog was not there, but Caroline told Richard about meeting him the first time and how he led her away the second time. This time, Caroline led Richard along the narrow path. They had to walk single file in most places, at least until they would get to the old forest.

'Over here it's going to cross the creek and then you just wait,' she told him.

The creek was still low. It would be low until early winter when the rains would bring it back up. A frog hidden somewhere in the bank was making a noise but stopped when they came down the bank. They crossed on the stones that were above the water level and climbed up the bank on the other side.

'It's over here somewhere,' she said. 'The path gets obscured for a while and then, when we get into the pines, it gets better again.'

She walked fast. She reminded Richard of how she was when she'd run out of the beach house ahead of him and jumped in the sound to swim across. She had that same abandon and excitement, only this time, instead of standing on the reedy bank above the waterway, he was right with her.

'The whole time the dog, Jeep was his name, the whole time Jeep was walking along in front of me, I thought, now are we going anywhere? Are we really going anywhere at all?'

'That's what I was just thinking,' he said.

'I know. That's why I said that. Jeep used to know when I would get to thinking that again because he would always stop and look back at me and wait for me to catch up.'

She stopped then, herself, and turned around and kissed him a long, good, hard kiss. She hugged him tightly while she kissed him, and she felt the baby between them. She wanted the baby to feel the kiss, too, and know all about love and happiness even before it was born.

'These are awful-looking cutover woods here,' she said as they continued on. 'I wonder whose land it is?'

'I was just thinking the same thing. We're way west of our land, but I'm not sure whose place this is.'

'It gets better, though, real soon,' she said.

She lost the path but she didn't tell him. She was in a tangle of slash and limbs and treetops that had been left after the timber and pulpwood had been taken out. Here and there were deep ruts left by the huge log skidders. She did not remember any of this from the last time through.

'Are you sure you're going right?' he asked.

'I was, for a while. I'm afraid I'm not now.'

'Well, where is it you're trying to take us?' he asked.

'It's this forest of absolutely original-growth pines that are just as clear and beautiful underneath as those redwood forests you read about in California.'

'I didn't know there was anything like that left around here.'

'That's what I wanted to surprise you with,' she said.

'Well, do you remember which direction it was?'

'It was west. We were always going west. I thought I was doing the same thing. We walked less than an hour before we came to it. We were walking slowly, though, so you and I should have been there already.'

Soon they got out of cutover woodland and onto someone else's land. They knew they had crossed onto another piece because between the two sections of woods there was not only the abrupt clearing of the thirty- or forty-year growth of the new land, but there was a rusty barbed-wire fence between the two. This new piece they were in must have been cut over sometime just after World War II when so much of the South's woods were cut for lumber for the housing boom that happened then. It had grown back well, though, and by that time the old brush had rotted and gone back to the soil. They had a clear walk, then, but they were no closer to the old forest than before.

'I've messed up,' she finally said. He had diligently and dutifully followed her the whole way without complaining. Now he could see she was about to drop from either fatigue or despair.

'Damnit all, how could I mess up like this. After all the planning I did in my mind to take you there and now I can't even find it. Damnit oh damnit oh damnit,' she said and sat crosslegged on the ground. 'I do not know where I got off the path. It must have been after we crossed the creek. I can't believe this. I mean, when I came back from their place, the people who lived in the cabin walked me back part of the way, but I didn't think they'd taken me back so far that I couldn't find it myself if I had to. This is awful. What are we doing to do? I feel like crying. I swear I do. I had this great surprise for you and now I can't even find it.'

'It's all right. Let's rest awhile and then look around some more.'

'I mean, it's like hiding a present for someone and there they are sitting there waiting for it and you can't remember where you hid it. I mean I feel like bamming my head into that tree. We didn't even bring anything to eat or drink. We might die out here.'

'Well, Caroline, sweetheart, we're not going to die out here. I can get us back home. All we have to do is go directly south, and sooner or later, and probably sooner, if I remember what I'm thinking about correctly, we'll come to that state road that goes off below our house.'

'You mean just below Lucille's house?'

'Sure. It's right over there somewhere.'

After walking a bit longer, Caroline gave up and Richard led them out toward the road. Just before they got to the road, they came to a field. The field was the first clearing they'd seen since they started in the woods, so they climbed over the fence and started across.

At the house at the other end of the field, Edgar and Lucille were standing in the yard looking at the garden. The sweet corn was finished and the stalks were brown and dry. Behind the garden was the field, and as they looked in that direction, they saw Richard and Caroline appear out of the woods.

'Look over there,' Edgar said.

'Who in the world is that?'

'I believe it's Caroline.'

'It is?'

'Just look how she walks and her red hair. I'm sure that's her.'

'Is that Richard?' Lucille asked, and watched in wonder as Caroline appeared with Richard, as if she had gone off in search of him in the woods and found him and brought him back.

'That is Lucille's place,' Caroline said.

'There they are, too,' Richard said. 'They see us.'

'Don't tell them about what we were doing. The people who live at the cabin don't want anyone to know they're there.'

Lucille and Edgar gave them something cold to drink and then they all had lunch. Caroline felt like she had ticks all over her and wanted to get home and take a shower. Her skin was crawling and every time a breeze tickled a hair on her skin she grabbed at it as if it were a tick about to take a bite.

Back home, then, Richard had to check out every inch of Caroline's skin to see if she really had any or not. She didn't even have one, but in checking her out like that, and then in her doing the same for Richard, they ended up forgetting all about the ticks and made love and slept the rest of the afternoon.

Caroline had a bunch of happy dreams but she still felt foolish when she woke up. Richard tried to help her and told her he'd ask around, just in general terms, about an old uncut forest with a little cabin in the middle.

Chapter 30

Richard did ask around, and what he found out was not what Caroline wanted to hear.

'It's the old Jones place,' he told her. 'The family lives in Raleigh and some of them live in New York, and it's been tied up in some kind of legal or family trouble ever since anyone could remember.'

'Is that why the timber was never cut?'

'Well, I don't know about that. I mean, I haven't seen it, but if the trees are as big as you say, then the decision not to cut them was made a long time ago.'

'Oh yes,' she said.

'Anyway, the guy and the woman who live there were putting you on in some way.'

'How?'

'You said they'd been there for years and all that and that they walked in and out this secret path and all this baloney, but the person who told me about the place said there was an old driveway that came in from the other side about halfway and that they had a car they drove in and parked and then just walked the rest of the way, and the reason they freaked when you walked in on them and told you not to tell anyone about them was because they're growing dope back there.'

'Oh no they're not,' she said.

'Yes, they are. They've got an acre of marijuana back there spread out all over the place and that's why they don't want anyone coming back there.'

'That is absolutely and positively and one hundred million percent wrong,' she said. 'Who told you that, anyway?'

'Somebody I've worked with who knows them. He said

he's been there before. He's seen the whole thing.'

'I don't believe it. He's talking about someone else. He's talking about another place. It can't be the same people. It can't be the same place.'

'Well, it is.'

'Well, it isn't,' she said.

'I'm sorry, Caroline. I asked around and that's what I've come up with. You don't have to believe it if you don't want to, but it's the truth.'

'WELL, DAMNIT,' she screamed. *'IT IS NOT THE TRUTH.'*

'Just calm down,' he said.

'I'm sorry. I'm not supposed to let myself get like that. I'm sorry.'

'It's all right.'

'It's just that I know whoever told you that is telling you the truth about somebody and someplace but not the place I found.'

'Well, maybe not then, but I think it is.'

'And I tell you it's not,' she said.

'Well, either way, it sounds like a beautiful place and I'd like to see it sometime. The way the fellow described it to me, it's a pretty amazing location.'

'It is that,' she said.

'I'd like to see it sometime. I really would.'

'Then let's go now. If there's a way to drive there and you know where it is, let's go now.'

'No way. The guy who told me about it said that they'd be about to harvest the stuff now and that we'd be shot or killed if we went snooping around there now. We can ride by and I'll show you the beginning of their driveway if you want, but we can't go down there this time of year. We can do it in the winter, if you want, when they'll probably be gone.'

'Crap,' she said. 'I don't believe it. I just don't believe it is the same place. The people I met were not like that. You're talking about someone else. It's just as clear as anything to me that the place I found is not the place you are talking about and I'll go out and walk those woods until I drop to prove it to you. I swear I will. I don't care how long it takes. I'll show you I'm right.'

'You're not, sweetheart,' he said, 'but don't worry about it. It doesn't matter.'

'It does matter. It matters a lot. If they were dealers, how come they didn't shoot me.'

'I don't know. You got lucky. I don't know the answer to that. I just know it has to be the same place.'

She pouted and stayed mad most of the day but then tried to pull out of it because it wasn't going to do any good and because she didn't want the baby to feel it. She got it out of her system and slept well and the next morning, which was Sunday, she and Richard watched television.

Chapter 31

It was not the usual Sunday-morning television show. It was something special. Far across the ocean to the east, there was going to be a wedding. Some famous and beautiful people who had the history of western civilization in their royal blood were getting married. Caroline was excited about this wonderful event and Richard was watching it just to be doing something with her.

The wedding was on television for everyone to see. It was broadcast all over the world at the same time. People in South Carolina were going to watch it. Eskimos were going to watch it. Cannibals dressed in the bones of last night's feast (what a set of legs that woman had) were going to watch it.

It was a sultry day. It was still summer. Soon school would be back in session. The children would settle into their 180-day depression, and the parents would spend money on books, clothes and anything else the precious little ones asked for. It was only right to make life as easy and rewarding as possible for them. They hadn't done anything wrong yet. It wasn't their fault, whatever it was that had happened since the wedding that no one saw on television brought them into this world.

Somewhere near town a couple of teenagers had discovered how good it felt to kiss on the lips. The boy and the girl had just turned fifteen and they thought they'd discovered something that no one else knew about. They kept it secret and practiced it as much as they could.

It was late in the summer around that time as well when an ad appeared on television that showed an old couple kissing. They were in a motel. From the music and the voice-over and the looks of the room, they had just checked in and were alone. They didn't know anyone was watching. This ad showed the old people kissing. It showed the dry wrinkled lips lightly touching and then mashing into each other quite hard. The ad made some people uncomfortable. The two teenagers who had discovered kissing were completely and totally grossed out.

It was a strange thing to propose that old people might kiss with that much passion and force, and there had to be some reason that the idea had been made public. People weren't used to seeing old folks getting down and mashing all over each other like fifteen-year-olds.

It was a signal of some kind. It was confusing, though, as to just what the message was, and, once received, how to act on it.

'It's the old-people ad again,' Richard said. 'They're showing it all the time now.'

'I know,' Caroline said. 'I saw it last night.'

'I think they only show it on the things they think old people watch, like the news and Sunday-morning shows and that kind of stuff.'

'Well, we're not old, are we?' she asked.

'That's true,' he said.

The cannibals did not see this ad for the old people, and if they had they might have misunderstood it worse than most people. After all, a kiss could consume another person if that other person was not careful. It happened all the time.

'This is going to be beautiful,' Caroline said.

'It looks nice,' he said.

He was just watching. It could have been anything. It might as well have been a stock-car race. He was sitting there being with his wife and watching television and that was about all, until the procession arrived and the music began.

Then, quite by accident and in much the same way that the presence of another person in the same room might be felt before you looked up, and in much the same way that the absence of the person you love might be felt in the night, in your sleep, as that person slipped out of bed and away from you, Richard began to be overcome by what he saw on the screen.

It happened slowly and it happened quietly as he watched these two people standing together and heard the words and the music of the wedding march and saw them walk down to meet one another, and just as slowly and effortlessly as the events on the screen overcame him, he began to feel horribly blue.

It was possible that many other people besides him were affected strongly by what they were watching, and that men and women all over the world were shifting in their chairs or changing their positions or leaving the room for a moment in order to get control of themselves, and it was just as possible that the same number of people were sitting or standing where they were and letting the tears flow, just like Richard, as he unexpectedly began to cry.

He cried without a sound. His face became as wet as if he'd been sprayed with water. He shook all over and his teeth chattered as if he were cold and the tears flowed and flowed and dripped off the end of his nose and down his cheeks and over his lips and he could not understand how it all could have happened the way it did.

The attraction of doing wrong had been so great. The allure had been so strong. The promise of the new life had been so real. It would have been nice to change entirely, and never be the same again.

He could barely make sense of how wrong he'd gone and how much of a mess he had made of things and how easily and painlessly he had been able to ignore what had happened over the past three months, and so, as he wept while sitting beside Caroline, who at first did not notice, he was forced, as he watched the charmed beginning of this royal marriage reflected in the faces of the man and woman, to consider his own life and where it had gone.

Nowhere in their eyes or in anything else did he see that they knew what they might do to one another, and it grieved him terribly to think about it.

He took a deep breath, and when he did, Caroline looked over at him.

'Oh my goodness,' she said. 'What happened, baby? What is it?'

He could not answer. He just shook and sobbed and stared straight ahead.

'Gosh, I can't believe this,' she said and went over to him. 'Is it the wedding? Is that it? Oh, I bet it is. It must all be coming to you now, isn't it. I'm so sorry. I really am. Let me get you a damp washcloth.'

She went to the bathroom and ran the cold water into a cloth and squeezed it out and came back and wiped his face. The cool cloth felt good and she stayed behind him and held his head.

'You poor thing. You must have been keeping it all bottled up and now it's come out. I'm just so sorry. I really am. I'm just so sorry all of this had to happen, but it did, and there's not much we can do about it but just go on, okay, my baby?'

He nodded yes.

'I know you're sorry, too, baby. I know it now for real now, because I have never, ever seen you cry before. Do you know that? You didn't even cry when your mother died. I just always thought you were one of those people who never cried. I thought, well, anyway, I cry enough for both of us. That's what I thought. But now I see, baby, it's all been inside of you and you couldn't get it out. I love you, my sweetheart,' she said. 'I really do.'

Eventually he stopped but she stayed behind him and kept the rag on his forehead and held him against her breast and they watched the wedding and the saying of the vows and the kiss and saw the faces of the people flash back and forth around the world rejoicing in this event.

'It's going to be all right,' she said. 'I'm not ever going to be mad at you again. And I'm not going to be mad at myself or anyone else, if you know what I mean, ever again. Everything's going to be okay. It's going to be you and me and our darling little baby and we're going to make it just fine. The rest of the world doesn't matter. We know that. We've always known that. We're going to make it just fine,' she said.

'I've changed so much that you haven't had time to see it all yet. So much has happened to me. I'm going to be so good to you, sweetheart. I really am. I'm going to be such a good mother you won't believe it. And I won't forget you either. Don't ever worry about that.

'And you know what else,' she said. 'You will be a great father to this baby. A wonderful father. I know you're scared and all that, but I've seen you around children. I've watched you with them all your life. You love children. I can see it in your eyes. And you're going to be just fine. You're going to be the best father any baby ever had,' she said, and went on to tell him more about their life, about what would be, and he stayed right there in the chair, like someone who could no longer walk, who had lost the use of his legs. He remained still, and Caroline stayed behind him like the person's attendant would stand behind the wheelchair of the poor soul, and she told him all of the things that were to come in their life.

Chapter 32

A whole week went by and everything was as perfect as it could be, but on Saturday afternoon Richard began to notice Caroline acting funny, a little withdrawn, a little pouty. He didn't know what it was, but something was cooking inside her and he wanted to diffuse it before it went too far.

'Let's go somewhere,' he said.

'No.'

'Come on. Let's take a trip for a couple of days. I've got those jobs coming up and I'll be really busy and glad of it when I start, but right now we can get away for a few days and have some fun.'

'I don't want to,' she said. 'I want to stay home.'

'Okay, then. We'll stay home. Have you written your resignation yet?'

'Yes.'

'Have they answered you?'

'Not yet.'

'It'll be good for you to get away from all that. It really will.'

'I know. I was thinking about that, and this will be the first time in my life I haven't worked. The first time.'

'You've earned it,' he said.

'Maybe.'

'What do you want to do, then?' he asked, still trying to get that look out of her eye which he knew too well.

'Talk,' she said.

Uh oh, he thought. Here it comes.

'About what, sweetheart?' he said.

'Don't call me sweetheart right now, okay? Just don't for a while.'

'All right.'

'Because even though I said I wasn't going to get mad about anything or let anything about what has happened bother me or upset me there's just something I've got to get out of my system before I settle down. Like you put off everything until it just came out, this is something I've been needing to get out as well.'

'Well, go on then and tell me.'

'I'm trying.'

'Okay.'

'It's difficult.'

'Well, wait awhile then. We can talk later.'

'No. I'm just trying to find the right words to use. Just give me a second, will you.'

'Sure.'

'What I want to know is what, you know, what it was like with her.'

'Like with her? How do you mean?' he asked.

'I mean, what was she like when you were, you know, alone with her.'

'Alone when? Or where?'

'GODDAMNIT, YOU KNOW WHAT I MEAN,' she screamed. 'I mean, what was she like in bed, stupid. I have to know. It's driving me crazy thinking about it.'

'I don't think I can answer that. I don't think I know how to answer it.'

'Yes you do. You just tell me, that's how you do it. I want to know what she was like. I have to know. I won't get upset. I promise. I won't even yell at you again. Just tell me and it'll be over. I'll sit here and listen to you and then we can quietly and so forth and so on, you know, go on about our life. But I have to know. I will literally go mad if you don't tell me, if I don't find out if you liked her more than you like me. I can't stand the thought of you two together but I have to know what it was like. I have to. Just tell me. I promise I won't get upset. Okay?'

'But there's no way I can describe what you're asking. I don't even remember it, all right? It's something that happened and now it's over and I don't want to remember it, if you want to know the truth.'

'Don't lie to me, Richard. Just don't do that. I can't take that. Me and my cousin,' she started to say when Richard interrupted her.

'You and your cousin,' he said. 'You know you don't have any cousin named Marlene. I don't know how you expected me to believe that junk.'

'I do so. Just because you've never met her doesn't mean she doesn't exist.'

'Baloney.'

'Now you are getting me mad.'

'You said you wouldn't get mad anymore.'

He was desperate to change the subject. He knew if he said anything at all about what Cynthia was like, he was done for.

'I'm not going to. I'm not going to get sidetracked about Marlene, either. I just want you to tell me what I asked you and I want you to do it now.'

'You want to know?' he asked. 'You really want to know? All right, then, I'll tell you.'

Now that she was about to find out, she wasn't so sure she wanted to know.

'Well, wait,' she said.

'Wait nothing,' he said. 'This is what she was like. Okay. This is it. She was like a tiger, see. She was like this wild beast who would fight and scream and moan and lose her mind and it would just go on all night and all day and then again all night,' he told her. 'Is that what you wanted to hear? Do you like that?'

She shook her head no.

'Because I can make up some more. I can make up as bad a stuff as you want me to. Do you want to hear some more?'

'No,' she said. 'I mean yes,' she said, and then shook her head no again, as if to cancel out the yes.

'Okay, baby,' he said and went over to her. 'It was like something that didn't really happen. No one in the world is as good as you are. No one. You're the best kisser, the best lover, the best everything. You've got the best lips, the best skin, the best everything. Okay? She was nothing compared to you. Nothing. All right?'

She nodded yes and managed a tiny smile.

'I've got to go to the bathroom,' she said, and patted him on the arm as he walked by.

Things were quiet in the bathroom for a while. In fact, the whole house was unusually quiet. It was, of course, the calm before the storm, and soon there were the sounds of things being broken, the sound of things being torn loose, the sound of metal being forced to do things it never had done before.

There was the sound of glass breaking, and then there was a pause and then the sound of something like a toilet being ripped loose from the floor and the sound that a tub might make if it had been kicked so hard the porcelain around it had shattered into dust and the cast iron itself had been recast into a new shape and there was the sound of copper pipes being stretched.

The pipes made a kind of *SQUEEEEEEEE* sound as something pulled on them and stretched them into little pieces of tan-colored taffy and then there was that horrible popping sound that towel bars and toilet-paper holders make as they are jerked off the wall, leaving their anchors dangling from the Sheetrock like tendons from a brutally fractured arm, and last but not least there was the sound of someone screaming with a hand over her mouth. The scream was powerful. It was frightening. It went through the walls and right up into Richard's feet and legs and all the way up to his heart like an earthquake would feel as it stopped just short of bringing down the whole place.

Then the door opened and Caroline appeared looking rather fresh and happy and she smiled at him as she walked by on her way to get the broom and dustpan.

'Hi,' she said, and waved and wiggled her fingers, just a little bit embarrassed, but much happier, he could tell, at least for a little while.

It would be a good night, anyway, and a good night with

a happy wife was about all a man could hope for in these modern times full of rich and beautiful people who roamed the land searching for mates, who beckoned from the doorways of grand houses and who offered, in a manner that seemed nearly impossible to refuse, everything you could have ever wanted.

These were difficult times and even the most honest and good-hearted men and women made terrible mistakes. People slept with their eyes open and the lights on. Once it became dark, unborn children haunted the air and men swelled up like boiled hot dogs, splitting open noiselessly while their wives talked for hours without stopping.

These were confusing times, and people living alone sat by the phone, by the radio, in front of the television, hoping to hear something that would tell them what to do, how to live, what to say. They turned the dials. They picked up the phone to see if it was still working. They changed the channels. Figures moved across the screen. The woman selling the necklace was still there. She was saying something. Her voice had become weak. It was hard to read her lips. Her lips had distorted like the fighter pilot's. The people listened and watched. Maybe buying the necklace was the answer. The phones began to ring. The woman on the screen began to smile again. Something good had happened. Everyone felt better.

Lights appeared on the horizon and people set out to discover what they meant. It was easy to get lost. Along the way, strangers waited in the shadows. Every now and again, someone would disappear and then just as quickly reappear, looking the same, but changed forever.

Old Silas had been right. It was best to stay away from the confusion until things settled down. It was so easy to go wrong in these modern times. It really was.